ILLUSIONS

A NOVEL

by

Rodger Christopherson

Copyright © 2012 by

Rodger Christopherson

ONE

Los Angeles was far behind him, almost eight years now. But that didn't stop him from thinking about it. And her. Jodi. That long afternoon walk on Venice Beach where it all began. The two bottles of champagne and the evening in her hot tub, followed by a long weekend in Morro Bay. What would life have been like if he had married the woman instead of walking away as he had felt so compelled to do at the time? What then? To be sure he could only try to imagine it. But it was over, so why go there?

No matter how hard he tried to push them aside, however, his thoughts kept coming back to her as he laid in bed trying to get some sleep, but nothing seemed to work. He stayed there anyway and before he realized what was happening, he went from thinking about her to dreaming about her, all in one smooth flow.

He was in bed with her again, snuggled up against her warm, soft body, her skin smooth and enticing, his arm over and around her waist. Then, spontaneously his hand came up and cupped her breast. Still half asleep, she responded by rolling over onto her back and the rest was automatic. Ardent and passionate, it was the most lucid dream he had ever had in his life and oh so very, very real. And then, when it was over, she told him that she was glad he had decided to come home a day early, turned over again and went back to sleep.

He laid there for a few moments afterward, then carefully slipped out of bed and went into the bathroom. Then, almost immediately, he noticed the old familiar bronze tray that was there, full of rings, bracelets and other bits of her jewelry. In particular, he saw the small silver brooch that she had often worn pinned to her jacket or sweater. The one he had given to her back in the early days of their relationship. Instinctively, he reached over, picked it up and looked at it closely. Then he looked back up at himself in the mirror and nearly went into shock.

One second he had been dreaming the most vivid dream of his life and the next he was standing in front of his own mirror in his own bathroom back in his own house and realized that he was fully awake. But when he looked down at his hand and opened it, there was that small silver brooch, still there, all intact and real. Or was it? He looked at it again, touched it with both hands, held it up and examined it in detail. It was as real as it could possibly get. But how could that be? It was technically impossible. Wasn't it? But there was more. He could also still smell her perfume and the scent of her body on his own and remembered the distinct sound of her voice when she had spoken his name.

Overwhelmed by the extreme reality of it, he got dressed and went outside, thinking that the fresh air might help clear his mind. Regardless of how else he might have felt about it, something very bizarre had just occurred. Somehow he had just transported himself over four hundred miles away and then back again. He had somehow been to the house on Patricia Avenue where they had lived together those several years almost a decade ago. Back in the upstairs bedroom with the fireplace in the corner and that same deep, thick, wine colored plush carpet on the floor and the same king sized bed they had slept in together and all the rest. Even the bathroom, just as he remembered it. And now he was back at his own home, the little silver brooch still in his hand. God! If he ever needed a strong drink, he needed it now.

TWO

Four days went by before he felt he was gaining control. Then he drove up the hill to the post office to get his mail, something he hadn't bothered to do for a while. Once there, he found a slip in his PO box that said he had an item to pick up so he went to the counter to retrieve it. The woman took the slip, disappeared for a few minutes, came back and handed him a small rectangular shaped, slightly heavy for its size, package. Outside in his car, he looked at it. The brown paper it was wrapped in looked old and discolored, the packaging tape was wrinkled, dried and curled up at the ends and the postmark was blurred but legible. It had been sent from Los Angeles, no return address. Tearing off the wrapping, he opened the box and stared at the contents, recognizing the object immediately. Inside was a very tarnished silver goblet.

Originally there had been two of them. They had always sat side by side on the shelf of the china cabinet in the dining room of Jodi's house and on Sunday evenings they would get them out and share a bottle of champagne over dinner.

Carefully, Reed removed the vessel from the box and looked at the bottom of it. Sure enough, there were his initials, right where he had scratched them into the metal several years ago, along with the date.

The whole thing went round and round in his head. Then something else occurred to him. He reached for the package again and looked at the hand written address on it. It too, was faded and old looking but it was clearly original. None of it had been crossed out and a forwarding address added and that was exceptionally odd. He had only had this particular PO box for less than a year. But was it Jodi's handwriting? He thought so, but couldn't tell for sure. It had been too long ago. Then he got out of his car and went back inside the post office.

"How long was this package here?" he asked the woman who had given it to him before.. "Can you tell when it arrived?"

"Maybe," she said. "Just a minute," and pulled out a stack of yellow cards from under the counter.

The one he had received was still on top of the pile and it had a date on it, the day the notice had been placed in his mail box. She showed it to him. It was the day after his dream adventure. Reed shook his head in dismay, thanked the woman and was about to leave when, overcome with a hunch, asked another another question.

"You're right," she responded. "That's the day we put the notice in your box. But if it makes any difference, technically it had to have come in on the route truck the night before."

"Really?" he replied, quite astounded. "Any chance it was after midnight?"

She gave him an odd look and told him, yes, the truck always arrived about one in the morning. It was a dismissive reply but it was good enough, so he left. What would have been even better was the truth. She actually had no idea of how or when the parcel had gotten to the post office. All she knew was that when she had come to work that morning, there was that old looking package sitting on her desk and no one seemed to know how it got there, leaving her with nothing else to do but put the notice in his box and put the item on the shelves where it belonged to begin with. Regardless, the package had arrived at some point during the night when he had gone to sleep and ended up in Jodi's bed.

Back outside in his car again, Reed picked up the wrapping and again looked at the postmark, this time more closely, careful not to smudge it any more than it already was. No doubt about it. It was mailed somewhere around the time he had left the relationship with Jodi. He could check the dates later, but what did it matter? He was still living in California then and had no idea that he would ever be moving to Arizona. That decision had come much later. But again he was baffled. Certainly her sending him the goblet was very symbolic regarding the end of their relationship, but damn! It had been mailed eight years earlier and had just now shown up at a place where he would never have been able to predict he would be at, at this point in time. He groaned, started his car and drove back down the hill towards home.

THREE

Well, there was absolutely no way he could leave it alone now. He either had to understand what had happened or end up in the psycho ward. Except for the silver brooch and the silver wine goblet, he might even have committed himself. But now there was no middle ground. The laws of physics had been completely violated. So had his common sense and everything else he had learned about normal reality. But where did he begin?

It was like having had a bona-fid UFO encounter. Who did one share it with? He didn't have a long term, close friend he dearly trusted. But even so, considering the story he would have to tell, that kind of friend probably didn't even exist. And if such things actually ever happened to other people, they probably weren't talking about them either.

Alone with his desperate need to comprehend, all he could do was to keep going back over everything that had preceded the event to see what specifically might have caused it. In all honesty it was a lonely time in his life. Somewhat new to the area, he was living a solitary existence in a big old house that sat back about a mile off the highway out on a ridge by itself, down the mountain from an old mining town that had gone from copper bust to tourist gold. Interesting as a location but so far, that was about it. A herd of antelope that sometimes grazed along his driveway, a pack of coyotes with a den nearby, a huge white owl living in the abandoned mineshaft out back and a resident road runner that insisted on waking him up at the crack of dawn by pecking on his bedroom window but no new human acquaintances in his life as yet to fill up the rest of it. No wonder he had gotten hung up in his thinking, looking back with some regret as to what he had left behind. A full time woman in his life. Damned if there wasn't a lot to be said for that, regardless of the complications.

It was exactly where he shouldn't have been letting himself go, however. He had obviously been feeling sorry for himself, had allowed himself to get overly sentimental about the good times, obsessing even, and in the process lost sight of why he had made the decisions he had at the time, overlooking all the compromises that would have been necessary if he had stayed with his old lady friend, Jodi, and all the rest.

Regardless, the review had been a good exercise and his sense of objectivity had finally returned. He hoped. Partially, at least. Leaving Jodi had been a major decision point in his life, one that seriously changed his lifestyle and standard of living but also one with deep emotional ramifications. Deep enough to trigger what had just happened, however? Maybe. Maybe not. But it might be a clue. So. Had there been other comparatively difficult times in his life? Of course. A lot of them. But, they were further back. Back when there wasn't much time left over for personal re evaluation and self analysis. A marriage, a career, another career, family difficulties, life's exigencies, this and that.

But now it was different. His life was his own and he needed to begin taking better advantage of it. A crack had opened in the wall between space and time and had given him a glimpse of something beyond that, that he was now unwilling to let go of.

It was one thing to consider all those odd little subconscious decisions people make every day of their lives, himself included, and some have a significance all their own. Like the people in the church choir in the south who had been coming to practice on the same night of the week at the same precise starting time of six in the evening for years, with it being extremely rare that even one person was ever absent. Not until one particular night when everyone was late. Everyone. But it was not by plan or done with outward, conscious intent. One person couldn't decide what to wear and took a few extra minutes to get dressed. Another made a detour to drop something off on the way. Still another just had a difficult time getting organized and out the door. And so it went for all nineteen people involved. None of them made it to the church on time. As a result, none of them were inside the building when the leaking gas heater in the basement blew up and completely demolished the structure.

The stories about such things are countless but for the most part are simply written off as coincidence. But nineteen people who should have all been blown up in an explosion? And the airline flight he had so stupidly missed for no clear reason which then went down in the snowstorm and killed everyone else aboard. And the one morning when the second cup of coffee is skipped so you are ten seconds ahead of where you might ordinarily have been on the freeway where an accident occurs right behind you with multiple injuries. And what about that time when they were out on the boat of the California coast and... Blind fate, coincidence, just plain luck or whatever, they were all significant in their own ways at the time and they all sparked his interest. But this one? Ending up in bed with Jodi. This was different. This went way, way beyond any of that.

FOUR

The initial list he made of other turning points in his life was quite long. Once done, however, he looked it over carefully. For the most part he had zero interest in finding out where this path might had led. Or that one, or this other one, or .... But a few remained and he reviewed them carefully, wondering about the possibilities if his choices had been different there too.

One item on Reed's list was the question about medical school. What if, after completing his pre-med work, he had gone on to med school instead of switching his major to physics? It was a financially driven decision at the time, but still...Then he would be a doctor practicing medicine somewhere. But what kind of doctor would he have made? Would he have been able to 'practice' medicine? And how happy would he have been doing that? Indeed, what would his life have been like then in all the other aspects too? More importantly, was it possible as some have proposed, that at such major decision points in life those other paths split off and we actually experience all possibilities on some level. Another side of self goes down that alternate route too, just like he must have done with Jodi. Somewhere, somehow he seemed to have stayed with her, and was still living in that same old house, having that life together also. If not, how else could what had happened ever be explained? Much as the idea offended him, it couldn't. With that he got up from where he had been sitting on the couch, went into his own bathroom, found the silver seahorse brooch and pinned it on his sweat shirt as a reminder, went to the kitchen, found the silver goblet, washed it out and poured himself a glass of red wine and drank it just to reassure himself. If it happened once, what the hell, maybe he could make it purposely happen again.

With that goal in mind, he began going over that point in time more intently. The one where he might have decided to go to med school. Forcing himself to remember it in as much detail as he possibly could, that portion of his life once again regained much of its original vividness. For one thing, he certainly remembered zoology. Having to sacrifice all those cute little frogs to learn what? Some obscure point derived from cruelty that could just as easily have been made some other way. Then there was anatomy and organic chemistry and medical terminology and, and. He went back over everything he could that had happened during those three years and went on to think about what medical school would have been like. He had been accepted so the path was clearly there. Finally, after days of effort, he went to bed fully clothed. Laying there in the dark he led himself into a state of calmness. Then as he began drifting off into a pre-sleep, hypnogogic state, he started repeating his thought out list of self hypnotic suggestions and tuned into that earlier portion of his life as clearly and realistically as possible.

Then suddenly, some time later, he found himself fully awake, lying somewhere on something that was not his bed in some dimly lit room somewhere. Holy jeez, he said to himself and sat up, only to realize that the only place he had gotten to was the couch in his own living room. Not all that unusual. It had happened before without all the complicated effort up front. What a bummer, he thought as he went outside for a look at the sky and then to the kitchen for toast and hot chocolate before going back to the bedroom, undressing this time, and back to sleep. The next day he started all over again, and the next and the next, determined to achieve some sort of results with the, exactly what, not so clearly defined. But nothing came and he gave up, realizing that a change of place and scenery might be good for him.

In that regard, Sedona was not that far away, the land of red rocks. Long Canyon. Boyton, Fay and Secret Canyon. Sterling Pass, Wilson Mountain, Westfork, the possibilities were almost endless and they were all on his to-do list. Oddly enough, however, the one place that was not on it was Sycamore Canyon but it was the one name that kept coming back to mind, interfering with the rest. Why, he didn't know but he finally yielded to it and soon found himself down at the end of the twelve mile long, rough dirt road.

It was early morning and mid week. His old Chevy Blazer was the only vehicle in the parking lot. He slid into the straps of his day pack, slung the big canteen over his shoulder and walked down the steep winding path to the bottom. Half a mile in he thought he saw movement on the twisting trail ahead. He stepped off the path and waited. Damned if it wasn't a woman. And alone, wearing jeans, boots, a faded shirt and toting a small back pack. Odd, he thought. Where had she come from? And then, when she was closer, he would have sworn that it was Jodi coming towards him. The body, the build, the way she walked. But no, the hair was different. And the eyes, different too and suddenly Jodi was the furthest thing in his mind. He nodded at the woman who appeared to be about his own age and smiled when she was closer, not wanting to alarm her with his male presence. She slowed and studied him quickly before coming nearer.

"Good morning," he said neutrally enough and stayed where he was off the trail so she could feel safe in going by.

"Hi," she finally said in return, after looking at him again, then smiled as though satisfied about something and kept on going.

"Well, damn," Reed said to himself, upset. He had just let her go right on by. But then he turned and called out to her.

"How far does this trail go on in?" he asked, grasping for something to re engage with, hoping it wasn't too late.

She stopped, turned to face him and answered him like he had to have been some kind of idiot.

"Farther than you want to go with what you're carrying," she said. "There's at least fifty miles of forest land straight ahead. And if you don't mind crossing highway 40 when you get to it, you can go all the way to the Grand Canyon."

"Sorry," he said, somewhat embarrassed and got back on the trail. "Really dumb question. My apologies."

"No problem," she replied. "I might have asked the same question the first time I came here but I looked at a map before I put my hiking boots on."

Jeez, Reed thought. What had he done? Why was she giving him such a bad time? Somehow he had ruined it so he just put out his arms, shrugged and remained quiet. Then she apologized and somehow they moved a little closer together, she still a fairly safe distance away. Then it occurred to him.

"You're hiking out but there aren't any cars in the parking lot. Is someone coming to pick you up?"

She studied him a little more before answering, judging her response. "No. I'm going to walk into Cottonwood."

"Walk? That's at least twelve miles. Maybe more."

"I know. I've done it before."

"Really? Well... before..? You're not coming back out here too, are you? That's another twelve miles."

This time she was the one who shrugged an answer.

Reed looked at her in amazement and shook his head.

"Look," he said as he came a few more steps closer. "My name is Reed. I live half way up the road to Jerome and, ahh. I mean, can I give you a ride, or something? Really. I'll drop you off anywhere you want to go. Or, if you aren't going to be too long, I'll even drive you back."

"Why would you do that? You don't even know me."

"I know, but... I mean, you came down the trail from somewhere so you've been here a while. And now you're about to walk twelve miles into town. I find that very interesting and I'd like to hear more, ahh, but I don't want to intrude if...

"But you just got here. You're obviously out for a day hike and I wouldn't want to spoil that. Maybe some other time. Thanks anyway."

Okay, he thought. Her answer meant she wasn't totally turned off to the idea and that was good.

"No, no," he said. "Seriously, I could use the exercise but I'd trade that for a good conversation any day. Really. I would. So why don't I sit down here and wait while you go on ahead. If you think it's okay to accept a ride, yell to me and I'll come and catch up."

"Well," she said with even further scrutiny and the tiniest bit of a smile. "Why don't you walk with me a bit while I think it over."

Reed was still at her side by the time they had climbed back out of the canyon and he knew her name was Kyara, but that was about it. By then there was another car in the parking lot and a young couple was gearing up for their own excursion.

12

Seeing Reed and Kyara, they came over and began asking questions about what lay ahead and this time Kyara seemed more than willing to answer in detail. Once they were on their way she turned to Reed.

"Are you sure you want to do this?" she asked, knowing from the way he looked at her that he most certainly did.

Back in town he stopped at a grocery store. She said she needed honey and rice. He went in with her and got a few things for himself also. By then it was almost noon. He asked if he could buy her lunch and she consented.

"So," he said to her once they were eating. "It seems pretty clear that you are camping out. How long have you been in there?"

"Well, since you're obviously not with the Forest Service, I can tell you. About four and a half weeks."

"Four and a half weeks?" he said, quite surprised. "Really? I mean, I guess you have but, ah, what does the Forest Service have to do with it and how do you survive? Honey and rice? Is that possible? But, you look good so......"

It was then that she began sharing bits and pieces of her story, after she first apologized for being so rude when their paths first crossed. She was from California, had been a rich girl living with a suppressed sense of adventure until the day she came across a one paragraph description of Sycamore Canyon in a travel magazine. That was what she said anyway and with that she came to Arizona, bought camping equipment, some survival books and supplies and moved out into the canyon. Every week she walked into town for honey and rice to supplement her diet, bought a few books to read at the used book store and that was that.

Reed stared at her and shook his head in disbelief. Her she was, this, nothing rough or tough about her, medium sized woman living all alone out in the wild. A rather sketchy tale but it had to be true, considering the circumstances under which he had met her. Wasn't it? But, being by herself, did she at least own a gun? No, she did not. What for? He was dumbfounded to be sure. Clearly this woman was not stupid and except for current events which she had no interest in, she seemed more than able to hold her own in intelligent conversation. What an enigma. He needed to know more but wasn't quite sure how to go about it.

"I can lend you some books, if you want," he said, however, for lack of something better to start with.

"Maybe," she replied, considering the possibility. "What do you have?"

He tried to give her an idea of what authors and titles he had and they spent another hour talking about that. Then, being bold, he asked her if she would like to come up and look through his private little library and was pleased to have her consent.

"Nice house," she told him once they were there and she looked around.

"Well, you can help yourself to the shower," he offered. "Sleep on the couch if you want. If you're not in a big hurry to get back."

Reed made her coffee, which she hadn't had in a long time, and opened a pack of chocolate chip cookies which she helped herself to. Then she picked out five paperback books and asked him if he could take her down to the dirt road that led to the canyon and they left. But when he got there he refused to stop where she wanted him to and drove her all the way back to the canyon parking lot. It was during that drive that she began asking a series of questions of her own. How did he end up in Jerome? What did he do before that and a lot of semi personal stuff which he answered in good faith. And when she asked what he did with his time he told her he was trying to write a book, which was true but he also, almost told her about his mysterious experience and his desire to experiment further. He wanted to, but didn't. This woman seemed very intriguing, why spoil it.

At the trail head they got out of his old vehicle where she stowed her supplies and the books in her pack, slung it up on her back, looked at him and told him thanks.

"Well, damn," he said. "When do I get to see you again?"

"I don't know. What if I knock on your door one of these days? Maybe in a week."

"What if I came out and picked you up? I could meet you right here."

"It wouldn't work. Once I'm here I completely lose my sense of time. But don't worry. I'll see you. I have to return your books and maybe you'll lend me some more."

Well, damn, Reed thought again. Absolutely. Anything.

Back at home, he floundered, unable to settle down. His earlier obsession with what had happened with Jodi was diluted and partially pushed aside by this new face. Kyara's face. And what a lovely face it was. This attractive, intelligent, mysterious woman whose path he had so coincidentally crossed. But the idea of her being out there in the canyon all alone, sleeping where? On the ground, in a tent or maybe up in some alcove? What about wild animals? There were mountain lions in the area. And even more dangerous, there were always two legged predators out and around. And she didn't even have a gun. None of that made him feel very good at all. But, yeah. None of his business either so he had better try and get over it even though it was going to be a long week before he saw her again. If indeed she was being truthful about that. Meanwhile it wouldn't be a good idea to go back out there and go hiking. If she saw him she might think he was trying to interfere and resent the intrusion. Best to leave it alone. Go hiking somewhere else for now.

FIVE

It wasn't a week, just four days instead, before the door bell rang but it was still a long and thought provoking time, full of questions for Reed. Why would a woman Kyara's age want to spend all those weeks out in the wild, living, for the most part, off of the landscape? Eating what besides rice and honey? He'd forgotten to ask. And doing what besides reading a few books during all those days by herself? What kind of a quest was she on, anyway? Or maybe it wasn't a quest at all. Just some suppressed desire for adventure finally coming to realization in a unique way. Or maybe just an escape. But from what? Or a subconscious desire to end her life in some bizarre way, maybe getting eaten by a wild animal? Jeez, he needed to stop thinking about it, he kept reminding himself. And then, there she was, waiting for him to open the door.

"You're early," he said with a smile as he did so.

"Want me to come back later?"

"Absolutely not. Come on in."

With that she entered and dropped her back pack by the door.

"How about breakfast?" he asked. "It's still morning."

She accepted the invitation but asked if she could clean up first so he showed her the guest bath, gave her soap, shampoo and towels and told her to take her time. Twenty minutes later she reappeared in a fresh shirt, face scrubbed and hair shiny, smelling like bath soap and he drove her down the hill to his favorite coffee shop. Once settled, he began asking her some of the many questions that had been on his mind, the answers to which he would have described as being rather illusive.

"I find it very freeing not to be owning anything," she finally said, however, after he had given up. "Not to be defined by possessions because when I'm out in the canyon I don't have any. Just a tent and a few clothes."

"Well. I guess if you know yourself, the rest doesn't make any difference," he blurted out, then apologized.

"But you're right," she answered. "That doesn't have anything to do with it, does it? Having stuff doesn't make you into more than you are. But not having it doesn't make you anything less, either. So, what about you? Would you say you knew yourself?"

He looked at her, took a drink of his coffee, looked out the window and then back at her, something he was trying to avoid because he always ended up staring into her eyes and had a hard time breaking away, not wanting to embarrass himself at this point. Then he scratched his head and looked back out the window.

"Yeah, well. Actually, there was a point where I thought I did. But now I....," he said with a shrug. "Not...ah, nothing seems that simple anymore."

"What do you mean?" she asked, looking back at him with genuine curiosity.

It might have been an opportunity for him to tell her about what had happened with Jodi because that sure as hell didn't make any sense. But still, it just didn't seem appropriate to talk about the sexual part with someone he was just getting to know. Especially this woman whom he seemed very attracted to and who he had by then decided he had been destined to meet. Dumb as that sounded it still seemed as if there was some pre existing connection between them.

"Well," he said. "I guess I'm still trying to figure it out. Anyway, how about you? Your life seems simple enough."

"Yes. And as you know, very basic. But still very rewarding in its own way. Lot's of time to think."

"Yeah. That's important, isn't it."

From there the conversation wandered a bit and then, for some reason, he was telling her about a re occurring clairvoyant dream he had had some years ago. Always a dark night along a narrow winding road. Red flashing lights, an accident scene. A warning. Not for him but for someone he worked with. But never enough clarity to follow through on.

"It was very disturbing at the time," he said.

"I can imagine. But seriously. What do you think a clairvoyant dream really means?"

"It was giving me a warning."

"Yes, but something else. What do you think makes it possible?"

"I'm not sure. I guess it just happens. What do you think?"

"Well, since it is a prediction about the future, then maybe the future already exists."

"Okay. That's an interesting thought. So something in the future sends a message back into the past and someone picks up on it."

"Maybe. Maybe someone connected to an upcoming event can see into the future and pick up on it."

"And in that case, me. But why me and not her?"

"I don't know. Maybe she had the same dream. Did you

ever ask her?"

"No. That never occurred to me. How about you? Anything like that?"

"Nothing sinister. Nothing that could even be called predictive. But there are those other little coincidences."

"How so?"

"That's what brought me here," she said. "Remember?"

"I do and I'm glad. Any regrets?"

"Not yet," she said with a smile.

"So, does that mean you believe in fate?"

"Like what? Higher destiny? Not at all. That would mean that everything is all planned out ahead of time, leaving us without choice and nothing to do but play out some previously laid down chain of events."

"What about blind luck? Do you think there is such a thing?"

"Do you?"

"Not at all. That is kind of in the same category as higher destiny because it couldn't be accounted for otherwise. No, I'm more inclined to go with that saying that says, nothing by chance except I don't mean higher destiny or fate. I guess I can't really express it very well."

"What if I said that I believe we are in touch with the universe in ways were aren't even aware of most of the time. But because of it we bring things into our lives, or not, that we wish to experience or not experience."

Reed pondered the concept for several moments. "Isn't that interesting. That says that we are then in charge of our own destiny. Is that what you mean?"

"Something like that, yes."

"Which is what keeps the person not ready to die from getting on the fatal plane that's going to crash, or, not going to choir practice on time?"

"Good. You're familiar with that story. Anything like that ever happen to you?" she asked.

"I missed a flight once that did go down. At the time I wrote it off as just being lucky."

"Not divine intervention?"

Reed laughed. "Hardly," he said. "God doesn't speak to me directly, either, like some people claim happens to them."

"Yes, that is a bit demented. Certainly delusional."

"I know. But now that you've said it, I guess I would have to agree that we are connected to the universe in more ways than we realize."

"So, other than missing a fatal plane crash and having a precognitive dream, have you had any other things happen?"

Holy, jeez, he said to himself. Did I ever, and thought about Jodi and the silver brooch he still had. But that experience was still far too absurd for him to want to share it with anyone just yet so he asked her to tell him about some of hers, instead. Clearly she had or it wouldn't have been a subject for discussion.

"I will," she assured him. "But first tell me some of yours."

"Are you sure? They don't seem so important. I'd rather hear yours."

"No. You first. Please."

"Okay, well.....Yeah. How about this one. A few years ago my ex wife and I were boating off the California coast, which we did a lot. This particular day it was late and we were tired. But, just as I was heading in behind the breakwater to go to the marina, this crazy thought came into my head. In essence it said, go to Port Hueneme, which was down the coast about a mile. Well, what did I want to do that for? It was just an old navy facility. A few rusting hulks of ships in repair. Went there once, never wanted to go back, but I asked my wife if it was okay and turned the boat around because it seemed urgent. Then, coming into the harbor there were a lot of people up on the inner breakwater waving their arms, shouting and pointing. The wind was blowing and the water was choppy so we couldn't hear what they were saying or see anything specific but headed towards where they were pointing and saw a man floating in the water. At first we thought he was dead but we finally got him aboard. He was alive but hypothermic and in a coma so I got on the radio to the harbor master and we rushed him back up the coast to where an ambulance was waiting. Another few minutes and he would have been dead, we were told, as his body core temperature was far into the danger zone. Minutes. Jeez. I always had a very hard time believing that that was all just coincidence."

"And now you know it wasn't."

"Well, probably not. I can't be sure. But I've always gotten intuitive bursts that just seem to come along. Do you get those too?"

"Of course. Most people do. The hard part is learning to listen and put them in practice."

"For sure," Reed said, and then he laughed.

"What? Tell me."

"Yeah. Now I call them, turn in here, messages."

"Which means what?"

"A few years ago I made a loop around the country in my old truck and ended up in Florida. And when I got there I decided I wanted to swim with the dolphins. Not in an aquarium, but out in the ocean. So, I was cruising down the road on the way to Key West, not knowing just how I'd make it happen, but confident that I could. I was on one of the big Keys, Key Largo, I think, when I got this message which literally said, turn in here. This little road off to the right. So, I did and it led to an old house but no one was around. But there was a boardwalk going off into the wetlands so I walked down it. At the end was a huge wire cage as big as a barn and several people rushing around inside, trying to catch wild pelicans. One of the women there looked at me and said I was just in time. Get busy."

"Okay, but why are we doing this, I soon asked. Well, a hurricane was coming. The place was a bird sanctuary and all the pelicans were rescued birds that had injuries of one kind or another. They had to be caught because they couldn't be left in the cage during the storm. Even if the wind didn't blow the big wire cage away it would at least blow the birds around inside it and injure them more or kill them. They had to be taken down to the house and put in the basement until the storm was over. So there I was, catching pelicans. And when we were done this same lady asked me if I had heard about the baby whale."

"A baby sperm whale had beached itself and was brought to another rescue group back down the road the way I had come. It was in the channel that crossed the island behind the Hilton Hotel so off I went. The whale was about twelve feet long, badly malnutritioned and couldn't stay afloat without the life preserver someone had made for it. A group of people were attending it, feeding it gallons of baby formula through a long plastic hose, rolling it over to burp it and moving its fins and tail to help keep it warm and to keep it from getting stiff. So, I spent the night taking turns in the water swimming with it and by morning it was somewhat better. The storm had also changed course by then and except for rain and light wind, had passed on by. I got a few hours sleep in my truck and then told the guy in charge where I was headed. He found a scrap of paper, wrote a name and number on it and gave it to me. It was a woman in Key West who owned a boat. She took me out in the Gulf where a whole pod of dolphins showed up and swam around me when I got in the water."

"That's a very interesting story."

"It was for me. Needless to say, but when something says turn in here, or its equivalent, I try to listen. And, actually, now that I think of it, that's almost exactly how I ended up in Sycamore Canyon and met you. Something kept telling me to go there. Must have been to meet you. Am I right?"

Kyara looked at him, smiled her cute little smile and shrugged.

"Is that what you think?" she asked.

"I'm beginning to. No. I'm sure of it. What do you think?"

"I guess we'll find out, won't we?" she said with a teasing look in her eyes. "Who knows? But I'm really glad you came," she said and that was the end of any deeper conversation.

The rest of their time together was chatty but superficial and ended out at the canyon parking area where he dropped her off. Before he could ask when she was coming back into town, she had her pack on and was moving towards the trailhead. There she turned to him and said, see you later, as she tapped her forehead and made a gesture towards him. Then she was gone.

When Reed got home he went on-line to see if any of the books she had suggested during their talk were available at the local library. Two of them were and the rest would be sent over from Prescott on the exchange program. With that he began searching for more information on the same subject, found a few articles and began reading. Later he had some dinner, watched the news and then sat outside until past dark. Then he went back inside to the dining table where he kept his computer and sat there for a long time thinking and leaning back in his chair. And then, what was that? He sat upright and stared. My god! Kyara was standing there, right at the end of the table looking at him. At least she seemed to be. He looked more carefully. It was Kyara all right. But a spooky version of her, not completely solid because he could also see through her to some extent. He shook his head in disbelief, trying to clear his mind. At this point she smiled at him, touched her forehead as she had done earlier out at the canyon, waved at him and disappeared. My god, he thought. This was too much. Now he was hallucinating.

Reed was up early the next morning and out the door, driving to the canyon. There he slipped into his day pack and headed down the slope. At the bottom he went about a mile, stopped and called out to Kyara. Then he walked some more and did it again. And again. Two hours later, having crossed the creek four different times, he had to have hiked at least five miles in and still no sign of her. Maybe he had taken a wrong turn. The canyon had branched off a long ways back but he figured that she would have chosen to stay somewhere along the creek for a source of water, so he kept going. Another half an hour later he was skirting a rock wall, being careful not to slip and go over the edge into the stream when she called to him from somewhere over his head. Then she told him how to find his way up.

It was not an easy climb but at last, there she was, sitting on the remains of an ancient wall built into an alcove at least sixty feet above the creek bed. She laughed when he finally came into view.

"I was expecting you," she said, "but you didn't have to tell the whole world I was out here. I could hear you yelling three miles back."

"I'm sorry. I guess I was afraid I wouldn't find you."

"It's okay. I just don't want the forest service to know I'm here. There's a two week limit on camping."

"Oops. I forgot. Well, it's not like you're easy to locate. This place is completely hidden. How did you ever find it?" Reed asked as he looked around. Inside the fallen structure were her few possessions, scattered about. Sleeping bag on the dirt floor, back pack, rolled up tent, food supplies, the books he had lent her and a small fire pit. It didn't get much simpler than that. For a moment he felt a touch of sadness as he looked at it.

"I guess I have good survival instincts," she said in response. "Sit down. Would you like some hot tea?"

"Tea?" he questioned, looking around. How was that possible?

"No problem," she stated as she quickly had a small fire going and pan of water over it that came to a fast boil. This she poured into a large aluminum cup with a tea bag in it.

"Hope you don't mind sharing. It's the only one I have," she said as she held it out. "Go ahead, have the first sip."

He took a small drink and handed it back, then unzipped his pack. "Almost forgot," he said as he took out a large zip lock bag full of already buttered English muffins and opened it. "Have one," he told her.

Two muffins each and two cups of tea later Reed looked at her and said, "Tell me that what I saw last night was real. Or am I going crazy?'

"I'm glad you noticed."

"You noticed that I noticed? So it was you. But how? That's not possible to...."

"Well, maybe not. But you were at the table using your computer. And if I wasn't able to notice that you noticed, why bother. It's pointless."

"Yeah. I suppose. But... Damn. So if I saw what I think I saw, how did you do that anyway?"

She stared back at him for a moment as if studying him.

"Okay," she said. "I think you're probably ready to take the next step."

"Really? What next step? What does that mean?"

"Nothing exactly. Just a comment. Have you ever been to Australia?"

"Three times, actually. But I never met any... ahh, ha. Is that where you're going with this?"

"With what?"

"Aborigines. Unfortunately the only ones I met were those who didn't seem to know who they were any longer. Beaten down by the whites, lost, drinking too much. Even the ones in the outback. I never got on a reservation, however. But I was always intrigued by the stories about them. Jeez, is that what you did?"

"What?"

"Project an image of yourself. Like they do when they are in trouble. Multiple images so some big white hunter doesn't know which one to shoot at or decides to leave them alone because he's afraid they might all be real."

"Well, it's not quite the same. They are just projecting apparitions. I projected both my consciousness and an apparition of myself which you were able to see."

"Yeah, but that's, ahhh... Seriously? How did you do it?"

"All in good time. First, do your homework."

"What... You mean the books you suggested I read. Some of them are in the library. I'll pick them up on the way home."

"Good. Just remember, however, they were all written by people."

"Which means?"

"Writer's have personal biases and mental and emotional limitations, so keep that in mind.

"For example?"

Many people are stuck with the idea that there is only one past which, if tampered with, would have dire consequences for the present."

"The, go back and do away with your grandfather so you never are born, idea?"

"Exactly."

24

"So why don't you just tell me some of this stuff."

"You're not ready yet."

"Really? Ready for what? Why not?"

"Well, I'm sure you took calculus in college. Could you have understood it without having had algebra first?"

"It's highly unlikely but how do you know all this stuff? You didn't exactly answer my question about how you did what you did last night."

"I know and I can't give you an explanation you'd understand unless..."

"Unless I do my homework."

"Something like that so why don't you let me walk you back to your vehicle. We can talk on the way."

Okay, Reed said to himself. She had just let him know that their time together was over for now. And what was happening here? Who was this person, anyway? Not exactly your ordinary little ex schoolteacher off on a nature trip. Except she did know a lot about the various kinds of plant life that was not only edible but also told him how to cook it and what it tasted like and what it was good for as a natural remedy. She also pointed out coyote tracks and the paw prints of a mountain lion which again made him feel for her safety which she in turn assured him was not at risk. Not convinced, he still let it go, however, because, who was he to argue with her? Obviously she knew a lot of things he didn't understand at all and before he realized it, they were at the parking lot. It was then that he looked at her in a very perplexed way.

"What is really going on here?" he asked. "I know that I know you from somewhere even though I don't seem to know you at all because we only just met. And why are you so much like my old girlfriend when you're not, and ..."

"Like Jodi."

"How did you know her name?"

"I think you told me."

"I don't remember it. But it doesn't matter except that must be why I want to kiss you so damned badly. What do you think?"

"Probably. But that will also have to wait until later," she said as she smiled up at him, put her hand on his check for a brief moment, then backed up, touched her forehead again like she had done before and said she would see him later.

SIX

Bleary eyed, weary and unshaven, Reed spent the next series of days reading and thinking. He completely lost track of time, forgot a dentist appointment, forgot to pay some overdue bills, almost forgot who he was. And in the end, what did he have? Nothing specific. Nothing he could put to use in everyday life. Not yet, anyway, but he felt something was coming together somewhere beneath the surface. Hopefully, in time, it would clarify itself. Time. What about time? An illusion?

Does all time really exist at once so that we only seem to move through it from past to present to future because our minds are not equipped to experience it any other way? But if it did exist on this other scale, why all the obsession about going back to the past? What about the future? That should be just as accessible. And what about sideways? Were there other dimensions to time, too. What if he could go off to the right or the left, whatever that meant in this context? What would a person find there? He was sitting outside in a lounge chair when all these thoughts reappeared in his mind and kept going round and round. It was late and dark out but a billion or so stars were all visible and he gazed up at them as his mind worked. Then he fell asleep and began dreaming of Kyara.

Reed stood on the ledge outside the alcove where Kyara was snuggled up in her sleeping bag. It didn't occur to him that it was very dark out but somehow he could still see her clearly. Then, somewhat shocked at what happened next, he saw her form rise up above the sleeping bag, turn in the air and float over to stand in front of him.

"Hi, Reed," she said. "I was hoping you would come. Sit down here on the wall and we'll talk."

As they sat, he turned to her.

"Wow," he said. "If this is a dream, it sure is realistic."

"It's not a dream, so please relax, try to enjoy the experience and I'll explain. Are you okay?"

"Yes. I think so. But this is really weird. Oh, oh. I think I get it. It's an out-of-body thing."

"It is. How does that make you feel?"

"Pretty excited. My first one."

"No, not your first. You do it all the time. Everyone does. They just don't remember it just like most people don't remember their dreams. Some people are so frightened by their dreams that the close them out and deny they even have any. But it doesn't change anything. The difference is that you have been reading about it and you were open minded enough to let the possibility in, all coupled with the strong desire to see me again. So, here you are."

"It was strong all right, but..."

"It's really something to think about, isn't it? Here you are. Your body is where? Back in bed?"

"Outside in the lounge chair."

"In the lounge chair. So, what about this? Your brain is part of your body, so are your eyes and ears. But you can still think, have awareness and see me and hear me. It's very dark out and since I'm not physical, I can't make any sound. So why is that possible?"

"I... I don't know but if I am here, fully aware, then this must be the real me. And since I am not my body, I have an identity independent of that. And if that is so, then what is my body if my consciousness is here?"

"Well, as you might expect, it is rather complicated. For now, however, let's say that your body is a psychic creation, projected into the physical universe by your intent. The pattern or blueprints, if you will, exist on a different level. You come into the world for a reason. It becomes a setting or a backdrop for working out challenges and hopefully evolving into something better. You do this through the time period you choose to live in, the parents you have, the social conditions in the country you are born into and a whole lot more."

"Sounds complicated."

"Yes, but understandable if you give it some time."

"Well, it clarifies one thing. If I choose to be born and I choose the conditions then I can't say I didn't ask to be born and use that as an excuse for bad behavior like some people do."

"No you couldn't. If people understood that and realized that if they are born into poverty or war then they have set those conditions up as a personal challenge for themselves and the goal is to work it through and learn from it. The objective is to experience more than one side of a situation. Rich, one lifetime. Poor another. Slave and slave holder. Black and white, killer and victim."

"Sounds reasonable but if that is the way it works, why the need to get so completely immersed in all those lifetimes?

"Because it's like the white man who dyed his skin dark and went to live in the ghetto for a year to see the other side of things. Certainly he gained some insight by doing so but he could never get the same depth of experience that a black person would have because he knew he was not really black and trapped in being black for the rest of his life. It's like having a role in a stage play. The more the actors can immerse themselves in the role, the better the performance, so, to gain the most from any one life experience you have to believe it's really, real. Which it is in its own way but most people aren't able to see that until after it's over."

"Well, speaking of something being over...."

"Jodi?"

"Jodi. Right. I never really told you about her but you still seem to, ah..., I mean.... there's a connection between the two of you, isn't there?"

"In a particular way, yes, so you don't have to lie to yourself about that. And I'm not trying to be difficult but I'll explain it to you soon. Someday when we are back in our bodies so you can understand it better. As for now, since you've done a lot of research, what else have you become interested in?"

"You, primarily. Other than than that I'm intrigued with the idea of being able to visit alternate realities to see what kind of person I would have turned out to be if I had made different decisions. Assuming they exist which I now think I do after....."

"After your Jodi experience."

"Damn. After my Jodi experience which you also seem to know about so.... jeezz woman. Was that an experience with some alternate of hers and is she somehow connected to you? How could that be?"

"You're very astute. I was hoping you would figure it out by yourself. But like I said, the rest will have to wait. As for your own greater existence, eventually you will become aware of all that anyway but in the meantime your decision to do it now will certainly have an impact on your present life. I hope you're ready for it."

"Me too. This thing about my brain and my mind being different things is also very astounding. But now that it has come up I remember what several, ah, physicists, philosophers, thinking people like John Bell, Bohm, Einstein, Bohr and others have said about such things. Like, beyond the brain is the mind. The mind is not physical. Consciousness creates reality, creation is an act of thought and the face nature shows depends on the questions we ask. That's all I remember right now."

"But it's a good start. And what are some of the implications of that? Name one."

"Okay. How about, when I die I don't have to have some butcher standing by to cut off my head and drop it in a flask of liquid nitrogen to preserve it so my brain can be reinstalled in some clone in the future so I'll be alive again. Recording all my brain wave activity and putting it on a CD won't work either. That's so damned silly because while the body may die, I still go on living no matter what. How did present day thinking get so far off track?"

"Because confused people keep inventing over simplified stories to explain things they aren't capable of understanding which a lot of other people then blindly accept because it's the easy way out. But, I still think that most people know what the truth may be in some fundamental way but just aren't in touch with it on the conscious level. Too bad because there are so many obvious clues as to what it's really all about everywhere one looks. But most people get so bogged down in trying to sort through all the other misconceptions, they don't see them. Or refuse to because they conflict with what all the gurus in their lives have told them, scientific or otherwise."

"Yeah. I've been there. But I can't say I ever liked it."

"Yes, but you're going back to take another look. Intuitively, you always understood that you were far more than just your physical self and now you are pretty well convinced that physical death is not the end of one's identity. And you will always keep searching. None of that religious mumbo jumbo for you. Or New Age nonsense. Or presumptuous, near-sighted scientific pronouncement. It doesn't work. This alone will allow you to head down another path with your life and you should continue to do well."

"Thank you. You sound like my my coach, my teacher, my mentor and my muse. Are you my muse?"

"Maybe. But if I am just remember that the student's job is to try and surpass the teacher."

"I suppose, but right now I feel like I'm so damned far behind. I'd just like to catch up a bit."

"Well, on some other level maybe you already have. You've just forgotten what you already know. Maybe your goal for now is to re-assimilate that knowledge so you can achieve some even higher level of achievement this time around. And get that other thought out of your, ah, mind."

"What thought?"

"You're wondering what it might be like to kiss me in an out-of-body state just like you've been wanting to do when we are together in body."

"Damn. Is it that obvious? I'm embarrassed. Since you can see me, am I blushing?"

"In effect, yes. It's rather cute."

"Cute? Jeez. It's just that you are even more gorgeous than ever, having the ethereal look that you do now and that's not meant to be a joke."

"Thank you. That's very flattering. Now I feel like I'm the one blushing. But it's also time you went back."

"Why? This is just getting interesting."

"I know, but it's not good to be away from your body for long periods of time."

"Really? Or are you just saying that to get rid of me

because I almost forgot I had one."

"It's true. Seriously. Without your consciousness in the body, the body lies in one position too long. The muscles get stiff and the circulation slows."

"Okay, I'd like to be able to move when I get there. How do I get back?"

"Very simple. But first, tomorrow when you get up, also start learning what you can about remote viewing and we'll talk about it the next time I come in. Okay. Now think about your body. What were you wearing when you went outside and sat down in the lounge chair?"

SEVEN

"All right. Let's see what you can do," Kyara told Reed some days later as they sat at his dining room table with paper and pencil in front of them.

"And don't worry. I'm not going to ask you to meditate and let your mind go wandering aimlessly around. Instead, simply close your eyes, take a few deep breaths to relax, shut off all the internal dialogue and remain still. Now, imagine yourself in a place where time does not exist and has no meaning. A place where your imagination is unbounded and you can do almost anything you can visualize. Okay, give it a try and nod when you think you are there."

Reed obediently closed his eyes, took deep breaths and shut down his thoughts. Not always an easy thing to do as he knew from experience but concentrated on the process anyway. Most interesting. On one level he was completely aware of gaining control over his conscious mind, stopping all verbalization and placing himself in a state of limbo while on another level, working away in the background, he was aware of that awareness. He nodded his head.

"Good," Kyara said. "Now think of the alcove out in the canyon where I'm staying. You've been there both physically and in an out-of-body state but this time it will be something still different. Like the aborigine, you can send psychic projections of yourself to other physical locations. If you know how to do it and they are intense enough, other people will actually be able to see them."

"Like I saw you here the other night."

"Exactly. But then, left alone, they continue off on their own or dissipate without returning. Additionally, as you now also know, you can go somewhere out-of body and return with or without conscious memory of the episode. Additionally, however, your consciousness, in and of itself, has its own mobility. This is what we are going to try today. The goal is to project your conscious awareness out into the canyon, stay connected to it, see what's there and be able to describe it here. Forget about space and time. They are necessary illusions that we need to function in the physical world. But your present goal is to transcend that, making space and time collapse into a medium through which you can travel simply by thinking about where you want to go, so think about that and nod again when you're ready to try."

Reed sat there for what seemed to him and extremely long time but what was actually only a few seconds. Then he nodded.

"Now," Kyara said. "Visualize being at the alcove like you're suspended in space a few feet away out in front of it and tell me what you see."

Reed concentrated and did his best at describing what he thought he might be seeing but Kyara interrupted him half way through.

"Stop. You're only working from memory. Keep your eyes shut and let yourself relax for a while. Then try again," she said and waited.

Finally Reed decided he was ready and nodded and she told him to begin. "Just allow yourself to be there for a while first and just look without verbalizing. Study the details, let it come alive without describing it to yourself. Hold yourself there for a moment, then, without being analytical, describe it to me."

Again Reed tried and again she stopped him.

"Do you have any coffee?" she asked him after he opened his eyes. "You must. Make it strong and put some sugar in it."

"How about you?" he asked. "Would you like a donut? I just bought them this morning. No, maybe not. I'm sorry. Let's see what else I have."

"A donut would be great. I haven't had one in months."
"Are you sure? I could at least have gotten some bagels."
"I prefer the donuts."

Two cups of coffee and a donut each, they were still sitting outside on the deck an hour later where they had gone for their break. Reed again tried to get her to tell him more about herself, but with little success. She wasn't rude about it, just hesitant, so he let it pass. She was there with him, what more could he ask. Not only did she seem to have the most beautiful voice he had ever heard, she was intelligent and quick and physically very appealing, even in her oversized shirt, jeans and hiking boots. Wow, he thought, and wondered what would happen if he tried to kiss her again. Well, maybe later, after they were done experimenting, he thought and squirmed.

Back inside, back at the table, sitting across from each other again, this time it was different for Reed. Very subtly and difficult to define, different. But there nevertheless, on the edge of things, barely discernible. What was it?
"There's something on top of the wall," he finally said out loud, surprised at his own words. "Something white."
"Are you sure?"
"Yes."
"Can you get a little closer? Just move in. Can you see it better now?"
"I think it's a sheet of paper. It is a sheet of paper. With small rocks holding down the corners. And... and it has something written on it. It says..." Reed stopped, opened his eyes, looked at Kyara and grinned at her.
"What?" she asked.
"You did it."
She grinned back at him, very pleased, because that was what she had written on the paper before she put it up there, hoping he might be able to find it. 'You did it.' And he had, except that he then became skeptical of his own success.
"How do we know I didn't just read your mind? You wrote it, so you knew what it was, and maybe that's what I picked up

on. I mean, I don't mean to sound critical but..." he said and then regretted it.

"You don't. By all means be skeptical and demand proof. But, be willing to accept it when you find it. That's why I think you might be good at this. You have a nice blend of openness and skepticism. So, just to make sure your projection was valid, let's try something else. Have you ever been to the Cottonwood airport?"

"I have."

"Okay, forget that. How long has it been since you've been inside a church?"

"Not long enough. Maybe twenty years."

"Good. Where's your phone book?"

Reed went to the kitchen and brought it back to the table. Kyara opened it to the yellow pages, turned to churches and ran her finger down the list.

"How about Catholic?" she asked. "Have you ever been in a Catholic church?"

"Not that I can remember."

"Well, maybe this is your chance. There's one at 927 Riordan Road in Cottonwood. Do you know where that's at?"

"No."

"So , let's try it. You sit at one end of the table, I'll sit at the other. Use the paper and make a sketch of what you see. First the outside, next the inside. Then we'll compare."

Reed watched Kyara shut her eyes, seem to concentrate, open her eyes again and almost immediately begin to draw. Jeez, he thought. He'd never be able to keep up to her. But he at least had to try so he picked up the pencil, held it over the paper, shut his own eyes, told himself to relax and when he felt his mind had cleared he repeated the address of the church to himself. At first there was nothing and he began to worry. Then he thought he heard Kyara telling him to stop, relax, and try again. He did and immediately after the break something actually happened. He wasn't out-of-body, he knew that. He felt as if he were viewing the scene through a telescope from above, instead, knew he was much too far away and moved in closer. And there it was.

A church, for sure, with a large cross up on the spire above the roof. Eyes still closed, he tried to draw but felt it wasn't correct. Then he concentrated with everything he could, determined not to lose what he had, opened his eyes and focused on the paper. His hand began to move as he made rapid, clear lines on it.

When he stopped drawing he heard Kyara tell him to turn the paper over and then go back to the site and go inside the church. He flipped the page without looking up at her, and shut his eyes again. It took him a while but damned if he wasn't there, just inside the front door, looking down the long aisle at the raised alter. But how would he ever be able to sketch it. Rows of wooden pews along each side, stained glass windows up front, on his left and, and, and. Great, but was there anything really significant and unusual that stood out which he might use to really validate his experience? He didn't see anything. Then he looked down at the floor. The entry and the aisle way were carpeted. And right there in front of him was a barely visible dark stain in the fabric. No, it was a badly worn spot instead, about a foot in diameter where the backing was beginning to show thru. With that he opened his eyes and started to draw.

Reed was a bit awed when they compared notes. His drawings were very basic in content while hers were more detailed but in general, they were very close. Did that mean he had succeeded, or had they both failed? The one really puzzling thing was a difference in their overhead, exterior views. She had shown a room extending out from the right side of the building while he showed it off to the left. How had he gotten that wrong, he wondered. He must have. As for the interior, they both had made floor plan like drawings where hers again had much more detail than his. That done, they got in his old truck.

"Well, I'll be damned," Reed uttered and shook his head in dismay once they were inside the church. "Look at that," he said as he pointed to the worn spot in the entry way carpet. As for the difference in their overhead, exterior views, they were both right and both wrong. There was a room extending out from both sides of the building. After they had checked out the otherwise correctness of their sketches they went back to Reed's house to discuss it further.

"How did you learn how to do this?" Reed asked her after he had made them more coffee and they sat across from each other at the dining table.

"When I was a kid. We lived out in the country and there wasn't anyone my age to play with so I used to sit outside on the porch in the summer and imagine myself going to all the places I had read about. I also used to think about what it would be like to go shopping at the mall in the nearest big town that I had never been to. It was just a fantasy game but the more I played it, the more real it seemed to become. Then, in the fall, my parents took me there because my father wanted a certain kind of boots he couldn't find elsewhere. When we got there they were trying to find the store directory but I looked around and told them I knew right where the shoe store was and walked toward it. And there it was, up on the second floor at the end. Fortunately they were quite open minded about the whole thing and before we left I was able to show them where the ice cream store was and a dozen other places. I even told them what flavors of ice cream they had and how much everything cost before we got to it."

"I was also very fortunate in that my father thought I was very gifted and always listened. Our ranch was several hundred acres in size, hilly, and a lot of it was pasture. One evening the cows didn't come back to the barnyard by themselves and he asked if I could tell him where they were so he wouldn't have to spend so much time looking for them. Strangely enough, I visualized myself up on the hill looking around and saw them. They were all milling around in a tight group like something was wrong and then I saw a black bear in the trees not far away. Needless to say my father grabbed his rifle and we got in the jeep. I think I was eleven at the time. My father sold the farm when I was twelve and we moved into town where he started a very successful business. Then I stopped projecting because my life was suddenly full of other people and things to do. Luckily enough, however, I never lost that ability."

"What about consciously going out-of-body? How long have you been able to do that?"

"Again, as long as I can remember. Sometimes I did one and sometimes the other. Both work for remote viewing but projection of consciousness is safer for the body in case it should come into danger. Anyway, you should be proud. You have done both quite adeptly."

"Looks like I did something, all right, but it seems so bizarre."

"So, keep practicing. You're on the internet. Pick some place you've never been before, like Perth, Australia and try to project. Look for aerial views of buildings or street layouts or a manufacturing complex. When you get something, go to the Google Earth website and check it out. The resolution is surprisingly good for satellite imagery."

"How do you know about satellite imagery?"

"Well, I haven't always lived so modestly."

"Okay, So how do you know I have never been to Perth?"

"You told me."

"I did? I don't remember doing that."

"Okay, doesn't matter. You haven't and it was just a suggestion," she said with a small smile. "You're going to be very good at remote viewing."

"You mean I have potential?"

"Something like that."

"Is that why you're helping me?"

"That's part of it."

"And the rest is...?

"Part of the rest is that you have an inquiring mind. The rest of the rest is, I'm not ready to tell you about it yet."

"Hmm. Well, what part of my inquiring mind do you like? I mean, what am I inquiring about that you think is so good? My growing interest in you? You're a very intriguing person and a damned good looking woman."

"Thank you but that wasn't what I was referring to. Other than that you seem very intrigued with mobility of consciousness for one thing. And I don't think that's something recent for you."

"It's not. I've been bumping up against that one for years."

"In what way?"

"Physical evidence. Experiments have shown that people can influence the decay rates of radioactive isotopes, the acidity of a solution, the roll of dice, things like that. Then there is the one where a house cat was able to control the on-off times of a heat lamp when he was cold. Beyond that there are places like Coral Castle in Florida where a hundred pound man was able to move multi ton rocks without the use of cranes or heavy equipment. And what about those, up to two hundred ton dressed stones moved into place centuries ago. The Wailing Wall in Jerusalem, the Giza Pyramids, Machu Pichu and that big ruin on the hill behind Cuzco. Someplace I ran across the explanation that the builders, 'sang them in place.' In other words used sound or mind power? So, why can't I make a pencil move across the table or consciously levitate my body? Seems like I should be able to do that. Somehow I managed to get my body to Los Angeles and back. Or did I? If you could just explain that one to me then I might be better able to understand a lot of other things too. Can you?"

"Maybe. Want me to try?"

"Absolutely."

"First, I'd have to ask, what causes your body to be here to begin with?"

"A fertilized egg," he said as a joke.

"Right," she laughed. "But we're not going to have a discussion about which came first, the chicken or the egg."

"I know. Sorry."

"It's okay. The fertilized egg is a necessary step in the process but it goes far beyond that. Which is why we need to get back to some things we talked about before. Since you are a conscious being and the conscious self can leave the body and come back to it and if consciousness can influence or affect matter, then what? How did you really come into the physical world?"

"By creating myself? Mind over matter?"

"And what is matter?"

"Certainly more than some form of coalesced potential

energy. An atom has to be more than a group of inert particles orbiting around other inert particles. If matter can be influenced by thought, then it must also have some level of awareness. Especially when it responds, not chaotically at some higher energy level, but in very specific ways, according to the desires of the mind trying to bring about the effect. And, since at the core of things, all matter is composed of the same building blocks, the awareness that it has is not a function of its atomic configuration but is a characteristic of matter on the most fundamental level. Which says that matter is composed of something else. Energy, in other words, since matter and energy are just different forms of the same thing, which really explains nothing because we run out of words to describe things with. At least I do."

"Well, maybe we could just say that everything is alive in some sense. Everything has awareness. And consciousness is the fundamental building block of the universe. A greater reality exists behind the physical one and conscious intent and desire convert the energy of this greater reality into physical form through power of mind and the cooperation of that which makes it up. Regardless, whether realized or not, statements about matter coming into or leaving the physical plane are an indirect acknowledgment that another plane, or planes, exist behind the physical one and that everything that exists in the physical plane has it origins elsewhere."

"I know you told me this before but I guess I didn't get the full impact of it at the time. What you are saying is that we are first of all psychic beings whose primary existence is in some other realm than the physical. Beings who are able to create physical forms for ourselves so we can immerse ourselves in the physical world and do it in such a way so that when we are here, our focus is purposely narrowed to the point where we see this as the only reality."

"From birth to death, yes, for the most part. But the more you progress spiritually, the more you become aware of what lies behind the physical world."

At this point Reed leaned forward in his chair so he was

closer to Kyara who sat across from him and looked at her very intently.

"Are you sure all you did was teach grammar school?" he asked. "Where did you learn all this stuff?

"When did I ever say I taught school?"

"I guess you didn't, but... My apologies. It's just that....well... ," he said and stalled out. He couldn't go on. Staring at her, he was falling into the depths of her eyes, feeling lost.

She stayed with his gaze, didn't look away but didn't say anything either. Not for several moments. Then she broke the silence.

"It's okay," she said as she reached across and held his hands. "And you're right. We have something very special between us. We have been together before."

"I know. Jodi. And now your alternate self is off living with my alternate self."

"That's true but it is such a minor part of it. And by the way, before I forget. You were right in leaving her."

"How so?"

"She made a mistake. She didn't think she'd end up falling in love with you like she did which is why she wasn't completely honest up front. And even if she had had the courage to apologize after it came to light, you would have had a problem continuing the relationship. But don't worry. It was devastating for her but she needed to learn."

"Really? Well, that certainly explains my feelings but why can't I remember the rest of our lives together?"

"Because this time you chose not to. You had other goals in mind."

"But when I look at you and when I'm around you my feelings are so strong. I just want to hold you and kiss you and, and.... dammit Kyara," he said as he got up and came around the table to her where she rose to meet him.

Their mouths found each other as fingers found buttons and bare skin met bare skin and passion rumbled and ecstasy rose and flowed through them, over and over where they lay on the thick carpet. At last, when it was over, Reed sat upright as she backed up to him, his arms around her, his face nuzzled into her long hair where he kissed her neck and held her close. A long time later she whispered quietly. "Unbelievable. It only gets better."

"Really?" he said, "because I don't know how it could get any better than that. But it's not fair that you get to remember something that good and I don't."

"Maybe not but I hope you don't forget this one."

"Never."

"Want to do it again?"

"Damn right."

The sun was setting before they were finally dressed and outside to see the sky create an appropriate grand finale to their eloquent, reenacted declaration of love. This time Reed sat in an over sized lounge chair with Kyara backed up to him again so he could have his arms around her. Then, after the drama in the sky had played itself out he began with his questions.

"Since you seem to know, tell me what my goals were this time around. And tell me how you know."

"Ask yourself."

"Ask myself what?"

"What you are doing here. Not in rural Arizona but in the now twenty first century in a country with a stable government and a high level of freedom. Why the parents you had and the economic level? What were the challenges that set up for you? Why not some barbaric country in Africa? Or in the turmoil and uncertainty of Palestine or high up in the Andes mountains. Assume that none of it was coincidence and ask yourself why. What is it that you could learn from your own specific situation? Were you friends with your parents or did they often seem like strangers? Were there deep conflicts that needed work on? With them and the people you crossed paths with along the way? What special connections, good or bad? This is where the answers to your questions lie. It's best if you try and figure it out for yourself."

Reed groaned.

"Well, not tonight," he said. "Want to try the bedroom for a while?"

"I thought you'd never ask."

EIGHT

"Actually I don't think I had a very specific goal in mind this time around," Reed told her in the morning while they were having a very late breakfast. "I didn't start out with a over riding desire to be a doctor or an opera singer or president, a business tycoon or a religious zealot like some people do. Nor was it to end up with a wife, a house on a quiet street, two kids, two cars, financial security and bingo in my old age. On the other hand, living to a hundred and twenty, ending up in a rocking chair on the front porch side by side with you would be a great way to spend the later years."

"Thank you. Is that a proposal?"

"Absolutely."

"I'll keep it in mind. But if we keep making out the way we're doing, we'll never live that long."

"That might be an even better alternative. What do you think?"

"I think that as soon as you finish your coffee, we need to go back to bed."

It was nearly dark before they finally showered together and got dressed. Then they went out to eat. It wasn't the best of places for intimate conversation but such a place really didn't exist in that part of the world either. But it was reasonably quiet and private and Reed still had a backload of questions on his mind. Where was she living? Didn't she say, California?

"Hollywood Hills. I have my own house and I live alone. Still single. And, like I said, my father was highly successful so I have a very generous endowment and don't have to work. But I did spend six years at UCLA although things have changed dramatically in the academic world since, ahhh, since..... hmmm."

"Since what?"

"Since, ahh, in fifty years since you... please, Reed. Don't be upset with me. I should have told you sooner. I intended to but we got so involved. Re involved, and..."

"And what? Am I not going to like what you have to say? Don't worry. Whatever it is, it's okay."

"I hope so because I'm from the future."

"The future?"

"Yes. Your future, this one."

Wide eyed, he looked across the table at her and shook his head to make sure he was awake. Then he reached for her hand and held it tightly.

"Well, that shoots the hell out of that idea."

"What"

"Well, if the future doesn't exist yet, then you can't really be sitting here with me. Can you? Except that being with you has been the most real thing that has ever happened to me."

"What? You mean the sex?" she asked, teasing him, not answering his questions.

"You're avoiding the issue," he told her and gave her a quick kiss on the cheek.

"I know, but maybe I'm still horny. What about that?"

"Looks like I'd better stop asking questions and pay the check so we can get out of here."

"Are you upset?" she asked once they were settled back in the living room at his house.

"Upset? God, no. I'm... really? How could I be upset? Wherever you're from, you're here now. But fifty years! What an idea. That's fascinating. But.... how is that possible?"

"Hopefully I'll be able to show you one day soon. In many respects it's similar to when you went to see Jodi. Except that was more of a side step in time rather than a journey through time."

"Yes. And it was purely accidental, or something. Because when I tried to do it again, it was a complete failure. Why? How is time travel different than what I did?"

"Actually, it's not. Like they say, time is an illusion. Time doesn't flow. Focus changes instead. It's a gross over simplification to say that all time exists at once because that makes time sound static. It's not. Every moment everywhere in time is alive and dynamic. You can bounce around in time just as in space, have an effect in some other reality and still not upset the over all reality you are living in now. Personally, however, that's something else."

"But the thing that still bothers me the most is, was I really there, in, ahh, bed, ahh, with her? But then, you're here. So if you are from the future and you are here now, body and all, then I must have really been with her, body and all and, ohh jeez," he stammered as his face got red.

"You were. Body and all. And you really had sex with her. But don't be embarrassed. That was an important part of the relationship."

"I know. But..."

"And now you're having sex with me."

"Yes, but it's not the same."

"I know," she said and hugged him tight. "It's love that gives it significance and you weren't in love with her anymore."

"Like I am with you."

"Like you are with me. But you were right to leave her when you did. I hope you know that, too."

"It seemed necessary at the time."

"It was. But like I said before, she really wasn't ready for what you could have given her and it would have been even more hurtful to you if you had stayed with her."

"Yeah, it was already beginning to. Trying to talk to her about anything serious was the hardest part. And the longer it went on, the lonelier I felt. A person shouldn't feel lonely in a relationship. I think that was worse than just being alone."

"I'm sure it was. You were trapped."

"But now that I have you in my life and no matter what happens, no matter how much time I may have to spend alone, I don't think I'll ever feel lonely again."

"I understand. But I was more fortunate. I always knew you existed and that one day we would reconnect. So did you, of course. Just not on a conscious level."

"But how did you find me back here in your past?"

"One step at a time," she said and gave him a quick kiss on the cheek.

"Okay, but I want to be able to do that too."

"I know. Popping in on Jodi like you did was an unexpected fluke. But that's what I like about you. Your immense curiosity. You didn't just write it off as some weird event. It got you started down a whole different path."

"Yeah, but so far not very successful. Visiting Jodi was one thing but ending up on the couch like I did when I tried so hard to check something else out wasn't much of an accomplishment. How about some help?"

"All right. How about a little demonstration as a start?" she said and got to her feet.

"Sure," he said and got up too.

"Good. Now just stay right here. I'm going outside and stand where you can see me while you take off all your clothes."

"Me? What about you?" he smiled and unbuckled his belt as she went outside, closed the sliding glass door behind her and also began to undress.

"Can you hear me?" she said in a loud voice once they were both nude..

"Hold that pose," he said back to her. "I like what I'm seeing."

"Good. Now pay attention," she said as she touched her forehead in that old familiar way as her image quickly became transparent and she disappeared, only to almost instantaneously reappear right in front of him.

"My god," he said after he jumped back a step. "Holy damn."

"Take it easy, Reed. It's really me. Touch me and see."

He did, and found her skin to be warm and soft as ever. He touched her face, ran his fingers though her hair and down her back, feeling all her curves, then kissed her on the mouth and bent down and kissed her nipples..

"Wow," he exclaimed. "You're real all right. How did you do that?"

"First things first," she said as she put her arms around him and pulled him down on top of her.

NINE

Reed had no idea how long they had been sitting there wrapped together in a warm blanket outside in the light of the rising, near full moon. It might have been forever and if he had to spend forever doing something, this would be it. Eventually he regained his awareness of the surrounding world to realize that the moon had risen from the horizon, half way to zenith. That would be several hours. But, coming back to reality, Reed still wasn't sure which he wanted the most. To just go on sitting there like they were, in their own kind of ultimate serenity or find out how she was able to disappear from one place and immediately re appear in another. It was then that a coyote began to howl from not far away. Then another answered from up on the hill and it wasn't long before at least a dozen had come together just down the hill and went through their greeting ritual of yipping, yapping, squealing and bumping into each other in hugging ways. After it was over he kissed her on the neck and they began to talk as he asked her the many questions that were still on his mind.

"Well," she said. "Let's see what we can agree on. As we started to discuss before, we are first of all spiritual beings who chose to come into the physical world for our own reasons. The mistake is in assuming that the physical world is the primary reality when it is not. I know this is repetitive but remember, behind the physical world is the psychic and psychological reality that makes the physical world possible. It does so through conscious intent so that if everything has awareness and consciousness, the entire physical universe creates itself on every level. Not only does it create itself, it constantly re creates itself, over and over through a massive cooperation amongst all it's components so that everything that exists in the physical world has a chance to evolve and change through participation in the grander scheme. From the atom to the ant, from the tree to the mountain to the human, a set of psychic blueprints exist which the energy of the universe then fills in and makes physical."

"That would have been a little hard to accept a few days

46

ago but now I think I get it."

"Well, ask yourself this. Does emotion exist? Love and hate, envy, happiness? Does an idea exist? You can't weigh any of these things, you can't put them out on the table and analyze them yet we all accept the fact that they do exist and have their own reality on some level. The same for the psychic blueprints we form ourselves from. If they didn't exist we wouldn't be able to grow from infant to adult and we wouldn't be able to maintain our health or heal ourselves from injury. On the physical level the information resides in the chromosomes so that the process can take place in the physical world but behind that, just as behind the physical brain is the mind, behind the code of the chromosome is the psychic blueprint, the spiritual form. Do you have a problem with any of that?"

"It's a long reach but, no. I guess not. Not really, what with everything else that's happened."

"Okay, it's a start but it's not anywhere good enough. All I can do, however, is go back to the same question we also talked about before and expand it a little. How do you become you on the physical level? Behind the scenes in the greater reality is your primary identity, your inner self or whatever one wants to call it. The you of you. This inner self is the designer and the director that creates and materializes your physical body. It does so with desire and intent through power of mind. The stronger, more intense and well developed the inner self, the more perfect the bodily creation, even if the intent is to create a perfectly imperfect body to bring focus to some particular experience in some lifetime."

"Humans have a different emphasis and viewpoint than animals and far more personal freedom than other forms of life, so that sometimes we also have a more difficult time with physical survival because humans also have the ability to create more problems for themselves. To aid in their survival, however, they have a well defined sense of self, or ego and are able to process information differently than most creatures. For the most part the ego, this outer ego, is largely focused in the physical world, and is very self centered and protective. Unfortunately, as you well know, the ego can become too strong, too fearful, too rigid, too protective and over developed to the extent that it can sometimes actually get in the way of the individuals own best interest and prevent the individual from seeing the bigger picture and short circuit spiritual evolution."

"The ego, in fact can become so overly fearful and protective that it blocks out tremendous amounts of otherwise valid information that the individual could other wise take advantage of. It blocks out any telepathic messaging the person may receive, it refuses to listen to the signals the body is sending to the brain as to what is, or is not good for it, believes it is smarter than the bodies wisdom when it comes to health and well being and actually sets the body up for unnecessary illness, improper functioning and premature aging. It can also become belligerent and paranoid which can, in the extreme, even lead to it's own destruction. Additionally, as people leave childhood and become adults, the ego gets the idea that it, and it alone, is the full self. And that, dear one, is something you will need to work on if you are going to be able to travel to the places you want to go."

"Hmm, really? Who says I want to go anywhere? I'm very happy just being here with you and I wouldn't mind doing re runs of this for the rest of eternity."

"That would be nice and that is what we have been doing. We reunite, help each other and separate, always becoming more than we previously were."

"So, what do you think will eventually happen to us? Will we have some sort of celestial wedding or something?"

"Possibly, but not knowing leaves the door open to some enchanting possibilities. Doesn't it?"

"Does it ever. In the meantime, however, we must at least be cosmically engaged. Do I need to buy you a ring?"

"Another session on the carpet would be better. Or in your bed. After we're done talking, that is."

"Right. About my ego."

"Yes, but not so much your ego. You are already a confident, open individual. You don't need to get your ego under control as much as you need to become more fully aware of your bigger self and reconnect outer with inner. Inner is always fully aware of outer but loses control when outer becomes too dominant. To do the things you want to do the outer has to relinquish some of its control and learn to trust in its bigger self. When that happens your conscious mind can ask for and receive help from the inner. And since the inner self is the source of power, it is what makes it possible for the individual to materialize in the physical world to begin with so that is what you must do, learn to trust more fully."

"That will allow me to do what you did? To disappear and reappear?"

"To dematerialize and rematerialize. The inner self as the source of power, pulls energy into the psychic form that is behind the body and allows it to exist in the physical world. But, as you probably realize by now, the stuff of the body, the basic building blocks of atoms and molecules is constantly changing. If atoms could somehow be tagged to prove the point it would be found that there isn't a single atom in your body now that was there a year ago, a month ago, a week or a second ago. Energy flows into the psychic pattern, materializes to form the body and moves on, constantly re creating. The key to doing what I did is to have a strong connection between the conscious outer ego and the inner self so my desire to dematerialize is brought into play by my inner self and my outer ego understands that it will not be annihilated in the process:

"Sounds easy but why is it so hard?"

"As I said, because of beliefs. To accomplish this you must one hundred percent, absolutely believe it possible to do so. You can't compromise. You can't say, well, I'm not sure but I'll pretend I believe it and see if it works. It's all or nothing. It's the same as with your health or any other bodily thing. You have to completely trust that your body knows what is best for it and not your ego, or the logical portion of your brain. Trust keeps you healthy, not some forced regimen of diet and exercise as dictated by some outside, self appointed authority. Trusting in the fact that you are far more than some physical meat machine will allow you to create and recreate your body at will. The reason you were able to go climb in bed with Jodi was because the desire was very strong at the time and you were asleep so your ego was out of the way. After it was over and you went into her bathroom and looked at yourself in the mirror and realized it wasn't a dream, your ego panicked and brought you home."

"Which must be why I have never been able to repeat the process," he said. "My ego gets in the way when I try to do it on a fully conscious level."

"Yes, because the ego almost completely identifies itself with the body. So if the body is disappearing and reappearing, which the conscious mind doesn't believe is possible, the ego steps in and prevents it from happening, proving to itself that it's true."

"So what's the answer? Re educate my ego? How do I do that?"

"Like I said. By believing what is really possible, is possible. And you have a head start because you saw me do it, so you need to let that in, intellectually. Don't let yourself believe it was an illusion. Or some other mysterious phenomenon divorced from reality. Also know and understand that if I can do it, so can you."

"So simple it's almost impossible."

"Something like that."

"Okay. What about defects? Would re materializing cure me of cancer if I had it?"

"What do you think?"

"I guess if my thinking and beliefs created my disease to begin with, then that would continue to be present. Am I right?"

"Just like that glimmer in your bright blue eyes and your sexy body."

"You're the one with the sexy body."

"Don't get distracted. Are you ready to try?"

"Ah, sure. What do I do first?'

"Get dressed and then go stand across the room."

"Why? You did it in the nude."

"Because it will demonstrate something else at the same time."

"That's it," she told him. "Right now your goal is to get your body from there to here without walking. And then we'll talk about an appropriate reward."

"Well, damn. That's the best incentive a man could ever have. How do I start?"

"Maybe begin with a light state of hypnosis for now. Later, when you become more proficient, it won't be necessary. So, shut your eyes and relax, then do what I tell you. Tell me when you're ready."

Reed did as told and nodded after taking some deep breaths and relaxing.

"Good," she said. "Now try to visualize what I'm saying and do as I instruct. First imagine yourself going inside of yourself. In there is your inner self or inner ego. It is your benefactor, the deeper source of your power and being. It is both formless and timeless but exists and is as real as any idea or thought, except on a far grander scale. The gestalt that gave you your physicality and allows you to exist in this world. This is the real substance of yourself. See yourself as a part of that bigger whole, not some isolated, separate thing. Let it embrace you as you embrace it and understand that if you trust it, trust in your deeper self, you will be able to go beyond everything you previously felt possible. Think about that for a while and feel the power and strength that is yours to use when you want. Surrender yourself now and allow your desire to be here in front of me take over. See and feel yourself here. See it, feel it. See it, feel it. Good. That's good.....that's...."

"Dammit," Reed said angrily. "What happened? I swear I was in the process of...., Jesus."

"It's okay, Reed. Take it easy. You almost did it."

"Are you sure?"

"Positive. It's that one last tiny bit of doubt you can't get past. And a trace of fear."

"My ego is still in the way."

"Somewhat. But hear me. Trust me, trust my voice and let's try it again," she said and had him go through the relaxation routine one more time."

It seemed better for him. He felt near to achieving his goal, however, but still failed.

At this point Kyara came over to him and gave him a big,

wet kiss.

"Well, maybe you just need more incentive," she said as she kissed again and went back to her place across the room.

Moments later, utterly shocked, Reed stood in front of her and smiled immensely. "Wow," he said happily.

"Yeah," she replied. "Fun, huh?"

"So, what kind of reward did you have in mind?" he asked.

"The one you would like the most. Except you have to relocate your body one more time to earn it."

"Please. Anything. Just don't tease me."

"I'm not. Think about your bedroom."

"I can do that."

"Okay. Take your clothes off and come and get me," she said and promptly disappeared.

TEN

In the morning, Kyara was up first and Reed woke to the smell of freshly brewed coffee. And when he came down the hall to the dining room, the table was already set. In addition to buttered toast and hash browns, there were his eggs just the way he liked them. But, best of all, there was Kyara, fully dressed, looking as mystifying as ever, holding a chair, waiting for him to sit.

He looked into her sparkling eyes, kissed her on the mouth and sat down as she went around the table and sat facing him. They ate and talked about nothing at all serious until their meal was over and Reed had cleared the table. Then he laughed and said,

"And all this time I've been feeling sorry for you having to walk twelve miles into town and back."

"I'm sorry to have misled you," she smiled.

"Yeah, but I think you could have really walked that twelve miles if you wanted to. You"re in such marvelous shape."

"Yes. And I did try it once. About two miles, however, and that was enough. But, speaking of being in shape, who was it that kept me up half the night?"

52

"Damn right. And... by the way. Did you really live out there all alone all those weeks before we met?"

"Of course not. But I did stay there over a week just for the experience. It really is very beautiful."

"And you didn't need a gun for protection, either. Did you? If a mountain lion came, all you had to do was disappear."

"Or a bad guy. I'm sorry you worried about me so much but it was necessary."

"Well, I'm certainly glad you didn't disappear on me there on the trail when I first met you. They would have had to lock me up for sure."

"As you must know by now, I didn't want to disappear at all. I just really want to grab you and drag you off into the bushes and rip all your clothes off."

"That would have been interesting."

"Yes, wouldn't it though."

"Okay. So what about now?"

"Now would be good, too."

"Want to disappear so I can follow you into the bedroom again?"

"What's wrong with right here?"

Much later, after they were dressed again and sitting on the couch, he reached for her hands and looked into her beautiful eyes. Then, with a wistful look, he said, "Why do I get the feeling that you're leaving?"

"Because I'm afraid it's true?"

"But why so soon? Having you here has been so absolutely wonderful. You know I love you."

"Yes. You have almost always been in love with me and I with you. But you are on your journey and I am on mine and there are things we need to do separately for a little longer."

"Like what?"

"Like you getting in touch with some of the other sides of yourself which you recently set out to do."

"Well, yeah. I thought it would be interesting but it's not that important."

"Not with me being here but ultimately, it is for you. And

if I stayed and distracted you it might be a problem later on."

"Well, I don't see how." Reed said, looking perplexed.

"Okay. Let me see if I can give you an example. Suppose you are going to take a trip to some place you have never been to before. There are several options for doing that. One is that you sign up for a guided tour and the guide leads you every step of the way, not only deciding what form of transportation you will go on but where you will stay, what you eat and what places of interest you will see while also subjecting you to running interpretations of everything you come across, all limited by this person's knowledge and personal biases."

"Next, you could do a lot of research and plan your own detailed, day by day trip. Read all the guide books and take their recommendations about lodging, restaurants and places of interest. Or, you could just get on a plane and go there, completely unplanned. You could avoid everything westernized and, as much as possible, experience the culture through the eyes of the native people. Lastly, you could travel any of these versions with a companion. Certainly that would be nice if the purpose of the trip was a getaway vacation, a romantic holiday, a honeymoon, or, who knows. The point is that this additional presence also modifies any experience you would have. Indeed, there is nothing wrong with this and for some it is exactly what they should be doing. But not you. If I were a full time presence in your life at this point I would deprive you of the freedom and flexibility you need to experience the full impact of your own life's adventure and what it is you feel you need to do to continue evolving as an individual."

"So I'm stuck with going it alone?"

"For the time being, yes. And now that you know how to consciously get from place to place in more than one way, the rest is up to you to figure out for yourself. It wouldn't be fair of me to stay because I would influence the outcome. You will also meet other people along the way that you will have relationships with. Some may be very intense, but that is all part of the bigger process, so don't ever deny yourself that."

He was silent for a moment, then nodded his understanding.

"But, damn," he then said. "I'm not ready to give you up just yet. Can't you stay a little longer? Please!"

"I could, but that would just make leaving even harder later on. "

Reed shrugged and looked as though he might begin to cry. He opened his arms and she came to him and they held each other silently for several minutes until he finally spoke.

"I'm damned sure going to miss you."

"And I you, equally so. But it won't be too long, I promise. One day I will leave a message and it will be your turn to come and visit me. Tell me that's okay."

"Absolutely."

"And don't worry. I'll look in on you once in a while in the meantime. And if you should need me, try to dream about me and we can meet out-of-body out in the alcove in the canyon. That will be our place."

"All right. But why there?"

"Because it's what you might call a portal or a doorway to and from certain other realms. It has a specific set of coordinate points that make it possible for me to be here at this time. When it becomes your time to visit me you will need to go there too, if you come physically."

"Well, you can certainly bet that I don't want to just see you in an out of body state. That was nice but I want the rest to. You make me crazy."

"And look what you do to me. God, isn't it wonderful?"

"It is. "

"But in the meantime don't bother to go out there because you won't find me. Please understand that."

"I'll try.

"Okay," she said as she stood up, got her back pack off one of the chairs and held it. "Love you," she smiled, touched her forehead in that familiar way and faded from his view, leaving him powerless to do anything except to stare at the spot where she had been until the tears came to his eyes.

ELEVEN

Devastated was not the word. That was the problem. He wasn't exactly sure how he felt. It was extremely complicated, mentally, emotionally and every other way possible. This beautiful, mysterious woman from some far away galaxy had set down in a space craft in his own front yard and let him fall in love with her. Except that he was already in love with her and she with him and she wasn't from some distant place far off in the universe, she was from out of his own past and his own future, the lost dream he had been chasing all his life, and found, and now she was gone again. Where? Some adjacent, parallel universe whose strands of time and unfolding reality were all intertwined and tangled up with the one he dwelled in? It seemed like it.

Having ended up in Jodi's house four hundred miles away in the middle of the night had already told him that he was living in a far greater and far more complex and mysterious reality than he had ever previously imagined possible. It also explained why he had never felt fully satisfied or complete in the relationship with her, or with any other woman for that matter, because none of them were Kyara in her present form.

And, yes. Looking back, his life had certainly been a quest. And he was on a journey, all right. Just like Kyara had said. Somewhere they had found each other in a different time and place but it was more than that, bigger than that and their final reunion had to wait. And even though he couldn't explain it and was completely unable to find words for it, somehow he still understood.

But, oh my god. He had held her in his arms, kissed her, and he knew she was far more than just a dream. His heart ached, unfulfilled. But if what she had promised were true, then he could wait. But for now she was really gone. He had seen her disappear right in front of him, but to where? Out to the canyon, to be sure. But not to stay. There was no reason for her to do that. Or was there? He still couldn't be totally sure. Well, he could and he was, but his not wanting her to be gone was such a strong feeling that he was completely unable to help himself. So unable that he got in his vehicle and drove out to the canyon and

56

hiked in the five miles to the alcove. Not only was it empty but there was not one single trace that it had ever been occupied. Not in years, anyway. Nothing.

Unable to let it go at that, however, Reed still crawled up inside behind the remains of the wall and sat on the ground and tried to imagine what it might have been like for her to live there, even if only for a few days. And where was the portal, the doorway she had come through to get here? If it existed, it certainly wasn't obvious. He looked around carefully, felt along the walls, went outside and stood on the ledge, scanning everything once more when, good grief. What an idiot he was. He hadn't needed to drive way out here and hike in at all. How dumb could he be? Stay home, concentrate, dematerialize there, show up here. Dematerialize here, show up there. Jeez. Well, at least he wouldn't have to hike back out to his truck, he told himself as he prepared to take the easy way back. But then he changed his mind. Yes, it was a long walk, but it was a bright sunny day, the canyon was spectacular in it's own right and maybe if he did the hike, it would keep him busy and tire him out enough so he could go to bed early and not think about her so much. But it didn't work.

It was dark by the time he got back to the house. He made himself a sandwich and went outside. After he finished eating he wrapped himself up in the same blanket he had shared with Kyara, laid down on the big lounge chair and looked up at the sky, so immense and so forever and tried to visualize their next time together. That and what seven or eight hundred more lifetimes together might be like. Or how many there were before moving on to something else even more fascinating.

TWELVE

Before living with Jodi there had also been a wife turned ex-wife in the picture. Would he want, for any reason, to try and find out what his life would have been like if he had stayed with her? Not really. Not only, not really, but, hell no. What a disaster. A very bright, very attractive younger woman. Someone he had known over two years before they were married, a seemingly stable and together person who slowly slid into a drinking problem that ended in divorce. And so much for that. What possible good could come of dropping in on that situation? He would probably have turned to drink himself, if he had stayed with her.

Okay, so what else was on this list? What if he hadn't gone to college? Where would he have ended up then? That might be interesting but how would he ever track that one? It was long ago and back in another part of the country. Where would he even start? He couldn't remember exactly when or where that decision had been made so it might be best to put that one on hold until he was more proficient at this. But that triggered another memory. Back then he had also always wondered what it would have been like to have a sea worthy sail boat to live on and sail around the world in. Even today there were times when it still seemed like a good idea. No car, no house, all this stuff. No taxes, utility bills or insurance. What the hell. But there was a catch. The ocean was a mighty big place. He wasn't concerned about the hazards, the question was, could he have done it alone? All those days and nights by himself? That would be okay for a while but as an on going life style? He didn't think so. Unless... Ah, Kyara. But Kyara wasn't available at the time and besides, she was much too much of a dynamic individual to be confined to such a life.

All right, what then, Reed asked himself, only to be interrupted by another memory. One that was suddenly very pertinent. Several years ago back in California he had been driving down the Orange freeway early one Sunday morning alone where, very unusually, there was almost no traffic at the time. Fully awake, no cell phone, no radio on, nothing to distract. He was in the center lane cruising along somewhere near the speed limit as he always did when he looked into the rear view mirror to see a car come roaring up behind him, the memory still very clear because at the time he thought he was going to be rear ended. There was a man driving and a woman beside him, both very visible through their windshield. Then, at the last second, as though finally realizing they were there, the driver veered to his right to go around him. But it never did. It disappeared. He was about a mile from the previous off ramp and the next one was still several miles ahead. Puzzled, he slowed way down, moved over into the slow lane and stopped on the shoulder. No, the car did not pass him, he was completely sure of that. Nor did it end up in the ditch, either. It was simply gone. And what did he say to himself at the time? Nothing. Like all such enigmas, he simply pushed it aside and let it go. If only he knew then what he knew now.

Parallel worlds coming together, criss-crossing briefly. But not always so clearly obvious and how would one ever know for sure when they did. Unless you knew them personally, how could you even be sure that the people who lived in a neighboring house were the same ones who were there last week? Maybe it wasn't even the same gas station down on the corner that was there either. Maybe different realities weaved in and out of each other all the time, sharing this and sharing that. What else could it be? How else could he account for his freeway experience. And, he thought, as that other even more significant enigma came back to mind. How else could he account for the package he had received from Jodi with the silver goblet in it, mailed years earlier to an address that wasn't even his at that point but arriving at the same time as he crossed paths with her in that other reality?

Later that day the thought of his being a doctor in some other reality came back again. Unfortunately, when he had tried to check that one out before, he had ended up on the couch, having failed miserably. But now, since Kyara had come along and made a game out of him chasing her around, he felt a little better prepared. At least with the actual process of moving from place to place in the same time period. As for going backward or forward in time, he wasn't sure but all he coud do was try.

A quick search on the Google Earth site showed that the library was still in existence back in Madison, Wisconsin in his own reality. Zooming in, he looked for a safe place to visualize as a destination and saw that the big fountain was also still there. With that in mind, Reed got up early the next day, picked up his already packed small bag of essentials, transported himself halfway across the country and, guess what? There was the same big old fountain out in the middle of the mall area, bubbling away just as he remembered it and for now, he was alone. Sitting down on a concrete bench he surveyed the scene. Everything there had an enduring, timeless look about it. Yes, this might be the place, he thought after a bit. The place to take the next step from into the reality he was searching for. He got up and walked slowly around to get a sense of it. What did he feel? Was there any one spot that felt any different than the rest? Did the paved area seem different than the surrounding grassy area? Maybe. Maybe just a little and maybe more so right up around the fountain itself.

By then there were cars in the street, a few people on bicycles and pedestrians. Students more than likely, some carrying books, many with their classical back packs. The library had opened. He went across the street to the Student Union cafeteria in the Alumni Center, bought coffee and an order of toast, took it all outside on the deck that looked out on the lake. The same lake he used to water ski on back when he was a student. A lot of years had gone by, to be sure, but things didn't seem to have changed that much. Still, it stirred up a lot of old memories. Nothing nostalgic and no regrets but it certainly did bring home the, what if, aspects of life and the reason for his being there.

Toast gone, coffee cup empty, he went back to the fountain area, again sat on the different concrete benches, walked back and forth, stopped here, stopped there and quieted his mind while trying to stay open to whatever might appear. Yes, the feeling was even stronger now, especially at a spot near the fountain on the south side. But still, the question. Even though that spot might also be some kind of portal, just how sure could he be that if he went through it, he would come out in the same location in some other reality? Then too, how many other possible realities or parallel worlds were there in actual existence of which the library area might also be a part? If there were multiple versions of it, how would he ever be able to get to the right one? It wasn't exactly like buying a ticket and walking through the right boarding gate at the airport.

He couldn't just drop in and expect to be okay, either. The

one thing he would need to take would be money. If he had the right money, anything else he needed he could come by. Gold or diamonds might work if he had them. Or, they might create suspicion. Best to go with cash, he decided. Hopefully, in that regard, the currency was basically the same as before and dollars were still dollars. But no sense in taking recent versions of bills with their more intricate, anti counterfeiting colors and designs. Find a bank, use his debit card, get sums of bills, sort through them for the older ones and keep doing it until he had as many as he could safely carry.

THIRTEEN

Too bad he couldn't just say Abbra Kadabra and get it over with, Reed thought the next morning, back at the fountain after having spent the night in a nearby motel. Sitting there, however, he was having a difficult time concentrating on his goal and agonizing over his lack of results. People were beginning to look at him with suspicion. What was this seemingly, totally preoccupied older man doing there? Maybe he was some confounded, self-absorbed professor lost in cosmic contemplation. While that might keep him from getting picked up for loitering, his awareness of students staring at him was completely defeating his own purpose. Then it occurred to him that his timing was obviously way off. Most of these kids were on their way to class. He needed to go get some coffee and come back when sessions were underway.

Much better, he thought, twenty minutes later as he sat on the concrete wall that formed the large pool of the fountain. Now, assuming that all the interweaving alternate realities involving earth would be revolving around the same sun up in the sky and that if he were able to jump realities successfully, it would be the same time of day in both places, he let his mind drift off into a state of limbo. As clearly as possible he tried seeing himself as having spent eight years on this campus instead of five, visualizing himself in a white jacket thumping people on the chest, listening to their hearts, looking down their throats, writing prescriptions and ..... He opened his eyes and looked up.

Something was different, wasn't it? But what? There were more students in the area for one thing. But that wasn't it. The clothing, maybe. The shoes, for sure. Not one pair of Nikes in the lot. The rest of their garments weren't as gaudy, either. He looked over towards the library. It, too, was different. The exterior stone walls had been recently sand blasted or something, making it appear newer and fresher. He got to his feet, turned around and viewed the fountain and pool. It also had been renovated. Then he looked at the students, none of whom seemed to be paying any particular attention to his presence.

What if they couldn't see him, he thought. Then what? With that he purposely walked directly in front of a couple of young men crossing the area and apologized when they veered around him. Good enough, he said to himself. He was really there. Somewhere, anyway. Time to head up the hill.

Well, Bascomb Hall was still where he remembered it to be and around on the east side of the building, there it was. The Records Department. He went inside, took a moment to orient himself and walked up to the counter and told the woman behind it that he would like a copy of his graduation diploma from medical school. She handed him a form to complete, along with a pen.

This was it, he told himself as he quickly filled it out and handed it back, almost shaking because he was so nervous and excited.

"I'll need to see your ID," the woman said after she had looked over the form to make sure it was complete.

Reed handed her his drivers license.

"Are you all right?" the woman asked as she looked up at him after checking his photo.

"Ah, yeah," he said, trying to remain calm. "Just one of those days. I had a hard time getting here."

"Oh, right" she said, looking at his license again. "Arizona. Okay, be right back," she said after handing back his license and went to a nearby desk and sat down at a terminal.

"Jeez," he said to himself, relieved that the woman hadn't noticed the date his license had been issued because, to her, it would have to have been faked with a date that was somewhere in her future. How far he wasn't sure of yet, but, lucky him. For now at least.

No flat screen monitors here, however, Reed noticed. But they weren't the old bulky cathode ray tube units either. Something in between.

A minute later she was back, handed him a document and asked for five dollars. He dug in his wallet and gave her a twenty which she squinted at briefly before she put it in the drawer and handed him back a five and a ten, which, except for the fact that a different Secretary of the Treasury's name may have appeared on them, still looked the same as always, before all the security minded changes. So his money was good. One more thing he didn't have to worry about.

Finally outside, Reed went around to the front of the building and sat on the steps. The moment of truth.

"Holy, shit," he mumbled as he looked at the copy of the diploma the woman had given him. "Holy, damn," he said a little louder, wanting to jump up and shout, I did it, I did it. I got to the right place and I did it on the first try.

"Wow," he said, completely out loud this time and began reviewing his accomplishment. Then he got up and began walking back down the hill towards the library, having already worked out a preliminary plan as to what to do next if he succeeded. Homework and research. Once he got down to Lake Street, however, he turned right instead of going straight to the library, thinking he had best find a place to stay in case it took a while to track himself down and, as he walked along, he tried to pay more attention to the everyday details in the new world around him.

Bicycles still had two wheels and some people still rode them on the sidewalk but automobiles were noticeably different. For one thing there wasn't a single vehicle that might be labeled an SUV. Coupes and sedans, a convertible, pickup trucks, an obviously new Jeep that looked very similar to the original World War Two version, and some station wagons. The most striking thing was that all of the assorted makes were distinctly different in styling and that was refreshing. All the old standbys were still there, too. Chevies, Fords, Dodges and whatever, but no cookie cutter, copy cat, non nondescript boring designs like back in his own world. And ... with the exception of what looked like a later day Jaguar, not a foreign car in the bunch. What was that all about?

Unfortunately, the motel on University Avenue he had stayed at the night before back in his own world was now an office building so he went inside and asked the receptionist where he could find lodging. Back down to Park Street and take a left, she told him.

All together, the staff very nearly had to throw Reed out of the library at night so they could close. He had read every issue of the Madison Gazette, the Washington Times and the New York Post that had been printed since he had graduated from there so many years ago. He had also gone through stacks and stacks of Life, Time, People, Variety and much more, as well as Scientific American, Popular Science and everything else that seemed pertinent and was still being printed in this reality. To say that what he had learned was fascinating would be a gross understatement. He was, in fact, so totally overwhelmed and caught up in what he was learning that there was no way he would ever be able to continue his mission until he had fully investigated the almost incomprehensible chain of events that had occurred in this other world, the most significant of which happened on November twenty second of nineteen sixty three in Dallas, Texas. Lee Harvey Oswald had missed his primary target. Jackie Kennedy had been shot in the chest and killed instead, but the President himself had survived with a flesh wound in his upper arm. Not only had he survived but he had gone on to serve a second term in office. My god! And that was only the beginning.

Thus far Reed had spent four full days and three evenings in the library and then gone back to his motel room to watch more TV, another surprise that expanded his view of that reality and added to his knowledge. Yes, television was still a commercial venture but an hour of viewing time was only interrupted on the hour and the half hour for maybe five minutes total. Delightfully so, there were no burdensome, fear inducing pharmaceutical ads either. Or cancer treatment center solicitations, weight loss remedies, dietary supplement promotions and the other, paranoia producing advocations of his own world. And, now that it came to mind, he couldn't think of having seen even one clearly obese person on the street or anywhere else he had been thus far. Might just be a fairly reasonable place to be a doctor in, Reed thought. Maybe not as lucrative as his own world but also not so many extreme individuals to deal with. That might be nice. Probably not so many people being maimed by unnecessary surgery either. But what else? Surely, there was something he was missing, what was it? He knew it was there, why couldn't he think of it? It was only later when he turned off the TV that it occurred to him. Of course. There was no AIDs epidemic here either. There wasn't even a single mention of it in all the papers and publications he had been through. It was as though the word itself hadn't even been invented. And then there was the rest of it.

At the same number of years later this world didn't have six, going on seven, billion people in it. It only had about three. Additionally, and of great significance was President Kennedy's survival. Putting it all together it seemed that the loss of his wife had matured him greatly. Marilyn Monroe was still dead but there were no more significant women in his life and he was now living out the rest of his life in Cape Cod. It also appeared that his firm stand during the Cuban missile crisis had taught him one thing and the defeat at the Bay of Pigs taught him something else. Putting it all together Kennedy seemed to have realized that, bottom line, the Soviets were just as afraid of the United States as the US was of them. Unintimidated by the military establishment, he refused to let congress and his military cajole the nation into further nuclear arsenal build-up. What purpose was there in having ten or twenty thousand atomic bombs when a dozen properly aimed ones would still keep things under control? Spend the money on propaganda instead and convince the Russian people that their leaders were taking them down the wrong path.

Not so surprisingly, Kennedy's strategy worked. The communist regime fell apart twenty years earlier than it had in Reed's world. Additionally, Kennedy was wise enough not to see Chinese communism as a creeping world threat to democracy and fifty eight thousand Americans did not die in Vietnam. Also in his second term, Kennedy put the pressure on Israel and the United nations and demanded recognition of Palestine as an independent nation. This act alone created an entirely new chain of events that put a much more peaceful slant on middle eastern affairs. Iran's leaders, however, continued to be a source of provocation to the western world that had never went away.

On the lighter side of things Elvis Presley didn't die of a drug overdose either, but was still out there at sixty nine, singing his heart out just like Tony Bennett was doing in Reed's world. Timothy O'Leary on the other hand, went on an LSD trip that ended in his getting shot by a policeman in a wild confrontation and the reclusive Neal Diamond was appointed Ambassador to Israel by President, ah, whomever. Too much new information to handle. And on it went, totally fascinating. Too bad people didn't realize all the different ways their lives could work out if they would let them.

Having forgotten to pack his shaving gear, Reed decided it was a good thing. He would let his beard grow just in case he ran into someone who thought they knew him as his other self.

"Ha," he said. Wouldn't that be something.

He also bought a floppy looking hat and a pair of sunglasses to aid his disguise and so far he was in luck. On Sunday, with the library closed, he slept late, had breakfast in the restaurant across the street and then went down to the lake. He stood on the pier a while and watched the sailboats skimming across the calm water. Then he turned away and strolled up the lake shore path. It was a perfect fall day, warm and sunny. The leaves were turning color but the lawns were still green and there was a mild and gentle breeze coming in off the lake. A hundred yards along the path he glanced up to see a familiar looking woman coming towards him. It was one of the librarians. A person about his own age. She smiled when she was nearer and said hello.

"Hello," he said and returned the smile.

"Well," she said when she was closer and stopped. "No homework today."

"Afraid not. But maybe that's good. I'm feeling a bit saturated."

"Really? I can't imagine why. I think you'd be sleeping on the library floor if we let you."

"Yeah, maybe I should have brought a pillow," he said and then decided that meeting her was an opportunity to sit down and have a real conversation with someone from that world so he asked her if he could buy her coffee.

"You are obviously not a student," she said, once they were settled at a table out on the deck of the student union.

"Why? Because I'm too old?"

"No. That part might work but you can't be going to classes when you spend the whole day in the library. Besides, the world should be so lucky to have students who worked even ten percent as hard as you do. And if you're doing research and there is anything I can help you with, please let me know."

"I will. And thank you. It probably would have been easier if you had internet service but I should be caught up in a few more days."

"Internet service? What's that? Am I missing something?"

"Ah, no," he said, backtracking. "It's, ah... something that was proposed a few years ago but nothing ever came of it I guess. Let everyone be able to connect their computers to each other so people can communicate and share information quickly. Electronic mail, that kind of thing."

"Oh, right. I believe the university has a project underway now but I have to say I'm overwhelmed with your devotion. It's like you must be from Mars or something."

"No. Nothing quite that dramatic. I'm from, ah, Arizona."

"You are? What part? Have you ever met McCain?"

"McCain?"

"The President."

"The President? Oh, right," he said, wondering how he had missed that one in his library venture. Jeez, McCain was President. That seemed a bit extreme for this society. He wondered how that was working out.

"No, never met him personally but I lived about a mile downstream from him once. His ranch, as he called it, right on Oak Creek."

"In Sedona. I was there about ten years ago. Beautiful place."

"It is. Or it was until the Chamber of Commerce destroyed it by promoting it as a major tourist destination."

"Really? That must be recent. It was just this tiny little place in the red rocks when I was there."

"Ten years ago?"

"About that. Yes."

Oops, Reed thought. He'd better be careful here so he pointed out the fact that McCain's ranch really wasn't in Sedona either. It was in a place called Cornville. But Cornville was, pardon the pun, a corny name so his public relations people always said he was from Sedona. As for himself, he now lived half way down the mountain from Jerome, where she had also been on her Arizona trip and loved it. Enough of that, he quickly decided and began asking her about herself and what brought her to the university.

It wasn't a long story and he listened carefully before asking questions that she didn't seem to mind answering. Then he shifted his questions to the more social and political aspects of this new world and made more mental notes to take home with him. By then they had talked their way clear into the middle of lunch hour so they went into the cafeteria and loaded up. Back outside, their meal over, she looked at him in earnest and said, "I have never heard anyone ask so many questions in my life. What is that all about? Are you sure you aren't from Mars?" she asked again with a friendly smile.

"My apologies," he said. "It's a bad habit of mine. When I meet new people I like to find out what they are interested in and what is going on in their heads."

"Oh, no. Please don't apologize. It's very refreshing. Most people just want to take up your time and rattle on about their problems. You hardly talked about yourself and this is the first really genuine conversation I've had in years so, thank you. And what else is interesting is that I feel like I have met you somewhere before but I can't seem to get a clear picture of the circumstances."

"Hmm. Well, I did go to school here. But that was a long time ago so, I don't know. Maybe."

"Well, you're certainly not my ex husband. I'll never forget that bastard. Oh, sorry."

"No problem. I have an ex wife in the same category."

"But you're not married now?"

"Is that a question? No, I'm not. And you're not either, I guess."

"Which is exactly why I'm inviting you over to dinner tonight."

"Really? Are you sure? You don't even know me. Plus, I'll only be here for a few more days. Then I'll be gone, probably never to return."

"My, you are so mysterious. I love it and that makes it even better."

"What? Being mysterious?"

"No, not coming back. That keeps it uncomplicated. I have a man friend I'm interested in but undecided about. I haven't seen him in couple of weeks so I could use a one night stand to help me clarify things. Maybe even two. What do you think?"

A bit shocked, Reed looked at her, surprised at her bluntness. As for what he thought about it, he wasn't sure. This woman wasn't beautiful but she had a very interesting face. Nice eyes and cute smile. Yes, and sexy too, now that he let it in. But what about Kyara? Before she had shown up in his life his response would have been an eager, automatic consent. Now, however, would being with this woman amount to some kind of infidelity? It was already beginning to feel that way. But then, what was it that Kyara had said to him just before she left? You will meet interesting people along the way, don't deny yourself the experience of the relationship. Something like that, and it seemed clear as to what that included. But still....

"Well, dinner would be great," he said. "We can decide about the rest of it later if that's okay."

"Fair enough," she replied. "Now you can walk me home so you know where I live. And, for the record, my name is Susan."

"I know. I saw the little sign on your desk at the library. And mine is Reed."

Well, there there he was having dinner with some woman from another parallel world, one perhaps spinning around in the same space as his own and yet she was every bit as much alive as he was. And then, the next day when he was back at the library digging through publications she put her hand on his shoulder when she went by, whispered a suggestive thank you in his ear and asked him if he wanted to do it again. So, as it turned out, two nights turned into three and, all in all, it was a very valuable experience. Most importantly it gave him an intimate look at life in this other world, psychologically, philosophically and physically. A more sedate, serene world with it's own peculiarities and approach to problem solving, still vital and full of life but without all the violence and the insanity of war and the mistaken idea that the only measure of success was money and power. A world much more appreciative of art, music and literature and human kindness. Not such a bad place to spend a lifetime in at all, one could be very happy there. But was he, his other self, happy being there, he then wondered? It was time to stop doing what he was doing and get back to the real reason for his journey. And where to start with that? Without an internet, he couldn't just Google himself. But they did have phone books and the library was full of them.

"Oh for god's sake," he said as he looked in the yellow pages and laughed out loud with an intensity that made everyone look at him. Even Susan looked up from her desk a good distance away with a questioning expression.

Reed smiled at her, shrugged his shoulders and framed a

silent, sorry, to her. Then he stared at the yellow page listing once more and there he was. A general surgeon with an office out on the west end of town, his own face staring back at him without all the new whiskers. Good grief. How could it have been so easy?. He had been here for almost a week when all along his reason for coming hadn't moved off to Florida or California or anywhere else. He was right there waiting the whole time. Jeez, he was lucky he hadn't run into himself on the street or something. Then he turned to the white pages section. No listing there so he came back to the yellow pages. Now what? Call and make an appointment? That would be a totally unfair, kind of sick thing to do. So, how would he be able to check up on himself in some discreet manner? If only he had a car.

Forgetting to close the phone book and put it back on the shelf, he went over to Susan's desk.

"What was that all about?" she quizzed him when he got there

He shrugged again and asked her where he could rent a car. She said she would be happy to take him somewhere after work if he wanted.

"I appreciate it," he replied, "but I have an appointment that I need to keep. Anyway, have you made your decision yet?"

"My decision?"

"Yeah. Your boyfriend."

"Oh, right. Well, I think I'll probably marry the bum but if you're still going to be here tonight..."

"Don't know for sure yet. Can I call you a little later?"

"That's not necessary. Just come by if you can. It doesn't matter how late. And I think there's a car rental right over on University Avenue."

Needing to get up and walk around a bit, Susan left her desk as soon as Reed was gone and went to the women's room. On the way back she strolled up and down different aisles and ended up going past the table where Reed had left the phone book. Out of curiosity, she scanned the two open pages and stopped, her eyes stuck on the picture. It was Reed without the beard. Wasn't it? Or his twin brother. It had to be. But with the same first name. That didn't make any sense. Oh my god, what was going on? Was he an amnesia victim? Was that why he had spent so much time in the library reading everything in sight and why some of his, so many questions, were sometimes a little off? With that she took the phone book back to her desk and dialed the number of the doctor's office. When it was answered, she asked if she could talk to the doctor a minute. Without questioning the reason for the call the receptionist answered.

"The doctor is in surgery over at Madison General. Let's see. He should be back here in half an hour if it went well. Can I take a message and have him call you?"

"No, that's fine. Nothing serious. I'll try back later. Thank you," Susan said and hung up. Then she quietly tore the page out of the phone book, folded it up and put it in her purse which she keep in her bottom desk drawer.

FOURTEEN

Reed cruised around the city, revisiting places, noting the changes, passing time until noon when he hoped his doctor self would be going to lunch so he could get a look at him before decided where to go from there.

Well, either the man wasn't in the office or he didn't go out for lunch so Reed went back to the campus and down to the boat docks where he rented a canoe and went paddling along the lake shore just like he had done so many times before in his other life back in his college days. Hours later he returned to the doctor's office building and sat in his car, staking out the parking lot. Then, sooner than expected, there he was. Jeez. Watching yourself in a video was one thing. Seeing yourself in person was something else. Nicely dressed, sport jacket and tie, no sagging shoulders or weight problem, Reed was happy with what he saw. The man got into a full sized, medium priced newer automobile and drove off, Reed following.

Ten minutes later Reed watched himself go inside an upper end, older home on a wide street he never knew existed before and then come out again a little later with the rest of his family. A wife, two little kids and a dog. They were on a walk down to the nearby park. But who was the wife? Was it...? It was. That very pretty registered nurse he had thought was so wonderful back in college but had never been able to quite connect with. Lucky man. And look at those two little girls, he declared as a wave of emotion swept over him. With that he started the car, drove on by them in their walk and found a pay phone.

FIFTEEN

Her doorbell rang promptly at six and there he stood, damn him, ready to take her out to dinner as agreed on when he called earlier, still leaving her without any idea as to what he was up to. Setting her concerns aside, however, she got her things and they left in the car he had rented and, being discreet for her own sake, she directed him to a restaurant in a neighboring town. Also being discreet, she completely avoided asking him any questions about the mystery that surrounded him and they had a very delightful time together. She still felt him to be very appealing and under a different set of circumstances might have severed her other relationship but the picture in the phone book had changed all that. As for later that evening when he took her home, she hadn't decided about how she wanted that to end just yet either. But then, just before leaving the restaurant, he ordered a bottle of expensive wine to take with them and whispered in the waitresses ear about something else. And that was that as they left the restaurant with Reed carrying two packages.

Much later, when the wine bottle was empty, she took the torn out yellow pages from her purse and showed it to him. He looked at it for a moment and at first she thought he was going to cry. But he just stared back at her with the most embarrassed, helpless look on his face and shrugged his shoulders as though unable to speak.

"Look," she said as she reached out and put her hand on his cheek. "It okay. I really have no idea who you are or what this is all about or why you are here. So far none of it makes any sense. Not one small bit. But, you know what? It doesn't matter. It doesn't matter because I'm not sure I'd be capable of understanding it if you did try to explain it to me. All I know now is that you came along at a critical time in my life and you were very, very good for me."

"Thank you. And you have been more than good for me in so many ways. But now, looking back, I most certainly hope I haven't done anything to upset you and if I have, I truly apologize. In some respects I should have known better but your charming proposition caught me off guard."

"Any regrets?"

"None. How about you? Are you okay?"

"I am," she told him. "And what has become clear to me is that what I want in my life is some ongoing stability, especially after my first marriage. And that is why I decided to get back together with my old boyfriend. His name is Jim, by the way. He's a good man and he can give me that and I love him for what he is. But I needed what you gave me first. And no matter what you think of me you will become that happy memory that will be there to warm me up when I'm older, sitting in my rocking chair. For now, however, it's only about eight thirty. You can stay until midnight."

"Fair enough," Reed said as he picked up the second package he had brought along and gave it to her, a bottle of the most expensive champagne they had in stock at the restaurant. "I'd be very happy if you drank this at your wedding and then maybe I'll come back and check up on you in ten years or so."

It wasn't midnight when he left, however. It was seven in the morning. Then he turned in the rental car, checked out of the motel and set out for the library mall on foot so he could stand by the fountain and think of home.

Six days. It would be good to be back in Arizona. Sit out on the deck up on the ridge in the evening, watch the landscape's changing hues in the dying light and be able to see off into the distance, miles and miles away. Think about all the things far too many people were too busy to be aware of, dream about the future, some far off reunion with Kyara. Damned if he wasn't feeling a little guilty though, even with all things considered. No sex, he had only slept with Susan as mutually decided. But still. Well, he could deal with that later. Right now he needed to concentrate on getting back home.

SIXTEEN

Something was not right. He sensed it immediately. Something was not right at all. What the hell? He wasn't back home, he was still standing right by the fountain. Well, that wasn't good. So, stay calm, take a moment to relax and.... Why was it suddenly so noisy? Why were there so many people around, he wondered. Not students but .... men in black uniforms, all with sidearms? How could that be? Holy damn! And then a loud shout. He had been noticed.

Before he could even react, Reed was roughly seized by two men who jerked him around and started dragging him away. And then he saw it. The swastika. Completely stunned, he stared at it. Up high on the stone wall of the library building was a shocking, bright red swastika at least ten feet high. A swastika. Not some hate group, sloppily spray painted on figure but a precisely constructed one, bolted to the building. He dragged his feet trying to get a better look at it and then to see the faces of his captors but they were obviously very offended by his being there so he stopped resisting and did his best to cooperate.

Then he noticed the fence. Out by the street, along the sidewalk, was a very high chain link fence and there was a manned guard gate where the walkway came into the library. Furthermore, as he would later learn, the fence encompassed almost the entire block. What in hell was this, he wondered, as they pushed him up the steps into what obviously was no longer the library building. No bookshelves inside, either. The structure had been converted to an office or headquarters of some sort. Here he was forced down a long hallway and into nothing less than an interrogation room right out of a police movie. A metal table, a few chairs, a one way mirror along the back wall, otherwise barren.

One of his captors pulled out a chair and said, "sit," as the other one threw his small packed bag on the table in front of him.

They were both young white men, serious and self

important in their uniforms but in a fair fight Reed was sure he could have beaten the hell out of both of them. But, no point in going there. Thus far he hadn't said a word. And he wasn't about to, either. He'd wait and see what happened next.

As expected, the door to the room soon opened and an older man entered, also uniformed. Some serious decorations were pinned to the chest of his jacket and there on his shoulder, as with the others, that damned red swastika patch also glaringly apparent. The man went around to the opposite side of the table and, still standing, told one of the men to open Reed's bag and dump it out. Then he sorted through the contents that contained nothing but clothes. He scowled at Reed and ordered the men to search him.

Together they pulled him upright as one man kept his hand on Reed's shoulder while the other patted him down and put his only possession on the table. His wallet. The Commandant, as he turned out to be, seemed a bit perplexed by the limited extent of Reed's possessions and scratched his head before telling the two others to leave the room.

"Sit down," he said quietly enough and motioned, then sat himself.

Now Reed was even more perplexed. The man's English was good enough but in keeping with the bizarre circumstances, it did carry a trace of accent. What else but German, he decided as he watched the man go through the contents of his wallet. What there was of it. One hundred and twenty three dollars in old bills and a driver's license with Reed's picture on it.

Calmer now, Reed almost laughed out loud, knowing how puzzling that might be for his interrogator. Instead he stared back at the man with curiosity and continued to wait.

"Well, Mr. ah, Reed, is it. We will skip the formalities. Just tell me what you were doing here inside the compound so I can decide what to do with you."

Reed didn't have to try and sound innocent. He was even more confused than the Commandant. But how to answer the question without creating further problems. Finally he shrugged and spoke for the first time.

"Quite honestly I'm as confused as you are. I thought I was, ah, but, it's not. I mean, I thought I was at the University library except it's obviously not a library anymore and, I don't know. I'm sorry, I just can't explain it. "

"You can't explain it? But you are obviously here. Or are you going to deny that too?"

"No. Not at all. I"m here all right. But it's not where I thought I was going."

"And where is that?"

"Back home to Arizona."

"Really? So what were you doing inside the compound? Do you realize that you could have been shot?"

"No, and I assure you I am not here by choice. It was a mistake, or something. I don't have any idea what went wrong. Nor am I sure about any of it. Last thing I knew this was Madison, Wisconsin, United States of America, early October, two thousand and twelve."

Offended, the Commandant's voice rose in pitch.

"This is not a time for jokes, Mr. Jahneke. Whether you realize it or not, you are in serious trouble. If for no other reason than the fact that you are from Arizona which makes you at the very least, a spy. So, let's stop playing games and for your own sake, confine your answers to the truth. Or do you have some other kind of problem? Are you taking medication for some mental condition? There are were no drugs in your bag or on your person."

"I'm sorry," Reed stated, actually a bit surprised by his treatment so far. Not the stereotypical Nazi arrogance he had first expected. But then, what should he be expecting? And being called a spy! Holy jeez, back where he came from one could be shot for that. Until he found out where the hell he was at and what it was all about, he had better try to keep it low key.

"I can certainly see I am in trouble and the last thing I'm trying to do is upset you. I"m.... I don't know. I just don't know. But may I please have my money back?"

"Of course not. Do you think you will be able to buy your way out of here with that? Is this another part of your joke? That currency has been worthless for over sixty years."

"Sixty years? No... I..."

"Enough," the Commandant said and took a cell phone like thing from his pocket and spoke into it, telling whoever answered to locate Dr. Gerhardt and send him in. Then the Commandant leaned back in his chair and stared at Reed.

Reed refused to stare back at him this time, however, not wanting to aggravate the man any more than he already had but shut his eyes and concentrated as hard as he could instead, hoping beyond hope that the shoreline path along the lake front was still there and that the big old tree he had once sat under was still alive in this, whatever in hell's name, reality this was. God almighty, damn. Then, when he felt he would succeed, and so as to not alarm the Commandant, he quietly reached out and pulled all of his belongings to himself.

This time Reed really did laugh out loud. God, what he wouldn't have given to see the look on the Commandant's face when he had disappeared. But his relief was short lived when he thought of his bigger predicament. What had gone so horribly wrong? The German Army occupying what? The University campus? That certainly did not make any sense. Not by itself. It had to be bigger than that. Much bigger. What could have happened? Did Hitler somehow win World War II in some other reality, namely this one? Was that even possible? Not having been much of a history buff, he didn't know, but maybe. Everything was possible. But if that was the case, then what was he doing there, here? He hadn't even been born until the war, as he knew it, was over so how could he then have had another self or counterpart alive in that world. This world. He couldn't. So, wow. Some cosmic wires had gotten seriously crossed somehow.

But then, thinking about it further, he had to wonder if that was really true. Maybe not. He was on a self structured quest for greater knowledge and understanding. What if it was that and that alone that had gotten him here. The library mall fountain area was a portal, no doubt about that and if one knew how to get through it why couldn't it have taken him to exactly where he was now? Along with lots of other places. So, for the time being, as long as he was here, why not take advantage of it.

But in the more practical sense, what a dilemma. Badly out of date currency that might get him in trouble if he tried to spend it, a few extra clothes and no motel room for the upcoming night.

The first thing Reed did was to stuff all his possessions back into his small bag and then walk in the opposite direction away from the library area up the hill behind him, then cut down through the campus and out on to University Avenue. Clearly there wasn't anyone out searching for him and it was a relief to learn that while the city might be under military control, it wasn't under siege. Nor was it under complete martial law. It was evening and there were people out on the streets, along with motorized traffic and only rarely, a military type vehicle. It was also a relief to see that his dress and appearance weren't that much different than most of the people who were there. Instead of going south on the avenue, however, he went north, back towards the library, but with a purpose. If he was in luck, the large grassy area at the corner of University and Lake where people always gathered in good weather would still be there. And since it was an almost perfect, warm fall evening he might just find what he was looking for.

It was even better than he could have hoped. The area was packed. Young people, old people, alone, in couples and small groups clustered around, standing, sitting on benches, sitting on the grass, leaning against the trees. Perhaps not so odd under the circumstances, most of them seemed rather subdued and somewhat lifeless, however, like people without much hope. No loud talk, almost no laughter, no open expressions of joy or strong emotion. It was a disheartening sight but fortunately, most of them also shied away from paying him much attention, either, as if that alone might be crossing some boundary and getting them in trouble.

Taking his time, Reed began sauntering through what was essentially a public park. Finally he saw an old man sitting alone on the ground and went up to him. But when he was near and the bleary-eyed oldster looked up at him, he simply nodded and kept moving, leaving the strong smell of alcohol behind. At last, about to give up, he found an older woman sitting on a concrete bench alone. Grey haired and simply dressed, she saw him coming, made eye contact and held it as he approached.

"Would you mind if I sat for a while?" he asked when he was near.

Taking a closer look at him, she told him it would be okay so he sat down and purposely maintained some silence for a while, hoping she would see him as non threatening. After some moments he commented on the beautiful evening to which she responded in kind. That having gone well, he continued, hoping she would be receptive to his needs. He started with an appeal.

"I'm sorry to bother you," he said, "but I have a problem and I wonder if I might ask you some questions?"

"Well, I guess that would depend, wouldn't it? Are you with the security police?"

"What? The Gestapo?"

"My goodness. I haven't heard that term in a long, long time. Where are you from, anyway?"

For lack of a better answer he said, "Arizona."

"Arizona?" she whispered and looked around to see if anyone was within hearing distance. "Arizona? How did you get across the border into the east?"

"The east? Here? Well, this may sound pretty stupid but in all honesty, I'm not really sure. I'm sorry but I really could use some help. And the one thing I beg of you is that even if you decide I am completely crazy, please do not call the, ah, security police or whatever they are."

"Don't worry about that. I wouldn't call them even if you made a pass at me. Which you had better not, by the way. So, what exactly are you looking for?"

"Several things. First of all I find that what used to be the University library is now a headquarters building or something with a big fence around it. So, what I'm wondering is if there is another library or even a museum, some archival facility that is open to the public where I could go to catch up on my history, say from approximately nineteen forty until now."

"Do you want the truth or the new version as our conquerors have written it? Of history, I mean."

"The truth, of course, if there is such a thing."

"There is, but you won't find it in the school books or any other such place."

"I was afraid of that. Any suggestions?"

"Yes. You would have to find someone old enough to have lived through the those times who trusted you enough to want to share it with you."

"Any chance that might be you? If I had the right kind of money, I would certainly pay you."

"What does that mean? The right kind of money?"

"Unfortunately not this kind," Reed said as he reached in his pocket and pulled out some of the bills he had been able to rescue and handed her one. "But it's all I have."

Taking it, she looked at it with a shocked expression and stared at it for a long time as a few tears came to her eyes.

"Oh, my god," she said and looked away, off into the distant past. "I had almost forgotten. It's so beautiful. We have lost so much." And then, after a long pause. "Where did you get it? It was all confiscated and burned, let's see, I think it was in fifty one, right after.... "

"After what?"

"After the country fell. Our part of it."

"That's why I was hoping you might be able to help me. That's the kind of information I need and I need someone like you who would be able to tell me what happened. So why don't you keep that bill. It's only a dollar. And I can give you a little more if you want. I would also like to know if there is some safe place I might be able to exchange it for whatever they, you, are presently using for currency."

"I don't know. How much of it do you have?"

"Unfortunately, not much cause I purposely spent most of it before I, ah, came here not realizing, well ..." he said and shrugged.

No sooner had he finished his sentence than from somewhere off up on the hill there was a siren like burst about ten seconds long and then another.

"What's that?" he asked.

"Curfew begins in half an hour. I'd better be going home."

"Oh, oh," Reed said. "Just a couple more quick questions

if you don't mind. How much video surveillance do they have here in the city"

"What's video?"

"Television cameras."

"Oh, yes. Of course. Not much after the big demonstrations back in ninety nine. The put down was so severe and so many people were killed that everyone is afraid to do almost anything anymore, even in small ways so they have gone into disrepair. Everyone knows that but they are all still too afraid to do anything even slightly suspicious. But I would think you should know that even if you are from the outside."

"I'm sorry but I didn't. And is there any chance I could meet you again tomorrow? Any time and anywhere you want that I can walk to."

"Hmm, maybe. Would you give me another dollar bill if you have one?"

"Absolutely. Most gladly."

"Okay. And this might still be the safest place to meet, what with all the people who come here. Say, six o'clock. But if anything happens, I will deny I ever saw you. And stop carrying that bag, or whatever it is, around with you. It draws attention."

"I will. And thank you. I mean it. Thank you, and I'll see you tomorrow."

For lack of something better, Reed had spent the night sleeping in the bushes down along the lake shore and cleaned up in one of the restrooms up in Bascom Hall in the morning. As he found out by doing so, the university was still a university although the student population seemed about half of what it had been for him back in his own world. He had seriously considered trying to find a hotel or motel and transporting himself into one of the rooms, hoping it turned out to be vacant but decided against it. If he messed up and was reported it would call attention to the fact that he was still in the area. Of course he had no way of knowing what story the Commandant had been forced to invent to explain his disappearance but there might well be an alert out for his apprehension. One thing was in his favor, however. The Commandant and his men had only seen him with his two week old beard. Fortunately he had also rescued his shaving gear with his other few items and with some difficulty and pain, he was able to scrape most of it off before he went to sleep, finishing the job the next day. Once that was done he felt relatively safe because most people made a habit of not minding other people's business. As for the police, who knew. Now if he could only find something to eat without having to steal it. Or steal it without getting caught.

There still was a library, however, as he found out by wandering around. It was now located in a converted Frat House just off State Street. The only problem was one needed a student ID card to use it so he spent most of the day walking around the downtown area of the city instead. Fortunately, for himself, he could view it in a somewhat objective manner. Unfortunately for those who were stuck there, it was a depressing, oppressive place. Only rarely did he see anyone smiling or engaging in something humorous. Many of the ongoing conversations he was able to eavesdrop on were unhappy grumblings about the quality and availability of goods. Mostly groceries. Well, why not see for himself, he decided with an ulterior motive in mind. Finally by about noon, he was able to pocket two apples in one store and some bread in another.

Purposely and rightfully so, he saved going up to the city square until last and was horrified and saddened to see the German flag flying from the mast over the state capital building with swastika banners hanging down the sides of the proud but defamed old structure. The only good thing about it all was that most of the clocks on the lamp posts around the square still worked so he was able to head back down to the university area and be at the corner by six o'clock. And then he waited.

Maybe the old woman wouldn't be able to recognize him without all the hair on his face. That might be a good thing if she had decided to turn him in. Maybe there was a reward out for his capture or something. Just in case, he sat down and leaned against a tree so as to be more inconspicuous and tried to be casual in his behavior. What must have been a half hour passed without his seeing either the woman, any police or other persons of authority before he decided to give it up and start looking for some other source of information. With that in mind, he began moving through the crowd. It was then that he finally saw her. She was standing a little further up the hill next to a group of older people talking together.

Cautiously looking around, Reed made his way slowly and circuitously toward her. When he was by her side he quietly said hello. At first she was a bit startled but soon realized that it was still him without all the hair on his face. The little smile she gave him told him everything was okay. They spotted an empty bench and went to sit on it.

"By the way," he told her. "My name is Reed."

"And mine is Marion. What's it like in Arizona besides hot? It must be nice to live in a free country."

"Definitely. And Arizona is far more than just desert. It has tremendous variety and some of the largest forests in the country."

"But do you get to vote and choose your own leaders?"

"We do."

"Well, things were that way here when I was a little girl. But as you can see, it has changed."

"God, has it ever. But when did the United States lose the war? Do you remember the year?"

Marion looked at him curiously. "How come you don't seem to know any of those things? Didn't you go to school?"

"Well, yes. I did. But it's rather hard for me to explain. So please be patient with me, like I just dropped in from outer space or something."

"Outer space? That's a good one. But, okay. I'll do my best. I think the British fell in forty four. Then the damned Germans dropped the atomic bomb on Washington in early forty six and began invading the east coast right after that so I think it was all over by forty nine. Of course as you know, they only made it to the Mississippi River and were never able to push beyond that. Now all we do is pray that one day we will be liberated again."

"Is the fighting still going on?"

"No. Not since about the mid sixties. I think what ended it was the forced conscription of our own young men so the opposing western forces didn't want to go on killing their own people. But now we have what is called the cold war. At least that's the news we get. But no one here really knows the truth. The propaganda is always so heavy."

"So Hitler's scientists were able to develop the bomb. That explains part of it. Have you ever heard of a man named Einstein?"

"No. Yes, maybe. Something about relativity or something. Nothing important I don't think."

"How about Roosevelt and Truman and Eisenhower?"

"Sure. Roosevelt was the one who was forced to sign the surrender. Truman was our Vice President and Eisenhower was the general in charge of the war and Hitler had him shot after the defeat."

"And what about the Japanese?"

"Wow. Such a long time ago. I believe the Japanese actually came ashore and invaded the west coast. I think they also held some towns north of Los Angeles for a while until they were beaten back. That was when our western forces also got the bomb and that's why the German's were never able to take the whole country," she said. Then she looked at him very seriously and continued.

"I just can't believe you don't know these things. Are you sure you're not trying to tease me or trap me into saying something wrong?"

"Gee. I guess I do sound a bit nutty and I'm sorry. But it's not a joke. I really don't know. I just wish I could find some way to explain why without making you think I should be put in an asylum."

"Here you'd be lucky to be in an asylum. Just don't get picked up by the security forces and end up in their prison."

"Is that what the old library building is? Is that the security police?"

"How did you know it used to be the school library? You are so full of contradictions."

"I know. My information is all scattered bits and pieces.

But my father went to school here," he lied, "and I remember some of his old stories."

"He did? What was his name? I used to teach social sciences until they brought in their own professors and started with all the lies."

"Reed Jahneke. The same as mine."

"Doesn't sound familiar but it's been such a long time. Is he still alive?"

They continued to talk until the curfew alarm sounded. She was a very accommodating individual but Reed wasn't sure he wanted to ask her to continue the conversation any further the following evening. He had slipped her two twenty dollar bills which astounded her because she said they might be rather valuable if she could find the right person to sell them to and she offered him some of her money in exchange. He asked her how much it would cost to buy various things like breakfast and dinner and a cheap room in a hotel and then only took enough to cover another couple of days. The last thing she did was to ask him if he had any papers.

"Papers? You mean identity papers? No, I don't."

"I didn't think so. So you had better be careful if you go wandering around. If they catch you without them they will lock you up for sure."

"Yeah. guess I never thought of that," he said. "But I don't expect to be here much longer, so I'll be careful."

"Do you have a safe place to stay?"

"Well, I was going to try and get a room for tonight but I guess that wouldn't be a good idea."

"Without papers, don't even think about it. Too bad I don't know you better, I'd let you sleep in my basement. It's all furnished and everything."

He thanked her and told her he would never put her at risk and, yes, he had safe place for the night. Then he thanked her again for all the help she had given him and told her goodbye.

SEVENTEEN

There had been a light rain during the night. Not much. Just enough so that Reed's clothes were damp. Enough to make him feel cold and miserable and unable to get much sleep. But the sky had cleared by morning and the sun warmed him once he had crawled out from his hiding place in the bushes. A brisk walk up the hill to use the restroom also helped and, except for the growl coming from his stomach, he felt better. He also had spendable money and once he felt halfway functional again, he set off for the cafeteria in the student union.

Sausage and eggs, toast and three cups of coffee. His first real meal in two days and it was good. But now what, he wondered as he sat there with his belly full. Maybe he had messed up. Maybe he should have somehow climbed over the fence into the compound in the middle of the night, gone to the spot by the fountain, tried to beam his way out of there and hope he ended up back home where he belonged because, what was the point in staying here any longer?

So what if he gathered more information about what had happened in this sad version of the world. What could he do with it, or about it? Well, maybe he could go down to Yavapai College and sign up to teach a course about parallel worlds and the other outcomes of World War Two. Somebody would believe him, that was for sure. But someone would also believe him if he claimed he had been sent there from the Ashtar Command space ship to transmute all their souls into higher dimensional vanaspace. Or whatever wild sounding nonsense might come to mind. This space ship, by the way, was rumored to be parked twenty seven thousand miles up in synchronous orbit around old mother earth somewhere over Missouri. Or was it Texas?

Okay, cut the crap, he finally told himself. None of this was about gaining some kind of perverse recognition for himself. Or financial gain. Or anything else except to increase his own personal knowledge about the inner workings of the universe. As long as he could remember he had always been unsatisfied with the easy answers and dumb, non explanations as to the larger scenario. Religion was so stupidly simplistic and appallingly unsatisfying that it was shocking to see so many people willing to give it acceptance. But as for science, it had its own severe limitations.

Certainly, relativity and quantum mechanics had opened the door into regions of more provocative thought. Experiment and string theory also hinted at the real profundity of the universe. Science, however, in it's bullheaded attempts to retain systematic scientific objectivity at all costs had so narrowed some of its own viewpoints to such a degree that a lot of what should have been intuitively obvious was banned from even the barest of consideration and comprehensively lost in the quest to achieve some greater understanding of the entirety of it all. As a result, mankind, for all of its sometimes greatness and grand potential, was severely limited by its own confusion regarding any higher purpose it might have beyond just living and dying. Science, in its pursuit of truth, had declared life to be an accidental happening and therefore meaningless by definition. A most depressing, demeaning and damaging paradigm. But totally wrong, Reed was convinced. Life was not meaningless at all. Life had a deeper purpose and greater meaning that extended far beyond the illusionary physical world. As a result, if people's personal philosophy encompassed some larger view of things, then their lives would be much more rewarding and satisfying. And that was the answer to his own question.

Of course he needed to stay here a little longer. If for no other reason than because of the fact that he was extremely curious as to how Germany could have won the war with a leader so insane and inept at battlefield strategy as Hitler. It didn't make any sense. But how could he find out? He certainly wouldn't be allowed in the library and his chances of meeting someone with that level of information were very limited. But, ah. The Commandant. What was his last name? He had heard one of the guards use it when they first apprehended him. Gerhardt? No, Gerhardt was the name of some doctor the Commandant had sent for whom Reed never got to meet because of his early departure. Probably a psychiatrist to check his mental condition. So, not Gerhardt.

Schmidt. That was it. So what did Commandant Schmidt do for lunch? Carry a brown bag or eat out? Maybe he just came across the street to the student union. There were still a couple of uniformed men there as Reed finished his coffee and suddenly realized how reckless he had been, even though he was sitting back in the corner somewhat out of sight. But, okay. So far he had been lucky and it was worth a try. Then he looked at the clock on the wall over the checkout counter.

It was only ten minutes after seven. He had been up early. But then, what time might a Commandant show up for duty? Eight o'clock, nine o'clock? Maybe he wouldn't have to wait until lunch time. Maybe the man ate his breakfast here also. If only he had a textbook to read or a notebook to write in to appear more like he belonged there, however.

Two tables over there was a girl with a stack of books on her table as she ate. Getting up, he went over and asked her if she might have a history book. No, she didn't. Just zoology, first year chemistry and remedial English. She was using her analytical geometry book studying for a test and after looking at him, wasn't about to share any of them. Okay, what else? Then he saw what appeared to be a version of a newspaper left on another table, now empty. Retrieving it, he went back to his own table and used it to hide behind, wondering if it wasn't a waste of time.

Waiting the way he was, made him nervous. Even if the Commandant showed up, what then? He needed some kind of plan to keep himself from being apprehended again because next time he might not be so lucky. What if some of these security police were gun happy and shot him without warning? Or just used their night sticks to beat him up before he could disappear?

By nine o'clock he was a nervous wreck. The commandant hadn't shown up and it was impossible for him to stay there any longer. Outside, he walked down to the lake shore and what appeared to be the very same lake as always. But the docks were different. Larger and longer, there were two patrol boats tied up to the piers with flags flying from the transoms. Black flags with red swastikas on them and he suddenly found himself feeling very angry. Somehow it seemed so very, very wrong and it took him a while before he was able to convince himself that none of this had anything to do with him. It was not his fight and the best thing he could do for now was to stay out of it. With that he turned around, went back to the campus and walked up the path along the lake shore instead. The same path he had met Susan on in one reality back, before something went wrong and he ended up in this shocking place. Well, nothing to do except keep walking for now and kill some time before going back to the cafeteria again.

Fortunately there seemed to be very little military or police presence on the campus itself and he was able to walk around freely and go into the buildings. He even followed some students into the auditorium of Sterling Hall and sat through a lecture for a thermodynamics course to use up some of his time. By the time it ended the clock on the wall said it was eleven thirty so he hurried back down the hill to the cafeteria.

After loading up his tray he went back to the area where he had eaten his breakfast because it was out of the way, downed his lunch and began thinking about how he might handle it if the Commandant did indeed show it, hopefully by himself because if there were other people with him, there was little chance of making contact without creating a problem. Then, before he could begin to think it through, damned if it wasn't the man himself, going through the serving line, apparently all alone. What more could he ask for.

Reed watched and waited to see where the Commandant would sit and was shocked to see him coming towards his side of the big dining area. Holy shit. And then, damned if the man didn't sit down at the very next table with his back to Reed. Was it just coincidence? He sure as hell hoped so. But even if it weren't it finally occurred to Reed that, having disappeared from right in front of him before, he probably had a tremendous psychological advantage over the situation. Waiting until the Commandant seemed to be done eating, he got up and went around the Commandant's table so that they were facing.

"Good morning, Herr Schmidt," he said, purposely ignoring the man's rank. "Would you mind if I joined you?"

The Commandant looked up with a scowl and stared at him without recognition. Then he almost spilled his coffee on himself. Without waiting for approval, Reed pulled out a chair and sat down.

"I only want to talk to you," he said. "So please stay calm and don't do anything rash."

It seemed quite clear that Reed's appearance had had a strong affect but any fear on the Commandant's part was quickly suppressed. But Reed knew he had interpreted the man's reaction correctly and pressed to take further advantage of it.

"Don't worry, Commandant. I didn't come here to harm you. But, at the same I don't want you to bring harm to me either. So, if we can have that kind of understanding I will behave myself and not make you disappear the way I did in your interrogation room, even though it is within my power to do so."

What the hell, Reed said to himself after he said it. It sounded good and what did the Commandant know about his limitations. After having seen Reed vanish from right in front of his eyes he would have to believe almost anything was possible. And apparently he did because after staring at Reed in confused silence for several seconds he finally nodded his head in agreement.

"Good," Reed said. "Now try and relax. Like I said, all I want to do is talk. Actually, all I want is for you to talk. As you must have guessed by now, I am not from your world, but a different one. So, stupid as it may sound, I need you to give me some historical information about the war and then I will be on my way and no one will know about our encounter except for you and me. And while I might consider you to be my enemy in some respects, I must also apologize for any trauma this experience may have caused you. That was not my intent but since your men had apprehended me and I was in custody, I felt I had little choice except to do what I did."

Even after the reassurance it took the Commandant a while before he was able to speak

"By all means," he said. "Whatever I can do to help. But why the war? It happened so long ago. Before either one of us were, ahh..... before I was born at least," he said with a sideways glance at Reed.

"Yes, me too. But I'm betting that as a part of your education, both as a German and as a military man, that your knowledge of German military history would be good. Even taking into account whatever distortions might have been added by the victorious. So, with that in mind let me say that there is one major thing I do not understand," Reed said and paused.

"And what is that?" the Commandant asked after a moment.

"Just this. From my understanding of Hitler and some of his, should we say limitations and peculiarities, and in spite of the fact the Germany was able to build an atomic bomb first, how were the Germans able to win the war?"

"And I am sorry, Mister Jahneke, how could I ever forget your name, whoever you may be, but I cannot see how it might have turned out any differently. Although it is true that Hitler had his limitations as you say, he allowed his Generals complete freedom to stategize as they wanted, which, for the most part, they did brilliantly."

"Well, maybe you are right but obviously I am missing something here so allow me to ask some specific questions because I'm .... well, never mind. First just tell me the outcome of your country's attack on the Russians."

"Germany never attacked the Russians. Nor did the Russians attack Germany. We have never been at war with Russia. It seems to be that both sides decided it would be a battle neither side could win."

"Does Dunkirk mean anything to you?"

"Of course. That's where the Brits suffered a major defeat when the panzers literally drove the British army right into the sea."

"They didn't halt their advance and allow the British to regroup and evacuate?"

"Of course not. That would have been stupid."

"Have you ever heard the term, D Day?"

"No."

"Who became the Commander in Chief of the German army?'

"Who else but Rommel. Right after he defeated the British in Egypt and captured the Suez Canal. A most brilliant man. One of the best strategists the world has ever seen."

"And how did Germany conquer the British Isles?"

"Actually it wasn't very difficult. We just increased the blitz and kept it up until London was completely demolished. The rest was easy."

"And what year did Germany have a usable atomic bomb by and where was it first used?"

"I'm not sure of the first date but it was used to blow up Washington DC in the summer of forty seven. And I really do not understand the need for your questions. You have enough information to ask them well enough but at the same time, how could you not know the answers. It's all a part of history."

"Yes. Your history as you know it. Where I come from it turned out much differently."

"How could it have? I mean .." the Commandant said and then gave Reed a disturbed look, suddenly realizing once again the uniqueness of the man he was talking with. Then he asked, "Is it possible...?" as his question made his mind spin with the implications.

"I assure you it is and I won't take up much more of your time. First tell me about the holocaust, as my world would refer to it. The Jews and the concentration camps."

"A tragedy of unbelievable proportions. I doubt that we will ever live down the infamy. All these generations later and we still suffer from it."

"Doesn't look like you are suffering too much. And I'm sure you never heard of a place called Israel."

"I have. We learned that the British were thinking of forming such a country, giving other people's land to the Jews."

"Other people's land? You can say that after your country over-ran half the world?"

"No. You are right but at the time ... You must understand how impossible that would have been."

"I think I do. So, how much of the world is now under German control?"

"All of western Europe, most of north Africa and the

eastern half of the United States. There was no reason to go into Canada or Mexico at the time and to attempt to do so now would be foolish. We are trying to present a new face to the world."

"How? By using your security police to suppress and intimidate the people it controls?"

"Well, that is a necessary but bothersome thing. As I'm sure you have seen, this area is now quite stable since the uprising ten years ago was put down but it is still a constant threat and vigilance is the necessary consequence. Americans are never content. Always demanding control over their own affairs, always creating disruption and turmoil, always sabotaging our efforts to maintain peace."

"But Commandant. What good is peace without freedom? You don't seem to understand. You have freedom, they do not."

"But I do understand. Privately of course. I have an American wife also, and I live with her concerns every day. But I am also in the military and I have my duties to perform."

"So there you go. Duty first, humanity second. Has not that always been the excuse for bad behavior? Of course the way things turned out in this world, you have never heard of the Nuremberg trials. Too bad."

"Nuremberg, yes. The trials, no. What was the significance?'

"To answer that, try and imagine a different outcome to the war. Difficult as it might seem, imagine that Germany was defeated and that after the war many German leaders who were responsible for all the horrific treatment of the Jews were put on trial and that almost every one of them pleaded not guilty because, because, mind you, they claimed they were only following orders and therefore their actions were excusable. The Nuremberg justices, however, came to a different conclusion. The conclusion was that it didn't matter. Humans must answer to some higher authority and if they are ordered to treat their fellow humans in some barbaric way, then it is their duty to refuse to obey those orders."

At first the Commandant seemed a bit astounded by Reed's statement and he sat in silence for a while, thinking about it.

"Well, I find that hard to argue with. And if only it were possible, the world would be a better place to live in."

"But it is possible. That's what you need to understand. There are times when one must put their own comfort and indulgence aside and do the more noble thing. Unfortunately, even back in my own world where this magnificent decision was made a point came where we had our own insane group of leaders. A situation where our own president, vice president, the secretary of defense and more, all should have been locked up for war crimes but were not and maybe never will be. Despicable, disgusting men without brains or conscience. So, what can I say."

"I would say that the world is not a good place for idealists."

"And you would be right. But without something to aspire to, what else is there that is really important?"

"So, Mr. Reed. You are not some super human who comes here from some greatly advanced society after all. And while you have either the technology and the backup that makes it possible for you to disappear from right in front of me, or you somehow have the personal power to do that, then I must surmise that there are limitations to what you can do. Am I correct?"

"Why do you ask, Commandant? Are you playing the role of soldier again? If you are then let me remind you of one thing. At this point I am still treating you in a neutral manner. But if we are adversaries my advice would be to remind you that the worst mistake one can make is to underestimate their opponent. So, keeping that in mind let me repeat what I said earlier. If you do not attempt to harm me, I will not bring harm to you. Is that clear enough?" Reed said in a strong, deliberate voice, playing on the Commandant's imagination and limited knowledge.

"Very clear. And my sincere apologies for playing soldier some more but you realize I spend most of my time intimidating people to get them to do what needs to be done. But, yes. Your philosophy is more advanced. There has never been much room in my world for idealism but I think it is something I could aspire to. I will certainly give it some consideration."

"And I thank you for that. One last question, maybe two, and then we are done. Tell me what you can about Hitler?"

"At the risk of losing my commission I would say that he was completely insane. So were some of his closest supporters. Fortunately, however, most of the military learned to defy him near the end or, as you say happened in your world, we would most certainly have lost the war. Hitler, meantime, got most of the glory but degenerated into nothing more than a figurehead until.. No one knows for sure but in, I think it was fifty one, he went with his woman to Austria on vacation. The Eagles Nest, they called it. A place up in the mountains which he used as a retreat."

"Yes. I have heard of it. What happened?"

"Nobody seems to know. He just disappeared and never came back to Berlin. Well, isn't that interesting. Did you or your people somehow intercede?"

Reed laughed at the thought. "Now that would be a simple way to keep peace in the world. Make tyrants disappear. Put them on some remote island together so they couldn't create problems. But then he answered the Commandant's question, adding some embellishment.

"No," he said. "Thus far our policy has been one of non interference. For the most part we feel that people must be given the chance to work out their politics in their own way. Only on rare occasions where the people themselves become too oppressed and atrocities take place, do we get involved. Otherwise we grant everyone the right of self determination, as much as possible, of course."

"I see. Most interesting. Now, if I might, I will share with you the flimsiest of rumors. Unfortunately, even if there is some truth to them it is not a question of honor, or noble cause, but solely one of practicality. Maybe you are already aware of it but there has been some talk about giving up the States of Wisconsin, Illinois, Michigan and maybe Indiana. Let them rejoin the western states. There are no real valuable natural resources here, just a lot of ongoing trouble. And it is always very costly to remedy trouble. So, like I say, it's not a humanitarian thing, just good economics. And if that is the case I would not dare to stay behind the way we are still hated. But, well, I would like to. Maybe there are amends. Time will tell, won't it?"

"Indeed it will, Commandant. And while I could keep you tied up for days with more questions, I must admit I have enjoyed my time with you and I appreciate the way you have cooperated. So, with that in mind I must prevail upon you for one last favor and trust you will grant it in good faith."

"Most likely. But again, only if it is not disruptive. I have also enjoyed our time together. And if I can somehow wrap my mind around how you got here and how you will probably be leaving, I may be okay. Certainly you have given me a lot to think about and perhaps, something to aspire to. So how can I help?"

"Just walk back across the street with me, bring me inside the compound with you and leave me alone at the fountain for a few brief moments."

The Commandant looked at Reed for a very long time, obviously thinking his way through a whole lot of things before responding. Some of them good, some of them not so good. Then he agreed.

EIGHTEEN

Damn. Now what went wrong, Reed asked himself as he looked around. He was back in Arizona, all right, but he certainly wasn't standing in the living room of his house like he had expected to be. Instead, he was standing in the exact spot where it should have been but the house itself did not exist. So what did that mean? As far as he knew, there were only two possibilities. One might be that he was still in the same world and time that the Commandant was in or he had returned to his own world but must have gone back in time. So, now what? Either way he wasn't about to try and fix it until he was sure as to when and where he was. It also made him realize that he needed a lot more experience bouncing around the universe before he got himself into some situation where he couldn't get back. What the hell, maybe he was already in one. And for right now, the only way he could find out where he was really at was to walk up the hill to Jerome and hope to hell the town itself actually existed. And if it didn't ...?

Well, thank god. What a relief. He could see old houses and buildings clinging to the side of the mountain as he made his way up the paved road and for the most part, the road seemed about the same as in his own world, except he had never walked it before. Then he heard a vehicle coming up the hill behind him so he got over onto the side and waited for it to pass. Instead of passing however, it pulled up alongside and stopped. It was a pickup truck but of a kind he didn't recognize.

"Get in," the driver told him through the open window.

Finding the door handle, Reed did just that.

"Thank you. I appreciate it," he said to the older man behind the wheel, a gray haired, solid looking individual with a strong voice who gave him a quick look over before he took his foot off the brake and stepped on the gas.

"You don't look like you've been down in the hole," the man said.

"The hole?" Reed questioned.

"You're not a miner."

"Oh, right. I'm not. I'm a, ah, a writer."

"Well, you came to the right place. This place is full of untold stories. Some of them are so bizarre I have a hard time believing them myself. But that's what makes life interesting, isn't it?"

"No doubt about that. I'm kinda working on one of those myself. Anyway, nice truck. Looks new," Reed said to change the subject.

"Last year's model but, yeah, I like it a lot and I'm glad they're finally back in full production."

"I heard that," Reed lied. "Where was this one made?" he asked as he finally saw the name in chrome letters on the dash. It was a Dodge Power Wagon. A name revived from the long ago past.

"California," the driver said and was silent for a bit. Then he began again.

"A writer, huh. So you must get around. You don't look

like you're from this part of the world. Any chance you have heard those rumors about us getting part of our country back?"

"You mean the upper Midwest?" Reed asked, now knowing exactly where he was. Still in the same world he had just left behind. The one he had no counterparts in.

"Right. Anything to that?"

"I think it's probably true," he agreed, seriously wondering how much he really cared. It had been a very interesting journey for him but did he really want to know the rest of the World War II outcome story? Not exactly. Mostly he just wanted to get back to his own time and place, but, how to do that?

By then they had made it up to the edge of the town and Reed asked to be let out at the big red brick buildings that looked out over the valley and which the signs indicated were still the school. There he thanked the man, waited until he was out of sight and started walking back down the mountain road. Once back at the place on the ridge where his house should have been, he tried again. Nothing. Then again, and nothing. So what next. The alcove out in Sycamore Canyon would certainly be there because it was hundreds of years old so he tried to transport himself there, and there he was. Good. Then another attempt to get home and that worked too. There he was back in his own house, seemingly also at the right point in time and with that he let out a sigh of relief.

Well, Kyara was certainly right about one thing. Access to some realms could only be gained by being at certain coordinate points and going through portals. Portals, for lack of a better name, were connecting points that intersected with other realities and linked them together. Like the alcove and the fountain back in Wisconsin. But whether or not they connected with just some realities or all of them wasn't clear. And what did, 'all of them,' mean? How many were there? An infinite number? If everything played itself out in every possible manner, there had to be. And then what? Was that another unanswerable question? Whatever it was, it hinted at some unending striving for continued evolvement and ongoing creation. Value fulfillment, to use the words from something he had read. Something to strive for without expectation of coming to perfection. Of necessity, an open ended system where there could be no ultimate perfection or end to things.

If perfection could be achieved, then perfection would be the end. There would be no eternal validity of the self or of anything else. Additionally, what was perfection? A concept or idea, but what does it mean in the bigger sense? Does it even have a meaning in those terms? It doesn't seem like it because perfection is, as the expression goes, in the eyes of the beholder. So then, is the multiverse (more limiting terminology), is the multiverse striving to reach perfection in God's eyes, assuming God is again some singular thing? And if that goal might eventually be reached, then what will happen to God? What will God then do to keep from going insane?

Or, was that how it all began to begin with? Was God dead ended in some state of perfection and on the verge of insanity so God blew himself/ herself/ itself up into an infinity of small particles that reached to infinity. Particles which were endowed with their own creativity and had the ability to recombine and unite in an infinity of never ending ways so that "God was and is a part of all things," human and otherwise, and becomes ever able to amaze and outdo itself by allowing a never ending ultimate freedom of choice. God, he hoped so. And now that he thought about it, perhaps that was what he had set out to do in some subconscious, poorly defined way to begin with, seeking some higher form of fulfillment. But not right now. Now he was feeling both very hungry and very exhausted and that over-rode everything else that was on his mind. He had also gone ten days without his favorite drink. Root beer.

None of it was a serious problem, however. Even though he had purposely ran the contents of his refrigerator down to almost nothing because he didn't know how long he would be gone, the cupboards were still well stocked so he dug out a box of pancake mix and went to work. Then, knowing that there should still be some sticks of butter in the refrigerator and some syrup because they both kept a long time, he opened the door, looked in and stared at what he saw.

100

Backing away, he shut the door and leaned against the counter. Then he looked again. Sure enough, he wasn't imagining it. Next, after shaking his head in dismay and for lack of a better idea, he went in the dining room, turned on his computer and went on line. Then he went to the Los Angeles Times web site, pulled up the front page of the newspaper and looked at the date posted on the page. How could that be possible, he wondered, his self confidence as a reality hopping traveler once again shattered. Not only did he think that the date was wrong, he had read the headlines once before. The same headlines. Then he took one more look at the date posted on the page, which was supposed to be today's date, one last time to be sure. How was it possible.?

Thinking back, he was quite certain that the day he had gone to Wisconsin was on the fourteenth of September. Yes, he was sure of it because it was his mother's birthday. Of course his mother was long deceased but it was one date he never forgot because she also died on her birthday. And what date was on the front page of the newspaper? August twenty seventh, over two weeks before he had even left. Forgetting for the moment that he was extremely hungry, he went outside for some fresh air and sat down on the low wall that ran around the patio area. Finally, however, his hunger got the best of him and he went back into the house and looked into the refrigerator again. He had already eaten all the eggs that were in the door tray once, but there they were again, seemingly just as fresh as ever, so what else was there to do but get out the frying pan and see what happened.

Eating the same eggs twice was enough to make a person crazy but they still tasted good. So did the toast and strawberry jam and the coffee. But just to make sure he was right, he went back on line after he finished eating and re verified the date with three other sources. After all that he felt totally exhausted and was soon fast asleep on his, better than the cold ground any day, big couch.

NINETEEN

It was a long nap and when he finally woke he was still a bit anxious about what had happened. But once he learned that his bank had not deducted the amounts he thought he had already paid out for his phone and electric bills, however, he was okay. Almost. Almost, hell. Where had the eighteen days gone? He had certainly lived them. He had the memories to prove it to himself. Plus, he also remembered, he still had some of the paper currency he had gotten from the woman, Marion, plus some hard change he had gotten back when he spent some of it. Those eerie coins with swastikas on them. And, so what? Who would ever believe where they had come from if he was ever foolish enough to try and tell someone. But, well, on the other side of things, he at least didn't have to run down the hill to buy groceries for a while since he had a second go at everything he had already devoured and that got him thinking along another line.

What if, he wondered, as he realized he now had a way to test a very important issue. The one scientists always brought up when people talked about time travel. Scientists, of course, always liked to take the most dismal view of everything possible, a mind set they seemed to enjoy as authority figures. But, why not? If they believed their own stories about the accidental creation of the universe that made life completely meaningless, they would always end up with negative conclusions. What else could it be when it was their own self imposed, stubborn refusal to acknowledge the vast sea of both physical and non physical evidence which surrounded them that kept them locked into a narrow, unimaginative view of any greater reality. Much as he might sometime love to be up on a stage somewhere talking to a large group of eminent scientists and disappear from right in front of them, they would only conclude that it was a carefully rigged magic show and they had simply been duped by an illusionist. So why go there. What he was going to try and find out was for his own information. This was for himself.

A stack of one hundred, one hundred dollar bills wasn't all

that thick or that heavy and he could certainly stuff it in his pockets. The only thing wrong was that if he succeeded in what he was about to try, he would have to come back down the hill all over again when it was accomplished because this time he would definitely need to restock his house with food. A minor problem, he thought as he climbed the hill in his old truck on his return home from the bank with a stack of cash. Once inside, he went to his computer to reaffirm the day's date, crammed the hundred dollar bills into his jeans and stood in the living room in the same spot where he had been able to transport his body before and thought of the date he should have returned home from his last adventure on.

At first he wasn't sure it had worked because he was still in the same location and nothing felt any different. But he had left his computer turned on, he knew that. And now it was off. So he turned it back on. Sometimes the damned thing was so slow in booting up, he thought impatiently as he waited. Maybe it was time to defragment again but then, there it was, the scene bright and waiting so he went back on line to see what had happened. Or had not happened.

Well, I'll be damned, he said to himself as he took a second look. He was back in his own present. Almost. Instead of being over two weeks early as before and still in the same place he was in when the day started, he was one day late from the time he should have returned in the first place. But close enough. And now, time to check the facts. The first thing was to get all the hundred dollar bills out of his pockets and count them, just to make sure. He did and it was still all there. Then he pulled up his on line bank statement and compared it to the last one he had received in the mail that he had dug out of his desk. Except for the two checks for his phone and power bills which had been paid when he had been back in Germany, as he referred to it for lack of a better description, the balance was the same. So there. Not only was he suddenly ten thousand dollars richer, he had proved something very significant to himself. Places in time all have their own separate integrity. That meant, contrary to all scientific speculation, that he could go back in time, find and kill his own grandfather and for sure still be alive in his present reality. A very minor detail, actually, when one considered all the other aspects of the situation because it also meant that some suicidal lunatic couldn't go back in time, blow up the world he was then in and put an end to this one. Not much of a relief when one considered that there were already far too many nut cases out there that would settle for just blowing up the present one if they had the means and opportunity. And so much for that, what he really needed was some R and R.

TWENTY

Not having to take his shoes off and go through airport security was a great blessing for Reed. He didn't have to drive to Phoenix, either. Or stand in line or waste all those hours on an overloaded flying contraption held together with bolts and rivets that was flawed with metal fatigue and poor maintenance. Pack a small bag, hold it close and end up at the Club Med in Zihuantanejo for some time on the beach. Except that they were entirely booked when he got there. He hadn't thought of that.

"What about Moorea?" he asked the young female clerk behind the reception counter.

"Moorea is closed," she said. "But Bora Bora is open."

"Can you check and see if they have an opening?"

"Of course. When would you be arriving?"

"This afternoon?"

"This afternoon? That's not possible unless you have your own private jet."

"I know," he replied and gave her his personal information and his debit card.

She looked at him a moment as if trying to decide if he were legit, went to the computer and filled in the reservation. Giving him back his debit card, she gave him another curious look.

"Thank you," he told her as he scanned the room around him where everyone seemed completely absorbed in their own affairs. Since she thinks I have my own airplane, I might as well have some fun, he decided.

"Do you have a brochure or catalog?" he asked, and when

she turned away, he disappeared, wishing he could have somehow also seen the look on her face when she turned back around.

Despite all the other disadvantages of flying commercially, this is where being in an airplane would have been worth the hassle, Reed told himself. Being able to see South Pacific islands and atolls from above. Spectacular shades of turquoise, blue and emerald. Black sand beaches on the main island, stretches of white elsewhere through the chain. But, okay. For now he was happy to settle for the sand between his toes in this special place.

A couple of sunbathers looked a little shocked at his sudden appearance but as with most anything that defies logic, they assumed he must have been there all along and they just hadn't noticed. Good enough, Reed decided and walked towards the reception center.

Inside, he went up to one of the bikini clad girls behind the counter and asked for Monique.

"I'm Monique. How can I help you?" she said.

"I have a reservation," Reed said and gave her his name.

She looked at him strangely before responding. "Yes. I just took it. But it came from Ixtapa in Mexico. I thought.... I didn't realize you were already here. Why didn't you...?"

"Well, " he said. "It's a long story and, anyway, it looks like I'm just in time for lunch. Is that okay? I don't mind paying extra."

"I, ah, think it will be okay," she said and started processing his information. "You'll be in cottage twenty three," she told him and showed him where it was on the small map of the resort. "Do your want to buy your beads now? For alcoholic beverages. Beads are our medium of exchange at the ...."

"Of course. Thank you. I know. I've been here before. So, let's see. Maybe fifty dollars American for now. Put it on my card."

She made the entry and handed him two strings of purple, snap together plastic beads and reminded him about being under the palm trees because the coconuts were ripe and falling.

He nodded, thanked her again and went in search of his cottage. Finding it, he got out his bathing suit, put it on, and tried to remember where the dining hall was at. Food first, sunshine later. Then, hopefully, a long, lazy, nothing much accomplished week during which he could rethink and review some of his previous adventures. Or not, as the case might be. For now it didn't matter.

The first three days were perfect. Lots of food and wine, swimming, snorkeling, afternoon naps in the sun, evening entertainment and a sky full of starry wonders south of the equator. On the fourth day, after filling his lunch tray, he looked for an empty place at one of the long tables, found one and sat down. And then, looking up he saw a blue eyed woman with her blond hair all stacked on top of her head looking back at him who then sat down. She brushed a few loose ringlets aside, gave him a small smile and began to eat once he returned the smile.

At first it didn't seem possible. She was old enough, obviously intelligent enough but just too damned attractive to make it seem like a proper career choice for her. She had spent time at Palomar, Kitt Peak, and the observatory on Maui along with others and now taught astrophysics at the university in Sydney. Astrophysics? Dr. Jill, PhD. Now wasn't that interesting, he decided, and would she like to go for a walk on the beach after they were done eating.

"Where's your husband?" he asked once he got past the way her white bathing suit accented both her curves and her newly acquired tan and he finally noticed the ring she was wearing.

She looked at it and smiled. "Probably at home," she said. "I just dumped the silly shit, if you will pardon my language. And this is my first holiday in two years."

"Good for you, I guess. And if you dumped him, it must have been for cause."

"Actually, nothing serious. Just exceedingly boring. Plus he started loving his latest little project more than me. I'm not sure he even realizes I'm gone."

"Boring is one thing. Brain dead is something else. He'd

have to be blind not to notice you and totally numb not to miss you when you're not there."

"Well, that's right nice. Or are you just being solicitous because you want to make out with me?"

"No. It was the most serious thing I've said all day."

"Thank you. That's really very sweet."

"Thank you. And what was it that made him so boring, if you don't mind sharing?"

"The end of the universe."

"Really? The end of the universe?"

"Yes. He became obsessed with it."

"How could... okay, I think I get it. Is he a physicist too?"

"He is. And he was my college professor. Ten years older than me but at the time I was quite impressed with both the man and the general subject of cosmology. For the first few years of our marriage I thought he was a relatively normal guy. And then his obsession got in the way."

"The end of the universe?"

"So much so that he gave up his professorship to work on it. For some reason he decided it was more important to know what might happen to the human race in a billion years or so when our sun overheats and makes the planet uninhabitable, than it was to explore life with me."

"Well, I'm glad someone took on the project because I've been worrying about that since I was a little boy," Reed said with mock seriousness.

Jill laughed. "Yeah, pretty threatening stuff. It should be a mandatory part of the elementary school curriculum. The sooner the better to start preparing the general public for that one."

"Except you couldn't live with his ..... ah, whatever?"

"Oddity, is the only way I can describe it. But I still might have been able to put up with it but he not only left teaching, he started sleeping in the spare bedroom."

"Well, at least it wasn't another woman. That would have made him an even bigger fool."

"Do you think so?"

"Are you kidding?" he said as he looked at her. "Absolutely."

"Thank you," she smiled. "But do you know what the most ridiculous part is? Once he was published there was enough interest in the subject to put him in demand as a paid guest speaker."

Reed shook his head in amazement. "My god," he said. " If people want to pay to hear about what might happen in a billion years, there is no hope."

"So what is there to say. Now he gets to travel occasionally and sleep with his computer so at least he's happy. So am I because he snored horrifically. Plus I was given his professorship. And someday I'll have a new man in my life."

"I'm sure you will," Reed agreed completely. "And a lucky guy he will be. Another scientist perhaps?"

"It's doubtful. I think I've had enough of over educated, tunnel visioned drones. I guess that's the thing that upsets me the most. What's that expression? Can't see the forest for the trees? And if I thought he was bad, you should have seen his older brother."

"Because?"

"It's a personal thing. If some person wants to spend their entire life examining the mating habits of a single species of grasshopper, I guess that's fine. It's an isolated field of inquiry. But if a study relates to humans I like to see people with a little more perspective."

"In what way?"

"World population recently hit seven billion and is postulated to keep on growing. In his eyes the only relevant problem is how to double world food production within the next several decades."

"And on the surface that would seem to be a legitimate concern. Except...."

"Exactly. Except it totally misses the mark."

"So you think the proper thing to do would be to determine how many people the planet could properly sustain first, try to limit its growth and then figure out how to feed them second."

"I do. Or at least be working on both problems at the same time. And straight away. Because if the population was in

108

balance with the environment, we wouldn't have to worry about feeding them. And forget the fact that about ninety percent of our other problems would automatically go away with far fewer people. But I think you already know that so we can change the subject if you'd like."

"Or not. I just like to hear you talk."

"Why is that?"

"Just something about Australian women. I don't particularly like the Australian males, hey-mate bullshit, but I find most of the women to be quite adorable, plus you have a very musical voice that has such a nice rhythm to it."

"Really? Well, thank you some more."

"My pleasure. And I know you're on holiday but what are your thoughts on parallel worlds? Is that part of the curriculum?"

"Cosmology?"

"Yeah."

"That interests you?" she asked with a rather surprised look.

"Sometimes. Parallel worlds, alternate realities, and if there are alternate worlds, what's in them and do we have alternate selves?"

"Well, thank god you're looking at the bigger picture. You didn't just ask me where heaven is located."

"No, I already know that. And that's the last place I ever want to try and get to."

"Get to? Would you like to go to other alternate realities if you could?"

"Well, pretty lady. How do you know I haven't already done that?" Reed asked as they came up to a palm tree where he looked up to make sure there were no coconuts overhead that might fall on them if they sat down under it.

"Hmm," she said as she studied his face once they were sitting. "You appear to be relatively sane. Is that where you came from before you landed here? Some alternate reality?"

"No. Nothing like that. I came from Arizona by way of Mexico."

"By means of conventional transportation?"

"Well, certainly not by UFO, so you don't have to worry

about being abducted."

"That's a relief."

"Good. But what about those theorists who say there may be something like ten to the five hundredth power of other universes out there that are hidden from view? That is an imaginative idea, don't you think?"

"String theory? Are you a physicist too?"

"No. Just a person with an overactive amount of curiosity. But the last thing I want is to bore you with my questions."

"Not at all. I like men with inquiring minds as long as they don't stall out and get stuck on a singular topic."

"Like your soon to be ex."

"Right on. And, yes, an idea of a multiverse is very interesting. Is there something about it that you want to discuss."

"Are you sure it's okay? Because the idea of multiple universe seems to open the door to a lot of wild possibilities. At least for me. So my first question is what keeps them hidden from view? And what are they made of? The numbers don't seem to agree."

"What numbers?" she asked.

"Well, let's see if I can remember correctly. Ordinary matter makes up only four percent of the universe. Twenty three percent is dark matter which has gravitational effects but does not interact with light, and the rest is dark energy. So if one took all the dark energy and converted it to matter and added it to the dark matter, there still wouldn't be enough physical material to create the huge number of universes the string theorists say could be there. So, where are they?"

"That's the problem with theory. It's easy to speculate and it takes a long time to disprove ideas when they are wrong. Meantime, we do the best we can. Make untold numbers of observations, collect stupendous amounts of data and then try to formalize the reasons as to why it turns out this way rather than some other. With all the advances in technology, cosmology has come a long way. But there are still far more questions than answers. As to where those postulated other universes may be, I don't know. Present ideas show our universe as finite so other universes would most likely be outside and separate from ours. I guess. What do you say?"

"I say, why some specific large number? Why not an infinity? If there are limits as to how much space exists then what is on the other side of that? Nothing? The concept becomes meaningless. But within what we think of as our universe, limited or otherwise, why couldn't we have universes within universes, not only sharing the same spatial field with each other but also material and energy. Maybe we are surrounded by, or living within other universes, or alternate realities as I prefer to think of them and maybe we weave in and out of them all the time without even knowing it."

At this point Jill gave him a curious look and paused before answering. "That's interesting," she said. "What else do you think about in your spare time. And I'm not making fun of you. It's a serious question."

"Okay. What about time? Is it just a psychological illusion or does it actually flow in a way where we move through it?"

"What are you really asking?"

"There has never been an experiment that actually proved the passage of time, so what are the ramifications of that? Wasn't it the Aspect experiment that proved that the past can be changed and have an effect on the outcome of an experiment in the present? Doesn't that prove that the past is not over but somehow still exists?" Reed asked. Even though he thought he already knew some of the answers to his questions from personal experience, he still wanted her opinion.

"Perhaps, but it's still not a view that is generally accepted. We like to think we are looking back in time when we observe the stars, which is true in the sense that we can only see them as they once were but have no idea of their present state. As for last week still being around, well, I can certainly entertain that idea. I used to love science fiction when I was younger and I was somewhat intrigued with the idea of time machines but I have no idea as to how one could build such a thing. If a tachyon is a faster than light particle moving backwards in time as Feynman said, maybe one could slow a large number of them down, build a capsule out of them, get inside and go back in time. Of course one would need a control system that would allow you to stop where you want or you would be on a forever ride back to the beginning of the universe. The other aspect of the idea of tachyons is that if they show up in what is our present, then they must have come from our future which implies that the future already exists too. Hmmm."

"Hmm, is right," Reed repeated after her. "But as for using that to visit the past, there is one thing wrong with that idea."

"I know. It would also require the existence of another kind of particles which are moving from the past into the future to catch a ride on in order to get back where you originally started. And, among other things, those haven't been discovered yet. and, besides that, the entire idea is technologically impossible."

All in all they talked for nearly three hours. Then at last she said...

"Well, as presented, your logic seems sound enough but as much as I enjoy a little fantasy, the thought of actually being able to jump around from universe to universe and also time travel is still too extreme for my scientifically indoctrinated brain."

"What does scientifically indoctrinated mean? That you are too skeptical?"

"Probably. But without skepticism we wouldn't have made the kind of progress we have made thus far either. In the field of science and technology, of course. But you brought up some very good points about a lot of things that are out there on the edge of mainstream science. Something to think about in my spare time,"

"Good. But more importantly, how long are you going to be here?"

"Two more days. Then I have to get home and prepare for my next series of lectures. But you don't have to quit. I'm really interested in some of the things you've brought up."

"I know but I don't want to become tedious. Any chance I could take you to dinner later? I heard this is free champagne night."

"Right. It's also guest night to put on a play in the rec

center. Will you be sending the limo for me? If so, tell your driver I'll be ready by six. I'll even wear shoes."

"It's the driver's night off so the best I can do is meet you at the dining hall entrance."

"Sounds delightful," Jill said as they both got up and brushed the sand off themselves.

It would have been the perfect opportunity. If he had wanted to, he could have literally destroyed all her present ideas about reality by disappearing from right in front of her. But who would he be kidding? Such a demonstration would be far more for the sake of his own ego than to expand her view of things so he said goodbye and then watched her hips swing as she walked away. Tempting as it was, it only brought home just how badly he wanted to be with Kyara.

TWENTY ONE

The first time Reed walked down main street in Tombstone, Arizona, he had felt very strongly that he had definitely been there before. And when he had turned into the Crystal Palace and had a beer, it completely confirmed what he felt. The memory of that visit came back to him now as he sat outside in the sun and looked down over the Verde Valley once again, after returning home from his eight days of diversion in Tahiti. Yes, he had definitely been to Tombstone before. City Hall, the Courthouse, the OK Corral, the church and the saloons. And something else even stronger. Damned if he couldn't almost feel the weight of that heavy old six shooter strapped to his leg and how slick and easy it came out of its holster and how big a roar it made when it went off. And when he had gone out to Boot Hill on his visit and had looked at all the tombstones, he was quite sure he had recognized the names of at least two men he had put there.

Hot tempered sons-a-bitches, always looking for a fight to prove themselves. Never willing to leave a man alone so he could go about his business. Maybe threatened by his indifference and refusal to participate in their drunken stupidity. But that was where he had had the advantage. He was just as

113

mean and ornery as the rest but he was also cool and calculating and unafraid and he damned well knew how to make his first shot hit the target. But he was also fair. Always fair and never went out of his way to pick a fight or hold a grudge and that had earned him a certain amount of respect. Something some low life bastards were always trying to take away. But it hadn't worked in that lifetime, he knew that beyond a doubt because he had never gotten sucked into the fray between the so- called Cowboys and law enforcement and he was minding his own business when that over dramatized showdown occurred at OK Corral in 1881.

Reed was also quite sure that he had had a mining claim out to the west of town, too, that gave up enough gold to keep him reasonably comfortable. He knew that he liked to come into town on week ends and spend the evenings in the bar rooms or down at the Bird Cage watching the women. And in the end Reed knew he had lived a long and insightful life that time around. So, yes, he might be able to go back there and look in on himself once again but somehow it also seemed that there was little more he could learn from such an experience and it might be best to just leave it alone. Okay, what then, he wondered.

He couldn't prove it had also been another of his lifetimes, but occasionally he had intrusive memories of what must have been another, totally different existence. One strongly evoked when he first read Fitzgerald's translation of the Odyssey, except that some of his personal recollections were far more dark and brutal than the story. Maybe he had ridden with the hordes of Genghis Khan as they swept across Asia and the Middle East, killing everyone in sight. Maybe he had himself been hacked to death in some gory assault. Maybe... Well, what did it really matter? None of it was that clear to begin with and even if it were, he had no idea where those things had occurred. Or even in what century, let alone a specific date, so how would he ever be able to connect up with himself there. It seemed quite impossible, so, what else? What if, for example, what if he hadn't gone to college? What might that have been like?

114

College had come late and was only possible because he had been drafted into the service, much to his own personal objections. Hell, he would have gone to Canada if it hadn't been for his mother. But that would have broken her heart. Luckily enough, however, even though he had gone overseas, he hadn't gotten himself all shot to hell like so many guys he knew. Shameful things, war. And except for World War II, none of them had anything to do with protecting American's freedom. What a tragic misconception. But if that was what some people needed to believe to justify such actions, who was he to take issue with it? At any rate it was still seven years after high school before he was free to go on to college, thanks to the GI Bill as it was called. But what if he hadn't used it or used it to go to trade school or put it to some other use? Off hand, the choice he had made at the time had been a somewhat arbitrary one so, quite possibly, he might just as well have made a different one. One that he should be able to check out if......

That "if," however, would require him to become as adept at finding locations in time as accurately as he was able to find them geographically and ultimately, to do it simultaneously. Plus, he just remembered, to stay within the correct reality while doing so. Jeez, how could he have forgotten how he ended up in German occupied American where it was impossible for him to have any alternates or counterparts. Better not forget that one.

Then there was the part about the ego. The ego was that necessary segment of the personality, primarily concerned with survival in the physical world. As a result the ego could often become very fearful, stubborn, overly protective and resistant to change. Additionally, since it almost completely associated itself with the body, it was very determined to be in full control of things on the material level and often felt highly threatened with ideas and concepts unfamiliar to it.

Looking back, it was one of the hardest things Reed had to overcome, just as Kyara had warned. To get his ego out of the way because, to the ego, dematerialization was akin to annihilation. No body, no identity. Moving about in the dream state where the ego was not in control was one thing. Doing it on the conscious level was something else. Without his love and fascination for Kyara as an intense motivating factor and total distraction that drove his desire for success to the limit, he doubted that he would ever have been able to achieve such control over it with conscious intent. But he had, for the most part, even though there were times when a light trance state helped subdue his fearful ego and made it easier.

Having been captured by the Germans was also an important step in improving his abilities. It was in that situation that his ego was fully forced to realize that the only way he would be able to save himself was to allow the body to disappear, and quickly. But it was those in between times where he still had some occasional difficulty. If he allowed his rational mind to take over he would end up thinking about all the unknown things that might go wrong, and that would put him in a situation where they did. Additionally, still at the very bottom of it at times, was the part about where in all of his experience did it ever say that people ought to be able to do such a thing in the first place. Everything one had ever learned said just the opposite. Such things were impossible and when that doubt was allowed to creep in it could still create a problem.

Practice makes perfect, however, he told himself. Almost. But close enough for what he wanted to do, Reed decided after a couple of weeks of intense jumping around in both time and space. There were some other underlying truths he also discovered along the way. First, when he went back in time he was still physically the same age as he was when he started out. He didn't begin at forty and suddenly become eighteen just because he chose a time twenty two years earlier. And he didn't disappear if he went back to a time before he was born. All time did indeed, seem to exist at once. It was just a matter of getting to where you wanted to go. And of foremost importance, he didn't lose a thing in terms of physical or mental ability in the process either. He would always be who he was, wherever he was. Knowing that, he decided to venture back to his old home town and arrive there a few years after he graduated from High School.

TWENTY TWO

Just in case he got there too early, however, and his earlier self was still around, Reed felt that the age difference would be significant enough to prevent such questions but if someone did comment on his strong resemblance to his younger self he could always claim to be his own uncle. Well, good, he said to himself as he materialized on the sidewalk right in front of the old City Hall where one glance told him he had gotten the time period at least reasonably correct. That was because the big sign was still there with his name on it. His name was there because it was a small town that showed some pride in its few citizens who had been in the armed services and had them all listed on this large panel on the city hall lawn. But from a personal standpoint he wasn't proud of having it there, just a little embarrassed when he looked at.

He was also a little embarrassed when a woman walked into him because he had appeared right in her path.

"I'm really sorry," he said as he caught her and kept her from falling.

She gave him a totally shocked look, backed up a step and looked at him again, seemingly very confused.

"Are you all right?" he asked her. But instead of responding, she quickly walked around him and kept on going as Reed looked to see if anyone else had noticed his sudden arrival. It didn't seem like it so he went to the corner and walked across the same tired old street as always and went into the drab old hotel he had never had occasion to stay at before and asked for a room. That also gave him a chance to look at the date on the registry form which told him he had arrived as planned time wise. Signing in, he paid cash in advance. One of the good things about the past, he remembered. No credit card required and no questions asked. Another was the fact that the essential part of main street was just a little over three blocks long. Walk a mile and you could cover that and everything else that was important in this small town, including a stroll through the park. He walked.

Even though the day had yet to reach its peak, it felt like the temperature and the humidity were both in the high nineties. There were cars parallel parked along main street but not many people out and about. At first Reed was tempted to go into the old drug store, sit at the fountain counter and have a good thick, made on the spot, chocolate malt but decided he was hungrier than that so he walked on past and went down to Maggie's Cafe on the corner across the street from the boarded up old theater. Along the way he also passed the 151 Club which brought back some interesting memories, and the bowling alley where he had drunk a lot of beer with friends when he was only sixteen. It was the real hot spot of the town. Maybe he'd go there later.

After eating, he went two blocks over from the main street to Howard Street and up four blocks to the house he had once lived in and suddenly, that was enough. Why he had detoured back to this part of his past was suddenly a mystery. He had thought having another look would have been more interesting but now realized he was only kidding himself. Sure, he had spent his last two years of high school here and hung around for another three after that and there were a few good memories. Nothing overwhelming, however, and some not so good ones too but the bottom line was that in retrospect and greater objectivity, this dumpy little town was in all truth, a rather depressing place. But, what the hell, his hotel room was paid for so, make the rounds a little later and then get on with it.

Thank god that was over, Reed said to himself the next day after he had moved on. He had run across two of his old schoolmates in the bowling alley the night before. They hadn't in any way recognized his resemblance to his earlier self and it was even further depressing for him to watch them, knowing that one of them had been killed in the Vietnam War and the other had later became the town drunk. And as if that wasn't bad enough he had moved forward in time to where he was now on his way to one of the drive in businesses his parents had owned back then and there was a fair chance he might get to see one or both of them. Provided that he was also in the correct alternate reality, of course, because the time was now past where he had made the

118

decision to go to college so if he had an alternate who had made a different choice, this was the way to find out. Unless... What if his parents had also made a different decision somewhere along the line in this reality and no longer owned the business? What then? Jeez, they might even be dead, or who knew what.

Well, here was the moment of truth, he thought as he walked up to the service window full of anxiety. His few days of beard, aviator sunglasses and dumb looking hat should help, however, and if he lowered his voice a bit ..... but, he need not have worried and, god damn, that was the spookiest thing he had ever done in his life. Seeing his own mother as she had looked all those years earlier. It was a good thing he was hiding behind sunglasses because all he could do was stare even though she seemed completely oblivious to what was going on. Later, though, after she had brought him his order and he began quizzing her about himself, she had looked at him in a rather perplexed manner before answering his questions. Reed had created a little story wherein he explained to her that her son, him, had once worked for him right after getting out of the service and he was wondering what he was doing now.

She accepted his story without question, however. And, never one to have been too deeply involved in her children's affairs, told him that he had gotten married and moved to California. But there was something about the marriage, maybe the tone of her voice, the inflection when she mentioned it that had a tone of disapproval to it. Or seemed to at least. And he was in Santa Barbara. Yes, she was sure it was Santa Barbara but they hadn't gotten out to see him yet. Probably this winter after they closed the business for the season. She could probably find his address but it was home so if he came back tomorrow.....

"No," he said and thanked her, saying it was quite a coincidence because California was where he was headed too.

Then, even though it was just one of those things that they had never done because there had never been that kind of family closeness, he wished he were inside with her for a moment because he would have hugged her and given her a kiss on the cheek. Instead, he thanked her profusely and walked away.

It wasn't Santa Barbara, however. It was another one hundred and twenty miles north at Morro Bay and it took some effort to find that out. When he finally did, he was a bit flabbergasted. Morro Bay was the place where he had spent one long and passionate weekend with Jodi in the early days of their relationship, the same person that launched this whole, mind altering adventure to begin with. But then, at last, there he was looking out at the huge rock landmark in the harbor and all the boats. Some of them very impressive in size. Which one belonged to his other self, he wondered. It had to be rather big if it was a commercial charter, deep sea fishing boat. Maybe he even lived on board. Wow, wouldn't that be something and it fit right in with one of those other subtle fantasies he had from time to time. Living on a boat like his old friend Mike once did for several years. A wistful day dream he might well indulge himself in if he had another lifetime. Which he now realized he had. And here it was. He was living it in this other time and place and he had to admit that he was just a bit envious at the moment. But, who knows. The reality of it might not be as idyllic as it sounded. And then, the other question, how to go about finding out?

As Reed had already learned, this reality wasn't all that much different from his own and, in fact, it seemed that the two not only shared the same topography but also a large part of mankind's constructions. Highway 101 still ran along the coast through the same towns on the way up from Santa Barbara and here was the bay and Morro Rock just as he had always remembered them, along with many of the same buildings and other structures. He was, in fact, even more surprised to be able to stay at the very same motel he had gone to with Jodi so many years ago. He even had the same room number for god's sake. What kind of extreme coincidence was that? And when he looked it over once he had checked in, the only differences he could see was new carpeting in the room and new fixtures in the bath but that would be normal under any circumstances. And then the question.

120

Was it possible the same mattress was still on the bed after all these years? Highly unlikely and he sure hoped not. Ugh. But even without that he would still be sleeping in the same room when he had spent a lot of delicious hours with Jodi. What if that caused him to start dreaming about her again? And if he did that, what if he ended up in bed with her again in that other reality? Or maybe an even different one? He hoped not. Not now, anyway. It had taken too much effort to just get where he was. He didn't need to get lost and have to find his way back in the midst of all this. In an attempt to avoid that he studied the reality he was in now with care and precision, focusing on the purely physical aspects of his surroundings.

In addition to the motel and all the rest of it, the two realities seemed to be almost identical with each other. Except for the fact that an I-pad was called an Apple-Pad, a Kindle was still a Kindle and every one was walking around with familiar looking cell phones. And while some automobiles had minor styling differences, they still had four wheels and gasoline engines and all the other basic features. Restaurants also served hash browns with breakfast too. Coffee tasted like coffee and on and on it went, which again confirmed his earlier conclusions. Alternate realities weaved in and out of each other, sharing both major and minor physical aspects which in this case was good because the actual adjustments he had to make were very few. Additionally, with his minimal attempt at disguising himself, no one seemed to mistake him for his other self either so he set out for the docks with some level of confidence. But, holy damn. He had met his own mother back in Wisconsin in this reality so how would he feel about meeting himself again?

Having consulted this reality's version of the yellow pages he already knew the name of the charter boat he wished he himself owned. Not so difficult when you know your own name. The ad in the phone book also said it was fifty two foot Hatteras so it shouldn't be too hard to find and it was called the Interloper. Very appropriate, he thought, if this side of him was anything like himself because he liked the name, wishing he had thought of it for the boat he had once owned but never seemed to get to use enough.

Down at the docks, however, the vessel was not in its designated slip and asking around, he found that it was out at sea for the day.

"Maybe you can catch them up at the Wharf later," another boat owner told him who looked him over fairly carefully but didn't seem to react to his appearance. "They go there for dinner quite often. Usually about eight."

"Okay. Thanks," Read said, feeling like he had passed his first test, and left. Time for a nap. Then, back in his motel room and just for the heck of it, he called the listed business number of the charter service and listened to the voice recording. It was a woman's voice. A very pleasant and enticing woman's voice and a voice that sounded very, very familiar. Who's was it, he wondered. He should know but when he thought back about all the other possible women in his past around that time he couldn't think of it. Well, no matter. He would find out soon enough but whoever she was, this reality's version of his mother didn't seem to like her very much.

At eight thirty, Reed walked into the Wharf, sat at the bar and ordered a beer. When asked what kind, he asked what they had. Three brands were also popular where he came from and three others were not. He asked for the one that was called Beer beer because the name was both dumb and clever at the same time. Tasted good, too. And after a couple of sips he swung around on his stool so that he could see out into the restaurant where he looked for, jeez, himself. And the woman he was married to. And ... my god. Alicia? Really? It had to be. But...?

And then he asked himself, well, why not? He had nearly considered it himself once, except at the time it was a little complicated. And very unconventional. No wonder his other mother was a bit piqued. She would have viewed it as crossing a forbidden line just as his own mother would have even though he had only brushed against the possibility in his own life. Alicia was a most gorgeous and intriguing female and there had been an undecipherable side to her that always came back to him in a haunting way. And, yes, he had loved her and he had let her go because she was, unfortunately, his own first cousin.

They had spent some time and more than a few nights together before they parted however, and it was very special. But then she had met a man with religion and had gone a different way. Guilt exacerbated by some relatives' narrow-minded opinions. Silliness, really. Albert Einstein had married his first cousin. And as for all the other stuff, new studies showed that even if cousins married and had children, the probabilities for their offspring's good health were exactly the same as for the rest of the population. Of course that wasn't saying much but... well, good for them, for him, for..... He was pleased.

Reed sat there and watched, trying not to be too noticeable but damned if they didn't seem to be happy enough together. He looked hearty and hale and she seemed to be as lovely as ever. They seemed to know a lot of the locals also and after a bit they were joined by another couple about the same age. But, jeez, it was so damned weird looking at oneself as if in a movie, except it was real. And to see himself walk when he got up to go to the restroom, that was very odd indeed but whatever it was, he still had a compelling urge to meet and experience this side of himself, even knowing that up until the point where they split and went their separate ways, they both shared the same history and memories. And, bizarre as it might sound, that included those times with Alicia. Furthermore, everything would be just as real to his alternate self as it was to him. Would his alternate self be able to wrap his mind around that, if it came to it?

"Do you know that couple?" Reed asked the bartender a little later. "Aren't they the ones who have the charter boat?"

"They are. Thinking to go out?"

"Yeah, but I couldn't afford to rent the thing all by myself."

"Well, let's see. Today is Tuesday so you're in luck. Wednesdays are open half days so all you have to do is be at the dock by six in the morning. Want me to ask them for you to be sure?"

"No. Maybe after they're done with dinner. What about

fishing gear?"

"Bring it if you have any, otherwise you can rent it on board. And remember, it's pretty chilly on the water that early, so dress warm."

"Oh, jeez. Hadn't thought of that. Anything open around here where I might buy a jacket this time of day?"

"Yeah. There's a CoMart out on the freeway. Get off at the first exist going north. It's on the right."

"Good. And if I could bother you one more time. Could you call me a cab?" he asked as he took another look at himself and his cousin. Tomorrow would be soon enough.

Bundled up in his oversized jacket and with a floppy new hat on his head, Reed felt reasonably secure. He also had hair on his face and was about twenty pounds heavier than his counterpart and didn't have the sun tanned look that came from being outside all the time. Besides that, who would ever be expecting to meet up with what amounted to be their identical twin when they knew they didn't have one? But from his own point of view, it wasn't all that easy either. His first major difficulty occurred when he came on board to check in and Alicia asked him his name for the log book and he had to invent one on the spot. God, he wanted to take in her face and look her in the eye but somehow he managed to avoid doing so. For the time being, anyway.

"Jack Wilson," he said, quickly enough.

"Cash or check?" she asked.

"Cash," he replied and dug out his roll of bills.

"Looks like you need some equipment too. Anything special you prefer? The bait is free."

"Whatever you have," he told her. "I mostly came along for the ride."

"Okay, Mr. Wilson. No problem and welcome aboard. My name is Alicia if you need anything."

I know, he almost blurted out but managed to thank her instead.

"Thank you," she replied in return. "Why don't you go below and have some coffee. We'll be heading out in about

124

twenty minutes."

The wind was up and there were sizable waves to deal with, along with large swells created by ships in the off shore shipping lane that rolled across the water. Fortunately, no one got sea sick and by the time they were six miles out the sun was well above the horizon and, except for a slight chop on the water, it was almost perfect. Further, up until the time they reached the fishing location, Reed's alternate had been busy in the cockpit and they hadn't yet crossed paths. Then his voice came over the loudspeaker.

"Time to bait up, folks. Squid or anchovies should work here. Hopefully you'll be pulling up red snapper or ling cod. Arnie is our crew man and either he or I will help you with your catch if it's too big and tag it for you when you get it on deck. We'll help you clean it on the way in if you like, too. If there is anything else you need, ask Alicia. Have a good time."

All together there were nineteen passengers. A grandfather and grandson, two couples, one group of five men, another of three and the rest were loners, himself included. Two of the loners were middle aged men, both beer drinkers and both trying to pick up on Alicia. One, just down the rail from Reed, kept making off color comments about her behind her back and Reed told him that if he didn't shut up he would throw his dumb ass overboard. The other one didn't go that far but Alicia soon told him she was married to the boat captain and that if he ever wanted to go out fishing again the best thing he could do was to cool it. Other than that the fish were biting.

The woman from one of the couples screamed when something big jerked her line and then screamed again after she pulled in a big rock cod only to find it's back half was missing, obviously eaten right off the line by a shark. Then, lastly, the most exciting moment of all when someone hauled in a blue shark. A good six feet long, it took the combined efforts of four men to get the hook out of its mouth and toss it back in the water. By then it was time to head back to land.

Reed made sure he was last in line to disembark. He

stopped and thanked them for an enjoyable time as he glanced from one to the other and ended up making eye contact with Alicia where his heart definitely skipped a beat. Or two. Maybe even three because she looked very much the same as he remembered, except older and more mature, more clearly defined as a person and he liked it a lot. There seemed to be some quick, undefined reaction on her part her also. But then she thanked him for dealing with the bad mouthed passenger .

"No problem. He was an obnoxious idiot. Anyway, great trip. I enjoyed it," he said.

Being near Alicia was one thing. As for being face to face with himself, that was almost impossibly difficult. Once he realized that what he was seeing wasn't completely the same as looking at himself in the mirror, however, the tension eased a little. Thanks to having gone down different paths for twenty years, there were enough differences in looks and mannerisms, as well as in speech to help him get past it. But there were also one big lot of similarities and half knowing what his other self was going to say in advance, before the words even came out, was a bit disturbing. And what if it was the other way around, he wondered, and was very careful not to just say the first thing that came into his own mind. Still, managing to feel relatively safe behind his beard, sunglasses and big hat, he did manage to ask them a few questions about their boat and their charter business, hoping to gain some insight as to what kind of people they were at this point in their lives. The deck hand, Arnie put an end to it, however, because he had finished hosing down the deck and broke in to ask what time he should be back the next day.

Okay, Reed decided. It was time for him to get out of their way too but rightly or wrongly, he didn't want to give it up just yet so he asked if they could meet for lunch later.

"I'm buying," he said.

His other self looked at him like he wasn't sure he wanted any further involvement and turned to his wife for some help.

"What do you think?" he asked her..

"Well, it's probably okay," she replied. "We don't have any

other plans for this afternoon."

"Okay, it is," his other self confirmed. "Why don't we meet you somewhere in about half an hour. We need to put the galley in order and lock up."

"Sure. Where?" he asked, already thinking he knew the name of the place that was about to be suggested, even though he had never been there before. "I've only been here two days."

"Betsie's Cafe? It's two blocks down Market Street if you're not familiar with it."

Reed arrived early and picked a corner booth in the back where there was some privacy. They came in about ten minutes later and Alicia ended up sitting in the middle between them. While this made it difficult to study his other self in any great detail, the benefit was that it also prevented the opposite from happening. As for Alicia, that was something else. While sitting beside her kept him from getting caught up in her enchanting eyes, the closeness created a different dilemma. One that he had been able to step around when they were out on the boat where there was more distance between them. But now...

Although she was still wearing the same clothing as then, he was acutely aware of that old familiar, extremely distracting feminine presence she had always had about her. Not only did it bring back some dear memories, it also evoked some strong feelings in regard to the intimacy they had previously shared. Regardless of what he was going through, however, they both seemed to be comfortable with his being there and he did his best to keep it that way. Part of doing that was to try and individualize himself by eating left handed and to pause more and stay a little off key when he spoke. All in all he felt it went well. Except for the part about picking up on his other self's thoughts all the time. He really had to work hard to keep from ending the other's sentences, but he managed. Then the meal and the small talk were over as Alicia finally asked him where he was from.

"Arizona," he replied and told them where.

"We went through Sedona on the way out here years ago," his other self said.

"And that old mining town, Jerome," Alicia added.

"Yeah, and remember," his other self said to Alicia. "We said we almost wished we were moving there instead? And what is really weird is that I often dream of being out in the desert and near all those red rock canyons, hiking and exploring."

"Well, sure. That I understand. But my thing is being out on the ocean like you are, and having a sea going boat. And then the California coast is just so damned beautiful, even in the L.A. area where I spent a lot of years until.... well, that's another story. But you said you have been out here almost twenty years but have only had the boat about nine. What did you do before that? I mean, if it's not being too personal."

"No, it's okay," Alicia said as she looked at her husband. "Isn't it?"

Reed's other self nodded his approval.

"After we got married we first moved to Garden Grove. Such a wonderful house on, what was that street?"

"Melody Park Lane," the other Reed said as Reed himself almost choked.

"Garden Grove was really nice back then," he managed to say, however. "I bet your street was lined with big palm trees. Most likely you had a couple of orange trees, too. Maybe a banana palm, hydrangeas, azaleas, Pampas grass, elephant ears, poinsettias and a jacaranda. Probably out in the front yard. And of course, there had to be some bougainvillea somewhere," he went on, saying it while exploring a bigger possibility by doing so. Could it be that they had somehow shared the very same house in both of their separate worlds also? Ridiculous! But no, not completely. He and his other self were both living in that part of California then and would certainly have been attracted to the same kind of house. Were they? Wouldn't that be something? Living in the same house for at least some of the same time period with your alternate but in a separate reality so that you were completely unaware of each other. This was really getting strange and maybe he was right because they both looked at him with awe and Alicia even said, "How did you...." and stopped.

"Sorry, I was rambling," Reed said, quickly coming up

with a complete lie. "I was just thinking about a house I once owned that had all those things that are so typical of southern California. Up in Chatsworth. Amazing. I can't remember the street but I believe the house number was 20085. Isn't it strange how stuff like that comes back to you sometimes?"

"Yes," Alicia finally said, seemingly relieved. "Ours was, hmm, 10503. Is that right?" she asked her husband who nodded his agreement while Reed himself was now totally astounded. Another beyond coincidence happening. They had lived in the same house on the same street with the same house number as he had in their own adjacent reality. He was absolutely certain of it because that was one house number he would never forget for a whole lot of reasons. But still...

Moving on, however, just as Reed suspected, his other self hadn't gone to college but he was resourceful and had become a highly skilled technician in the aerospace industry and worked his way up to a management position in the manufacturing area where they made sophisticated guidance systems for missiles. Alicia meantime, had taken some computer courses at community college and had gotten a job in data processing at the same company as her husband, all of this with a long term goal in mind. The boat and the independent life style it offered.

"It's not totally living the dream but most of the time it's pretty close," his alternate said.

"But, who knows," Alicia added. "Maybe someday when we retire we can go live in the desert. Then we can stop and see you."

"Well, you don't have to wait that long. Anytime would be very nice. Then I could take you hiking. I know some well preserved old Anasazi ruin sites you might find interesting."

"Really? I'd like that. But what I'm wondering now is why you seem so damned familiar? Have we met before? What do you think, honey? Don't you get the same feeling?"

"Somewhat. Yes."

"Maybe if you didn't have all that hair on your face."

"Well, who knows," Reed said. "Anything is possible. Maybe I'll shave it off before I leave and see what you think."

Then he changed the subject and asked how many days each week were half day fishing excursions, at first considering going out again. But he quickly dismissed it as not in keeping with what he hoped to accomplish.

"Tomorrow is a full day. All the top execs and wives from a Santa Barbara firm are coming up, so it's breakfast and lunch on the boat, a fishing stop and lots of cruising along the coast. For dinner we put in to the beach at Point Estrero for bonfires, food and music on the sand, provided by a catering company. Then the ride home under the light of an almost full moon."

"Sounds romantic," Reed said.

"And very lucrative," Alicia added.

"Plus we could probably use another deck hand if you're interested," her husband offered.

"Really?" Reed said, then stopped. On the surface it seemed to be a great opportunity. But they were going to be extra busy handling a large group of people who had to be high on their client list. If something went wrong and he were found out in the middle of that, what then? It would be a very difficult set of circumstances under which to try and make it come out right. That wasn't what he was here for, he reminded himself. The real question that he had to find the answer to was just how receptive they might be to who he really was and what he was doing there because, if they were open to it, he certainly wanted to share it with them. But if they had fixed ideas about such things, he was not about to infringe on their lives just to satisfy some self centered desire of his own. So, when they said it would be okay for him to call later, he changed the subject. What did they do in their off hours? Like on afternoons like this one after all the work was done?

"Guess you haven't heard the real definition of what a boat is," Reed's alternate said, however. "It's a hole in the water lined with wood, fiberglass or steel that you pour time and money into. Although we have been rather lucky in that respect, maintenance still eats up a lot of our time. Other than that, we go through a lot of books."

"We tried to put a discussion group together once but that didn't go anywhere," Alicia added. "Not that people here are stupid, they just don't seem open to new ideas."

Ah, ha, Reed thought to himself. Now we're getting somewhere. But unfortunately, by then it was also the polite time to part company so he picked up the check, put down a tip and said he had to leave. Outside, he again thanked them for inviting him on the next day's trip but asked if they couldn't meet for lunch on Wednesday instead because he had forgotten some other long over do things that he really should attend to before then. They said fine and told him that he would be most welcome on board the boat whenever it was convenient, so let them knew.

"Great. I will," he promised.

"Okay. See you Wednesday then," they both said. Something which enhanced his view of their relationship even further and also made him feel that it would survive his presence there even if he did something really rash. Like what he had just that second decided to do.

"Provided you still want to come by then," he then added.

"Well, why wouldn't we?" Alicia asked.

"I don't know. Just in case."

"I'm sure it will be fine. Isn't that right?" she asked her husband as she was prone to do, even though it was after the fact and she had already assumed he would agree. Whether it was presumptuous or not didn't matter, Reed thought that the very fact that they treated each other this way was still very respectful and a good indicator of how well their relationship worked and his heart ached a bit when he saw it. Regardless, his alternate nodded his assent as Reed already knew he would.

"Okay," Reed said at that point. "But if you're not here, I will understand."

"What does that mean?"

"Well, let's find out," he said and led them out into the middle of the large parking lot which was now almost completely empty where there was nothing to hide behind.

"Stand here," he told them. "And if you're willing to hear it, there is an explanation for this. So, hopefully, I'll see you day after tomorrow. Now just turn around and count to three before you look.

They both looked at him curiously, maybe even with a bit of suspicion but he smiled at them and shrugged. "Wednesday, then. And we can go from there."

With that they both did as he had asked and Alicia quickly counted to three out loud before they turned back around to find that he had disappeared.

The following morning Reed woke with some self reproach, hoping that in his own haste he hadn't done the wrong thing. Alicia and his other self had a long, busy day ahead of them and what he had done might well have been disturbing. After all, how would he have reacted if someone had disappeared from right behind him? At least before they had gone to sleep, ended up in a different reality and woke up to a whole new concept about life like he had? And then he remembered his latest dream. God damn. Last night he had dreamed about Jodi again. Jodi, here in the motel room with him. Fire in the fireplace, adventures in the bed. Oh jesus, not now. Let me get through what I'm working on first, he pleaded. Just one more night. Or maybe two.

For a moment he considered shaving off his beard before he went to meet them but then decided against it. On top of his disappearing, that might be too much of a shock. Let him try to explain some of the rest of it first, which, hopefully, was in the realm of possibility. After all, he and his counterpart were once the same person before they went their separate ways. That meant that they quite possibly still shared a lot of the same character traits and interests in spite of differences in education, vocation and intervening life experiences. And if his counterpart had also hung onto that ever present, driving curiosity and open mindedness that he himself felt, it should work out because that curiosity would have led to an on going exploration of basis philosophical issues, metaphysical phenomenon and more. Okay, good. So have faith in your other self, he told himself and laughed at what he had said.

Well, damned if he wasn't right about them because there

they were, sitting in the same corner booth as before, waiting for him as he walked over, said hello and slid in on the other side so that he somewhat faced them both. They each responded to his greeting but then went silent, apparently not sure as to where to go from there. But then, before any of them could get started, the waitress came, so they ordered instead. With that done, Reed looked from one to the other, searching for some clue as to where to begin. And since neither of them seemed to show any strong emotion about what he had done, he began to feel more relaxed. No awe, no fear or nervousness. No anger or upset over having their beliefs about reality challenged. Nothing like that. Just what seemed to be a very puzzled curiosity. But then, before Reed could find the right words to begin with, his counterpart looked at him and spoke instead.

"Well, Mr Wilson. If that is really your right name. That was really cute. Where did you learn how to do that?"

"Yes," Alicia said. "Whatever it was that you really did."

"My apologies," Reed said with a shrug. "I hope I didn't offend you in any way. I guess I might have gotten ahead of myself a little."

'Too late for that now. Just try and explain it to us."

"Do you think I fooled you in some way?"

"We don't know. Our eyes told us one thing, our reason another. I don't know about Alicia but if it was some elegant trick then I would be very offended to think you would try and do that to us. And, if it's not, then we'd like to learn how to do that."

"That's part of what I was hoping to be able to talk about," Reed said. "But I wasn't sure just how to go about it. So, I thought I'd try disappearing like that and see how you reacted. And, I can assure you of one thing. It was not a trick. Explaining it, however, might not be that easy. It depends on what you might be open to. But, damn, where to start?"

"Were you born that way?" Alicia asked. "Or is it something you learned how to do?"

"I guess... Okay, why don't I just tell you what happened. That might be the easiest."

"All right. Go ahead."

133

"Several years ago I lived in L.A. in the Beverly Hills area. I met this woman, ended up moving in with her and had a relationship that lasted over four years. There was a side to it that was absolutely marvelous but there were also some difficult compatibility issues. So, it ended and I moved to Arizona. Then, about six months ago I started having intense dreams about her. One night the dream was unbelievably vivid and ...... " he continued, telling them almost everything that had happened, including the part about the brooch and getting the package in the mail from her that was sent years before to an address he didn't yet have at the time it was sent. Then he stopped, waiting for some reaction, not exactly sure as to what the story was doing for them.

After some time to reflect, Alicia was the first to respond.

"That's really fascinating. Especially the part about you tracking her down right after your, ahh, adventure and finding out that she was actually married and living in an entirely different place than where you, ahh, are you sure about the brooch? I mean.... do you still have it?"

"I do. And the silver goblet she sent back, along with the package she sent it in with the old mailing date on it."

"So if we came to Arizona, you could show those things to us?" his alternate said.

"I could if...."

"If what?"

"Ah, nothing. If you could get there, I could show them to you," Reed assured them. And that part was the truth. The, how they would be able to get there, part was what he was hoping he would be able to explain. "And what was also really weird about this whole thing for me was that when I came here looking for you I ended up staying at the same motel that..."

"You came here looking for us? Why? What is this really all about?"

"Slow down. I swear there's nothing sinister about it. As it turns out, we're ..... ah," he said, catching himself too late.

"We're what?"

"Well, related."

"How are we related and how do you know that?" his

alternate asked.

Before he could respond, however, Alicia interrupted.

"Well, it doesn't surprise me. From my point of view there are some things about the two of you that are uncannily similar."

"Like what?" his alternate asked her in a skeptical tone?

"Same height, same build. Except he's a little heavier and even with that beard, what I can see of them, his features are much like your own."

"So what are we then. Long lost cousins?"

"No. You two are cousins," Reed blurted out before thinking about it, which caused them both to look at him with more unneeded suspicion.

"And exactly how did you find that out?" his alternate asked. It wasn't an angry question. Not yet, anyway, but it made Reed realize that his alternate was a lot like himself in another respect also. He wasn't one to put up with someone digging around in his personal life. Absolutely not, so, for now, he told them that he was her cousin too. More like a second cousin, he told them to give himself some room. Something he had only found out about a few months earlier so he decided to go looking.

"In the process I went through Wisconsin and met your mother," he directed at his counterpart, steering away from where things might otherwise lead.

"And I have to say that she is also very much like mine. Did you know that she thinks you two live in Santa Barbara?"

"No, but it wouldn't surprise me," his alternate said, allowing things to change course.

"I don't think she approved of what we did," Alicia then added. "Which is one of the reasons we moved to California to begin with. Her and some of the other relatives."

"Yeah. That could be a problem. And I had a cousin I was really close to once so I can understand what you did," Reed stated and felt they were beginning to relax again. But then the food came so they ate and talked about other things till they were done. It was then that Reed suddenly became very curious about something else that was subtly different about this reality. The economy seemed good and people in general, seemed more untroubled and happy than in his own, so on a hunch he asked,

"Does nine-eleven mean anything to you?"

After an uncomprehending look at each other, they both said no so he made some off hand remark and moved on. Much as he might be interested, this time he wasn't there to research what other paths society might have gone down politically and socially. But the lack of a nine-eleven at least meant that people in this reality had pursued a much more sane course of action than those in his own world and good for them. By then the restaurant was getting crowded, however, and there were other people within hearing distance so his alternate suggested that they go back to the boat to continue.

They sat out on the aft deck behind the main cabin and drank cold beverages and after Reed got them to tell him how their charter cruise went the day before, they pulled him back to where they had left off at lunch. Which still left him in a quandary. How to proceed effectively.

So far they had accepted his story about Jodi and his middle-of-the-night adventure without major objection and were being serious and reflective. Encouraged, he went on from there.

"Well, here you are, living this very independent life style. One that demands that you stay clearly focused in exactly what is going on around you, especially when you are out on the water. But when you're back here afterward, sitting in the sun, then what? You're clearly not religious. Or superstitious. Or seem to have some contrived set of beliefs to lean on to get you through the rough stuff. So how do you manage and what do you believe?"

It took some seconds before Reed got an answer and it came from his counterpart.

"I'm not sure we have ever given it that kind of consideration. We just live our lives for what they are. I think it's pretty clear, however, that we have a lot more control over how things come out, though, than we realize. It's not about being in or out of favor with God. It's being aware and in tune with what goes on around you. Learning not to bullshit yourself when something goes wrong. What do you think, Alicia?"

"I agree. And, no. We don't do a voodoo ceremony before we go out, or pray for some higher guidance to lead us to the place where the fish are biting or to protect us from harm, or, you know what I mean."

"Yes," Reed responded as his alternate then picked up and continued.

"We try and trust in our own good judgment to get us through the day, not some conjured up set of superficial beliefs. But beyond that? I think we work on that one all the time. As for me, all I know for sure is that there is one hell of a lot more going on than most people are willing to look at."

"Me, too," Alicia agreed. "The problem is, if you are searching for bigger answers, where do you go to find them?"

"Exactly," Reed's other self said. "It's easy to say, don't worry about it because when it's over you'll learn the truth anyway. But what the hell is that? Truth is not religious proclamation and my feeling is that if the real truth is available, why not seek it out. Maybe it would help us to have a more fulfilling life. Or at least to have a more interesting one. Like the way you disappeared in the parking lot. I find that very interesting. But I don't think you are one of God's messengers or some ET with strange powers or someone who came here to bless us in some way or lead us down the path of righteousness. I don't know about Alicia but it's clear you know something I don't and I'd like to understand it better."

"Me, too," Alicia said. "Because it was a bit of a mind jolting experience. But I don't think we have any preconceived ideas about how that might have been possible."

"Okay," Reed replied, thinking it couldn't get much better than that. "So, since you are interested, let me start somewhere else and back into it," he said, hoping he could explain it well enough.

Ultimately it was much easier than he had anticipated and he was amazed at the conclusions they were able to draw from what had been said. But then, after all, why not? That was himself he was talking to. And the other person that was once very dear to him. Still was. And maybe when he got back home again he would track down the other version of her who was alive in his own reality just to see how she was doing after all these years. But for now, however, the day was nearly over and he had to end it. If for no other reason than to keep them from overload.

Alicia apparently was feeling the same thing because she interrupted the conversation and offered to put something together for dinner. "Or we could go out," she added.

"Thank you, Reed said instead, " but I need to get going. Before I do though, just one last thing. You wanted to know how I disappeared so let's see if I can explain it well enough so that you can do it yourselves. If you want to, that is."

"We're listening," his alternate said.

"Okay. First go back to the idea of yourselves as being psychic or spiritual beings and that you are not just your body. Your body is a manifestation. Your creation of yourself in the physical world. It is not a static thing but a dynamic one that....," he said and continued, telling them what he had learned, both from Kyara and from his own experiences.

"I know it may be difficult but try and accept that for now. Understand that if you are creating your body to begin with and that you keep recreating it over and over, then, with the right kind of approach and control, you can also in the next moment, recreate it in some other place so that you seem to disappear from one spot and reappear in another. And it's not like you don't know it's possible because you saw me do it. So accept that. Don't be skeptical and say you'll try. It's an all or nothing situation and you have the power to do it."

"Okay," his other self said, not totally convinced but wanting to try. "So where do we start?"

"Yeah. Any suggestions? How did you learn to do it?"

"From a friend and... of course. Why didn't I ....? Jeez," Reed said and got up. "Look, you two seem to have a very warm relationship. You are always patting or hugging each other, sitting close together, happy with each other, so, since this is a double cabin boat, which cabin do you live in?"

"The one up front down below."

138

"Good. So here's my suggestion. Let that be your target destination. Go down there and look it over very closely then decide which one of you wants to be first."

"I do," Alicia said enthusiastically, and jumped up without even knowing what she was going to be first at. "What's next?"

"After I'm gone, check out the cabin. Find some unobstructed place where you might reappear that won't be a problem. Then, Alicia, you come back up on deck while he stays below and....."

"Wait," she said. "I think I get it. But I like the thought of him come to me instead."

"Either way. Then, depending on the mood you are both in, you can do something that would be enticing to him, like.." he said with a shrug.

"Like taking my clothes off," Alicia said with a mischievous smile.

"Exactly. Incentive is important. Especially in the beginning."

"Good idea," his other self asked. "And what do I do then?"

"Then you shut down your mind and concentrate as fully as possible on where she's at and what comes next. Nothing else. Don't demand, just allow it to happen. And with that I'll leave you alone. Are you going out tomorrow?"

"Another half day open fishing cruise. We'll be back by two so if you want, we could have a late lunch or something," Reed's other self said. "And since you're leaving, could you show us again, only this time let us watch?"

"Yeah, that would be okay," Reed said as he went over to the boat railing and looked down to the far end of the pier where it connected with the ramp that went up on shore because he wanted to make sure it was free of obstruction. Then he came back and stood in front of them.

"How about from here to the ramp?" he said as he shut his eyes and almost instantaneously reappeared on the ramp where he waved back at them and walked away. And that was that until the next day.

Again, they had made it to the restaurant and the same corner booth before him and when they saw him, Alicia broke out into a big smile. His counterpart also had a pleased look on his face.

"Well, I guess I don't have to wonder how that turned out," Reed said after he sat down and looked at them.

"Holy cow," Alicia said. "We were tempted to wait until you got here and then just, ah, pop in. But we decided that just because we know how, we should probably be a little careful about it."

"Yes. You don't want to end up sitting on someone's lap. Or misjudge the situation and find yourself in the wrong place like, ahh...anyway how did the rest of it go? Was it easy for you?"

"Anything but. And we kept changing places to see which one of us it was easier for."

"Yeah, she did it first on what, the seventh try?"

"Eighth, and then you did it right after that."

"And then, after... ah. Then we tried it together and it worked. Holy damn, I still don't believe it."

"Me either, which is why we were tempted to come here that way just to re assure ourselves it was true. But how do you know where it's safe to re appear? We thought of using the parking lot but what if there was someone there, a moving car or, you know?"

"That's why I cautioned you but, you're right. There is a safe way to check things out ahead of time, however. At least... Well," Reed said and scratched his head. "Yeah. I guess I'd better try and show you how to that, too."

"Besides the possibility of getting ourselves killed, we don't want anyone having a heart attack on our account either," his alternate said. "Or shooting us because we scared the hell out of them."

"Or invaded their privacy."

"Yes, but think of all the other possibilities," Alicia said. "We could even jump over to Arizona and see you. Or wherever. And we can come with our clothes on and not worry about being embarrassed. But what about other stuff? How much can you

140

bring with you?"

"I'm still experimenting with that," Reed confessed. "All I know so far is that I seem to be able to bring what I can hold onto. Like a small piece of luggage. But there are some other things you also need to be concerned about."

"That's what we were thinking. Which is why we decided to confine our adventures to the boat for now."

"Good idea. Or somewhere you know is safe. You don't want to reappear in front of a bus or something because you would end up just as dead as anyone else would who did the same thing. And then there is... remember what I told you about what happened to me on my first ... when I, ahh, found myself with my old girlfriend?"

"Of course. You ended up in bed with her."

"Well, yeah. But.."

"Are you ready to order" the waitress asked, suddenly interrupting him as she appeared at their booth, pad and pencil ready.

Reed looked at the other two and shrugged. They said okay and soon she was gone again.

"So what was the but you stopped with before?' his other self asked.

"Right," Reed said. "I guess what I was trying to point out wasn't the fact that I found her in her bedroom, but where her bedroom was. Where the house was."

"You said it was in Cheviot Hills in LA."

"Yes. But remember that afterward when I checked it out I found that she was really married and living in a new place down in Palm Desert and not in the old house we used to share. Someone else now owned it."

"Oh, oh. What are you saying? That you went into some other, what, parallel universe or something? Is that possible?"

"How else would you explain it?"

"I don't know."

"But it did happen. And it wasn't the only time. "

"So there are side by side worlds here in the same universe and you can get from one to the other? Are you serious?"

"Yes. And some of them are not necessarily safe places to be. But in general I don't think they are all that separate, either. I think many of them are intertwined and entangled and share a lot of the same features. I know this one ..." Reed started to say and stopped. But it was too late.

"This one, what? Shares? How do you know that?"

"Because... I wasn't going to go there yet but, ah, that's why it might be difficult for you to get to the Arizona I live in."

They both looked at him, letting the impact of what he had also said sink in.

Alicia was the first to respond and she did so by cautiously reaching over and feeling his arm.

"It's okay," he told her. "I'm just as real as you are. And if you stabbed me I'd bleed red blood. Not green or blue."

"I hope not. Otherwise ..."

"Well, here we go," the waitress said, interrupting again by placing their orders in front of them, then asking if she could get anything else before going away.

"Otherwise, what?" Reed then asked, continuing where they had left off.

"That's the problem. I don't know," Alicia responded.

"So, anyway," his other self said. "If what you say is true, then what's the same in our world as yours and what's different?"

"At first I was rather surprised because they seem to have more similarities than differences. At least physically. Same landscape, same ocean, same big rock out in the harbor and, I swear, the same motel I stayed in several years ago with my old girlfriend."

"The one you...?"

"Yes, that one. And the reason I say that is because, well, why I should remember some stupid thing like that is a mystery to me but whoever did the tile work in the bathroom must have run out of the right kind of tiles because there are two off-color ones down in one corner by the sink. Sounds dumb, I know and I didn't notice it until this morning and then I remembered. Jodi, that was her name. She had dropped some things out of her purse and when I helped pick them up I noticed that tile. And the one thing I picked up for her was her brooch. Yeah, that one. How odd is that? So, same motel with the same defects."

"But how could that be? Doesn't make any sense. Or does it?" his counterpart said. "I know this table isn't solid, so in that regard, it's a complete illusion. Which has to mean that everything that's physical is, in a way, an illusion too. And based on what you're saying, maybe we're sharing this booth with other people in some other reality, like yours. They're here but maybe just a little out of phase with us or something so we're not aware of them. Is that possible?"

"Maybe. So far I don't know how else to explain it," Reed said and, for lack of something better, used the analogy of an adjacent radio or TV station in the same frequency band as an example. It was a stretch but it seemed to work for them.

"So, jumping realities is like making a frequency shift. But if that's the case then how is someone in that other reality... how are we able to see you, and, as Alicia did, touch you and have you seem real? That could only happen if you are somehow bringing yourself into tune with us."

Damned good point, Reed admitted to himself. Why hadn't he thought of it? But then, technically speaking, he had. And with that he admitted its validity out loud also and then sat there for a moment analyzing the idea.

"Well," he said after a bit. "Maybe that's it exactly. If it is then it may make it easier to get from one world to another because getting here was no easy thing."

"How so?"

"Well, like I said. I'm still a novice so this is only the third alternate reality I've been in since I learned how to transport myself. The first time was when I went back to Wisconsin to the university where I went to college because...."

"You went to the university? Where? In Madison?"

"Yes. In Madison."

"What did you take? Did you graduate?"

"I first went through pre med, decided I didn't have the time or money for another four or five years and switched over to physics because I could transfer all my science credits and it was easy for me. So, yeah. I ended up with an MS in physics."

"Jeez. Isn't that interesting. I almost went there too. And I also thought I wanted to be a doctor. But then," he said as he reached and put his hand on top of Alicia's. "Then we got together and I decided I would rather be with her than go to college even though she wanted me to. But, things got complicated back there so we moved out here. No regrets. Not a one," he said and grinned at her as she leaned over and kissed his cheek.

And that is where we divided, Reed filled in mentally to himself. Where I divided, or he did, or something, and now we are two separate individuals leading separate lives, exploring two different probabilities. Well, three actually. Three that he knew of anyway, realizing that in one major respect the conversation was pretty much going where he wanted it to go except for one thing. Alicia. He had also slept with her just as his counterpart had before they each went their own way. How to deal with that? Better yet, how would she be able to deal with it psychologically if she had to face the fact that she had been in bed with both of the men she was sitting with. Not now but back then when there was only one of them. She seemed very strong willed and stable, but still. That would be enough to drive anyone over the edge. Or, if not, make her feel very uncomfortable about the whole situation. Quite possibly make his counterpoint feel very uncomfortable too. Damn, he had better be careful, he cautioned himself. Maybe he should just continue the charade, be someone from some other reality, let it go at that and leave. That might be the kindest thing to do, the one he was now considering the strongest, just as his other self spoke again.

"Sorry," he said. "I got you off track. Why did you go back to Wisconsin?"

"Because I thought that if I went there physically it would be easier to use that as a launch point. It actually worked quite well, too. At least for the initial step. At any rate, I was able to make the jump and find what I had gone there for. But, when I was ready to leave..... God, I still don't have a clue as to how what happened, happened."

"Not good, huh?" Alicia said, looking at him.

"No, it...." Reed started to say but stopped. What he was trying to explain was difficult enough. But a different outcome to World War Two? It might be best to wait on that one.

"Anyway," he said. "The reason I went there was because of how committed I was to becoming a doctor at the time. I wondered if what a friend of mind had said was true, about how all possibilities get played out somewhere so I decided to try and find out."

"But why would that happen. What's the purpose of going down all those other paths?"

"Well, maybe none, depending on your view of things. But if you are open to the possibility that it does happen, then it has its reason and you can't help but come to a different conclusion about what life is all about."

"Yeah," his counterpart said. "I guess that's where I'm at. I'm coming to a different conclusion about a lot of things since you came along. The problem is I'm not able to define it in a very concise way just yet. All I know for sure this far is that I have finally rejected that other view where dead is dead."

"Me too," Alicia stated. "Keep going."

"Okay. Good. So, for now let's say that we have an aware and infinitely creative universe, or multiverse, instead of a mechanistic one that will come to some ultimate, disastrous end, and go from there. This other multiverse then has a higher, evolutionary purpose. Not in the physical sense where the goal is to become increasingly better adapted to the physical world but in a mental, emotional and psychological way. How better to do that than by creating an illusionary world which we can choose to come to where all things are allowed to happen so that there are literally, an almost endless number of challenges we can decide to face so we can learn to become better beings. I'm sorry. I guess that sounds a little trite when I try and say it."

"No problem. Keep going."

"Okay. Well, as you can probably see, this illusionary world has to be a place which feels like some ultimate and final reality when we are in it so we have to take it seriously in order to get anything out of the experience. At the same time, behind it is bigger reality where, as you say, dead isn't dead after all. The real reality behind the everyday reality where there is such a thing as eternal validity of the spirit, or soul, as some would prefer. Where, for lack of a better word, we are spiritual beings and .... anyway. Enough of that. I guess simply put, the bottom line is that as individuals on this level, we go down all these different paths so that on some higher level we can explore all the possibilities and consequences of our actions. Without that there would be no emotional or psychological growth. But, in order to gain the most value from it we need a singular and highly concentrated focus in the immediate, ongoing drama as it is happening. Only later do we become aware of the bigger picture."

"That's one hell of a stretch," his counterpart said. "I'll have to think about that one a lot more. Anyway, did you have another side to yourself, however that might be possible?"

"And did you get to meet, ah, him? How did that turn out?" Alicia asked but by then they had been holding down the booth for a long time and it was getting busy so, as before on their previous lunch there, they left and again went down to the boat.

"Well, no," Reed admitted, once they were settled. "I didn't personally meet him. We didn't shake hands or anything. But he does exist and I followed him home and got some idea of what his life was like. Great doctor, married to a really special woman I once knew, beautiful kids and all that so I decided to leave it alone. I found out what I wanted to know, that other realities really do exist, so why mess with his life? I didn't think that would be fair."

"But what would you have done if he had been a totally despicable person?"

"I don't know. Left him alone, probably. We are still separate individuals."

"Jeez, I don't know," the other Reed said. "If we hadn't met you and found out how to disappear like you did, I'd say the whole thing was just a bunch of far out, crazy bullshit. Maybe it still is."

"I know. I was almost convinced I had totally lost it after what happened with my old girlfriend."

"But you didn't," Alicia said. "so, tell me how it made you feel. When you finally saw him? Yourself, like that?"

"A little shocking. More than a little, actually."

"But you said you didn't think it was fair to impose on..., him. Then you came here to see if I existed. Why didn't you just quit once you found that out?"

"Maybe I should have. I hope I didn't do the wrong thing? I guess, bottom line, I was being selfish. I felt I had a lot more to gain from getting to know you than I did from him, and then, after getting to know you a little I...."

"So, it's all right. I think you checked us out pretty well first to see if we could handle it. And after you did that disappearing act, we were hooked."

"That's a relief. What if it had gone the other way?"

"We probably would have convinced ourselves that it was some kind of trick and forgotten about it. Hopefully. What do you think, Alicia?"

"I'm just glad we didn't. That's all."

"Me too," Reed said.

"But there's something else we want to know," Alicia said. "Actually, there are several things. First, are you sure you're related to me? And if you came here looking for me that means I have an alternate back in your reality. So what was so unusual about her that led you to think she even had an alternate? And why did that make you go to all this trouble just to meet some alternate half cousin. I mean, don't get me wrong. I'm really glad you did but seriously I get the feeling there's something more you're not telling us. Am I right?"

Damn, Reed said to himself, good questions. These people were really sharp. And not about to be put off, either. Not good. But where to start? It could all backfire on him now.

"Okay, well, ahhh, " he said, starting out. "I am definitely related to you, that's for sure. And you do have an alternate back in my world, who, of course looks and is very much like you. And, I have to admit that just like here, I once had a serious crush on her too, so I was curious as to how things might have worked out somewhere else. As for the rest of it, you're right. There's a lot I'm not telling you. Some of it is because I haven't figured out a way to explain it yet," he said, trying to divert them away from the main question just a little longer. The real truth about his reason for being there.

"I only learned how to do this a few months ago myself so there are still a lot of things I'm still not completely sure about, either. For certain, I don't have the tiniest idea as to how another reality comes into existence. What the process is. Or, as we talked about, how one seems to weave in and out of others and apparently shares the same physical space. Or any of the rest of it. But at the same time on the conscious level, I don't have any idea as to how my body is able to process the food I eat and keep me alive and functioning, either, but I know that if I tried to handle all that on the conscious level, I would never make it through the night. And if I had to logically think through the process as to what the timing and sequences of muscles I would need to use just to be able to walk or talk, it would become impossible. But that doesn't stop it from happening. And, relatively speaking, those are extremely simple things in terms of the full range of what we are physically capable of. doing. So, what makes it all possible? Where does it start?"

"In the mind," his counterpart said as if he already knew what Reed was going to say next. Or maybe he did. "I pick a goal. I say I'm thirsty and off I go to get a glass of water. I don't have to go through the order of things it takes to get it, like, get up out of the chair, walk to the kitchen, find a glass, turn on the faucet and all that. Think the thought and the rest of it happens automatically."

"In other words," Alicia said, jumping in. "Concentrate on the goal and not the process."

"And get out of your own way," her husband said.

"What does that mean?"

"If you want a glass of water don't start out by worrying about your ability to go get it. Am I right?" Reed's counterpart asked him but didn't wait for an answer and went on.

"It's like he told us about transporting ourselves to some other location. You can't question your ability to do it. You have to accept the idea that's it's possible in order to make it possible."

"I understand. But if I hadn't seen him do it I'm not sure I would have believed I could do it," Alicia said. "But now that I also understand that my primary self is not my body but something beyond that and I won't be annihilated if I make my body disappear and reappear somewhere else, I'm okay. Better than okay. It's the most exhilarating thing I have ever done in my life. And, once we figure out how to find safe places to reappear at, think of all the driving or flying time we can save and how much fun we can have. We could just pop into the Hollywood Bowl for a free concert or, whatever, and still be back here in time for the late show on television."

"Jeez. Great idea. Why didn't I think of that?" Reed said. "But, until I get a chance to show you how to find a safe place to reappear at ahead of time and become good at it, go slow. Also realize that there are times and situations where you may not have the time or ability to know everything in advance and just have to risk it."

"We will. But, back to those other questions if you don't mind. I know you haven't forgotten them."

"No. Just not sure how to go about it."

"Afraid we might not like the answers?" his other self said.

"Liking them isn't the right word. And maybe it's not my judgment to make but most people I know wouldn't be ready for them if it applied to themselves."

"Okay, then let me put your mind at ease. And as far as I'm concerned there is nothing that gets me more upset than someone else deciding what I am or am not ready to hear, and how I might not be able to handle it. That may work for some people because sometimes they aren't strong enough. Or, as you say, ready, because something else is going on in their lives or, I don't know..."

Well, Reed said to himself as he listened because he knew exactly what would come next. He would be told that the truth was the truth and sooner or later you had to face it anyway, so put it out there. And besides, the sooner you knew it, the better

149

you would probably be able to deal with it. Get it over with. That was what he had expected to hear and that is exactly what his counterpart said, almost word for word. So, hearing it that way he asked himself what he would like if things were reversed. If he lied to these people now and got caught, it would be the end of it. He would have made an enemy of himself and this other dear family member. So, with that in mind he nodding his agreement, took a really deep breath and exhaled it slowly. Then he began, his words first directed at Alicia.

"You were born in Wisconsin and you lived in a second floor apartment while you went to elementary school. This guy," he said, indicating his alternate, "lived about two blocks away from you at the time and there was always this thing between you, right from the start. Your father was killed in an auto accident when you were eleven or twelve. A few years later your mother remarried and you moved to Cleveland. Over the years you and your mother would come back to Wisconsin for family events and funerals and you would hang out with each other," he continued as he watched her face turn serious. And then, after a long period of silence, she got it and the whole thing was suddenly obvious to her. She didn't go there directly, however. She asked another question first.

"All right. So tell me this. After we moved to Cleveland did you ever drive down to see me?"

"Yes," he said. "Once when I was on the way back east. But when I got there you weren't home. You were off somewhere with some guy you knew so I slept in your mother's spare bedroom and kept going the next day," he told her even though it was another lie. Something he said he wasn't going to do anymore. But for the sake of everything else that was involved, he still felt it necessary. And besides, for this one, there was no way either of them would ever be able to find out anything different.

Alicia looked at him as he said it, thought about it for a second and seemed relieved. Then she turned to his counterpoint and put her hand on his knee.

"But you did the same thing, didn't you? Only we got to see each other when you did," she said with an intimate look and warm smile.

Yes, Reed said to himself. That was where they first crossed the line. The time and place where it all began. That was another one of the things he would never forget. It was a shared memory with his other self but he couldn't think of any reason why his other self would ever need to know that.

Alicia also seemed to have accepted his version of how it had happened and, so far, so good.

"Tell me about my other self," she then asked. "The one you know back in your reality. How is she doing?"

"Well, like you, she's married. But... something happened. She met this guy from some off beat religious group and ended up with him."

"What? Me? Religion? Good grief. That's terrible. I hope she doesn't have any kids."

"No. No children. But she still looks good so there is still time. I'll check up on her when I get back."

"Too bad we can't just call each other on the phone. It might be interesting not have to wait until our lives are over to learn how it all turned out."

"So, who knows. Maybe there is a way to do that," Reed's counterpart said. "Maybe we could build a frequency shifting device that would work on the phone lines. Maybe on one of the microwave links. Wouldn't that be something. Having a hot line between two different realities."

Reed agreed and they all laughed. And then the killer questions from Alicia started again.

"When was the first time you saw us together?" she asked first.

"At the Wharf the night before I went on the fishing trip. I was sitting at the bar while you were having dinner."

"And...," she continued after an accentuating pause. "Were you shocked when you first saw us together?"

"You have no idea. A lot. But then I was really pleased. I thought it was great."

"So. Why would he be shocked?" his other self asked her. "That doesn't..." he said and stopped, then looked at Alicia and

151

then back at Reed and stared at him for a really long time. Then back at Alicia.

"Holy damn," he said to her. "How did you know? My god. Am I that dense? Are we... is ..." he said as he swore again and shook his head in disbelief.

"Well. You said you wanted the truth," she said and patted him on the arm.

"I guess I did. Looks like I got it, all right. How come I didn't see it coming?"

Then he looked back at Reed. "Pull up your left sleeve," he told him as he pulled up his own.

And there it is was, the indisputable confirmation. They both had a long wide, identical looking scar on their forearms. The one they had gotten when they were kids, messing around with a hatchet trying to chop a hole in the winter ice down on the pond near home. Reed's counterpart stared at the one on Reed's arm for a long time without saying anything. Finally Alicia put her arm around him and asked if he was all right.

At first he shrugged, then finally asked her how she was able to pick up on it before he did.

"Probably because I was able to sit and watch you both at the same time and compare. He did a good job of disguising himself at first. Even trying to make out that he was left handed instead of right. But there were just too many clues, even with the beard, long hair and different clothes."

"Goddamn," his other self said and got up and walked around before coming back to sit down. "Jesus," he said, shaking his head at the immensity of it all. But instead of making any direct comments as Alicia did her best to give him a hug, he said, "Well, I guess it might be time to show us how you check locations out before we try and go there."

"I am really, really sorry. I am and I have no idea of how it must make you feel to find something like this out but....well, there is no but, so I'm sorry."

"Don't be. It's not that. I like the truth and I wanted the truth and once I get more used to it I'm sure I'll look back and thank you for it. Actually, I already do," he said and patted Alicia on the cheek. "We never had so much fun in our lives, chasing each other around last night."

Reed looked at the two of them and felt relieved once again. It would be all right, so, time to show them a little about remote viewing and all that, something they were surprisingly good at, especially Alicia. And so, finally, that was it.

There were scattered clouds sitting on the horizon with the sun going down in a building crescendo of interweaving color as they now sat there in a long, protracted silence and watched the changing panorama together. Then Reed rose from the deck chair he was sitting in and stood up. As if sensing what was going to happen next, Alicia and his counterpart stood up too.

"If I can figure out a way to do it, I'll send you a picture of my house so when you get a little better at it, you will have something specific to visualize in case you ever decide to come to Arizona."

"Yes. Seeing myself in some other reality might be very interesting," Alicia said and gave Reed a long, hard hug. After that Reed put out his hand to his other self who shook it firmly and long. Then Reed backed up a step, nodded at them and disappeared.

TWENTY THREE

The first night after Reed returned home from Morro Bay he dreamt of Kyara. Kyara had stood by the side of his bed and looked down at him sleeping. Then she had bent over and kissed him gently on the mouth before she disappeared. It came back to him while he was in the shower and stayed with him all the time he was putting his breakfast together. And then, when he carried his plateful of food and coffee into the dining to sit down and eat, he found a sheet of pale blue stationary lying on the table right where he usually sat.

It said:

Hi, Lover. Welcome home. Hope you enjoyed the trip. For a completely different look at things go to Waynesboro, Pennsylvania. Early July, 1861. Find Bertram Hyer, 26, before the 15th. Your height and build. Black curly hair and dark eyes.

Do your homework and be careful. Remember, anything is possible. Kisses.   Kyara

PS. Your cousin here is in the midst of a nasty divorce. Give her some time, then she will probably call you.

Damn. Why didn't she wake me up, he said to himself. Or crawl in with me, he thought with excitement. But, yes, he was completely exhausted when he had gotten back from California. The kiss was real, though and he knew she had tried to wake him, gently enough, but he was just too out of it. So, bless her for letting him sleep, he guessed. Just wait until next time, however.

As for July of 1861. Hadn't the Civil War started by then? He thought so and as soon as he finished his breakfast, he Googled it. The lead up to the war was complicated. Negotiations, threats, ultimatums, secessions, minor skirmishes, murder and more but the actual official call to battle was given by Lincoln when he ordered the bombardment of Fort Sumter. That occurred on April 12, 1861. But why should he be there in early July? Did it have anything to do with the war itself. Or was there some other reason? After he finished his breakfast he drove down the hill to the library and came home with a stack of books.

American history, although compulsory back in High School, was not one of his favorite subjects and it was a lot of years ago. What still stood out in his mind, however, was that the Civil War was without glory, that it was extremely bloody and that Lincoln had somehow been elevated to the status of having been one of the greatest presidents of all time. Then he began reading.

Extremely bloody as a descriptive term wasn't even close. Older now and with a different perspective, Reed saw the statistics as completely appalling and if they weren't part of the historical record, almost unbelievable. Over six thousand soldiers were killed in one day alone at Antietam and over fifteen thousand wounded. Not with monster bombs and missile strikes but with very primitive weapons. As for the war itself, a war that lasted only four years, at least six hundred and twenty five thousand troops died in battle and another four hundred and twelve thousand were wounded. Over a million in all.

As for civilians, no one seemed to have kept track. Not of their lives, not of their homes and property, nor any of it. It was a time of hatred and madness and vicious cruelty almost beyond imagination as whole towns were looted and mercilessly burned to the ground where marauding armies and self appointed patriots vengefully destroyed everything in their wake. Everything, whether of military importance or not, in some insane rage as though possessed, taking sick advantage of war time opportunity because war is the prime time when defective, sick, demented and warped individuals are able to crawl out from under their rocks and rise to positions of power where they can unleash all their craziness on those around them without direct reprisal. War also provides opportunity to the unscrupulous entrepreneur, large or small, and to every other dysfunctional, warped nut case who needed to express themselves in perverted ways.

Worst of all and most difficult to understand was the fact that this was not a war fought to repel some mad, Hitleresque, foreign aggressor. It was brother against brother. Northerners and southerners equally guilty. But why? And over what?

For some odd reason historians seem to have taken the cowardly way out. In particular, American historians when dealing with American history. The war was fought to free the slaves. Emancipation! That's what so many have said. That is how it was justified. For certain it couldn't have been a time of mass insanity or over-riding stupidity. Nothing like that. It had to have some higher purpose, some ultimate humanitarian reason to justify all that slaughter. But was it emancipation? Was that the truth? No.

The war was not fought to free the slaves. Abraham Lincoln's primary goal had nothing to do with that. In the end, he didn't care about individual liberty and freedom. He was more than willing to compromise on those issues because his real goal was singular and limited. He wanted only one thing. To preserve the Union. No matter what, southern states would not be allowed to secede from the Union. The story as recorded, was a myth.

On the other side of the coin, however, America was born in revolution. It came into being because American colonists believed they had the right to self-determination, a right they fought for and won. A right which in the end, one man in particular, Abraham Lincoln said southerners land owners did not have and went to war over. He did not care that much about the issue of slavery. If he had and the war was really about freeing the slaves and granting those people the right of self determination, it might have been different. Regardless, none of it justified war. And most certainly not in the way the war was perpetuated. Lincoln was not a grand American icon who represented some ultimate in humanitarianism. Lincoln and all of his supporters were stubborn, ego driven, self righteous men determined only to prevail and impose their narrow ideological views on the rest of society.

Well, it was a sad and dishonorable chapter in human history and now he had a chance to go back and witness some small part of it for himself. A dangerous time to be sure, Reed told himself. As Kyara had told him, be prepared and under the circumstances he had damned well better be. And the best way to do that was to become as familiar as possible with the time and place he would be going to.

In particular, what had happened later in July in 1861 and why did he need to get there before then? And who, pray tell, was Bertram Hyer? The only thing he could find that was of any real significance in relation to the war at that time was that the first battle of Bull Run happened on July twenty first. But it took place just west of Centreville, Virginia, about eighteen miles from Washington, DC. and at least seventy miles from Waynesboro so maybe his reason for being there didn't have anything to do with the war directly. Well, whatever it was, it looked liked he would find out because, if Kyara wanted him to go, he was going.

So what about clothing? That shouldn't be too hard. If

need be he could just pop in to some Civil War museum back east and check it out. As for money, that was even easier. Going on line he found a site with fairly high resolution pictures of northerner currency, the only thing that counted at the time because the south hadn't created its own as yet. Downloaded and re sized, it came out of the color printer on some paper stock from the office supply store looking every bit as good as the real thing. Better, in fact. Something which stirring around in the dirt and some weak coffee stains made quite presentable. So, other than historical maps and emergency food supplies, what else did he need? Definitely a good hunting knife. What about a hand gun?

TWENTY FOUR

An instantaneous, bright flash of lightening and an immense clap of thunder almost blew him off his feet. He had materialized right in the middle of a muddy trail that served as a road during a severe storm where the shock of the lightning and thunder were immediately followed by a clatter of hoof beats and loud shouting as group of horsemen appeared almost on top of him. Reacting quickly, Reed jumped back, slipped and fell in the mud at the side of the road, only to be almost trampled to death by the horses. And then they were gone, down around the bend and out of sight as he picked himself up and ran for cover under the nearest large tree, hoping to hell it wasn't going to attract a lightning bolt. Too bad he hadn't put on the plastic rain poncho he had brought along before he started out instead of just putting it in his back pack. Wet clothes were not a great way to start the day off. On the other hand, however, he didn't have to resort to flint and steel to make a fire. He had at least had enough sense to have brought along a good supply of waterproof matches. So, fairly well out of the rain under the tree, he dug down under the cover of dead leaves on the ground and came up with enough dry tinder to start a fire.

By the time he had warmed himself and somewhat dried out, the deluge from the sky was over and the clouds were beginning to break up. The question now was, was he on the right road and with the sun still behind the clouds, which way was east. There was no GPS here but once he found it, his little compass got him started in the right direction. Towards Waynesboro. And because he was totally unfamiliar with everything there, it meant walking was the only safe way to get anywhere for now. Not on the rutted road itself but along the side, back in the trees a ways, just in case.

The thing he was the most happiest about at the moment was the fact that he had worn a pair of high top hiking boots. Damned mud. Obviously for those who grew up in this era, it was just a part of life. But for him, well, stop bitching, he told himself as he came plodding into the small town. At the most there were two hundred houses scattered about, clustered along the dirt streets, some of which were named. A combination of log huts, clapboard buildings, mud brick structures and a few built out of stone. There was even a town square, a livery, an eatery, a hotel and a bank. Elsewhere there should be a tannery, some grinding mills for grain and some kind of shop where they made steam engines. He stomped what mud he could off his feet, went into the hotel lobby and asked to be put up for a few nights. Thinking in terms of only seventy five cents a night was a bit of an adjustment, however, even without running water and private bath, but his currency passed its' first test and he now realized he was walking around with the equivalent of a quarter million dollars in his pocket. He could probably buy the whole damned town if he wanted to.

He should have let his hair and his beard grow a little longer before he had come there, however, he also decided because people looked at his clean shaven face with some suspicion. Maybe he could pass himself off as a businessman from New York or Baltimore in the meantime, until he became a little more scruffy. Another thing that might help would be a more appropriate wardrobe and with that went down to the general store where he bought a new jacket and some shirts. Not all that comfortable, but they seemed to help him fit in better. Then he went in the eatery, had boiled coffee and a slice of pie before he asked the woman proprietor if she knew a Bertram

Hyer. She looked at him blankly and shook her head no. After that he asked at the bank and the tannery and at the steam engine plant, all with the same response. Then, as a last resort, he went out on the edge of town to the grinder mill, a dusty, dirty, noisy place where the machinery was driven by a belching old steam engine fired by a dangerous looking boiler heated by an attached wood burning furnace.

Inside a lean-to kind of addition hung onto the main building, he found the owner. Not the happiest of fellows, the older man was shouting at one of the local farmers who was complaining about what he was being charged for the corn that had apparently just been ground.

"Pay up or leave it here," the farmer was told in a grumpy voice. "I got no sympathy for chiselers."

The farmer looked around to see Reed standing there over hearing the argument, then grumbled and dug in his pockets for the right amount of coins and handed them over.

"Well, could you at least help me put on my wagon," he said as he did so. "Or is that extra?"

"Might be able to do that if you get it up here," he was told in a milder tone, wherein the farmer went to get his horse drawn cargo wagon.

"What can I do for you, stranger?" the man then asked Reed, who had backed out of the small structure and was outside waiting.

"Sorry to bother you, but..." Reed started to say before he was interrupted by the farmer pulling his wagon into place in front of the open shed door.

"Just a minute," the owner said to Reed, then turned around and shouted in an overly harsh voice.

"Bertram! Get your damn black ass up here. Hurry it up." Then he turned back to Reed and complained about the quality of his help. But, before Reed could respond, a young black man came out of the main building, immediately saw what needed to be done and began throwing burlap bags of ground corn onto the farmers wagon.

A little shocked to see a man named Bertram as being black, Reed asked the owner if by chance Bertram's last name happened to be Hyer.

"Don't know and don't rightly care as long as he does his job. Why? Is he a runaway? One of yours? Where you from, Virginia? You're not from around here."

"Do you mind if I ask him?" Reed questioned, as the black man threw the last bag of corn on the wagon.

"I'm paying him and the day's not over until it's getting dark."

"Dark?" Reed said before realizing where he was at. In this time period people routinely worked fifteen or sixteen hour days.

"Git over here, Bertram," the owner then yelled, once the bags of ground corn were all loaded.

"You belong to this man?" Bertram was then asked in a gruff voice after he came and stood in front of them. "Wouldn't surprise me none. Can't expect anybody to tell the truth these days. Where'd you get those freeman's papers you showed me when I hired you? You been lying to me?"

"Wait a minute," Reed said. "Just a damned minute," he said to the man and then turned to the black. "Your first name is Bertram. Is there any chance you are Mr. Hyer?"

"Mr. Hyer?" the owner almost shouted. "You are calling a colored man, Mister?" and then he looked at Bertram and told him to get his black ass back inside and finish what he had been doing earlier.

"Hold it," Reed said in a much louder voice this time. "Let him answer my question first."

"Okay, boy. What is it? Tell him your name and be quick."

The young black looked at Reed, decided it might be safe to do so and nodded in the affirmative.

"How much you paying this man?" Reed then asked the owner who begrudgingly told him it was a dollar a day, which was probably a gross exaggeration. But Reed didn't care. All he wanted was a number.

"Fair enough," he said as he pulled a twenty dollar bill off his wad and held it out. "On one condition. I won't need him for more than a day or two so you give me your word he gets his job back when I'm done with him. He doesn't, I'll be making trouble for you. And, he goes with me now."

The twenty was more than convincing so Reed told Bertram to brush the dust off himself and they left. Bertram followed a few steps behind until Reed stopped.

"Please, he said. "Walk with me so we can talk, not behind me."

Bertram caught up but still hadn't said one word. Not to Reed or to his boss or to the farmer but then, for a black man in that time period, it was probably the safest thing he could do so Reed started talking instead.

"Do you mind if I just call you Bert? Is that okay?" he asked and got a consenting nod.

"Good. My name is Reed Jahneke. I would be pleased if you would call me Reed. But no matter what, don't call me mister or sir or any other ingratiating or subservient term. Can we be clear on that?"

"Yes, ah, boss, ah, yes."

"All right. Now the first thing I want to tell you is that you are not in any kind of trouble. I am not from the government or law enforcement or anything of that nature. I am just here for my own private reasons and I'm not an easterner or a southerner. I'm from Arizona. Do you know where that is?"

"Yes sir. It's in the south west. I..." Bertram said, clearly impressed and a little intimidated by the white man who had come to get him and obviously still a little anxious as to what it might be all about.

"It's okay," Reed said about having been called sir. "You'll get used to it. Let's see. What time is it?" he asked. After all the time it took to find Bertram, it had to be getting late. He held up his left arm, pulled up the sleeve a bit and looked at the cheap watch on his wrist. "Damn, six o'clock. Are you hungry? You must be the way you have to work."

Bertram didn't answer at first. He just stared at Reed's watch and it took Reed a second to realize why.

Certainly Bert had seen a watch before. Lot's of men had big pocket watches they carried around. But Reed's wrist watch was small and very thin by comparison and he let Bert take another look at it, an older model stem winder, because there weren't any watch batteries in this era. There weren't any other kinds of batteries either but he had still brought two miniature LED flashlights anyway, in case of some emergency. Then Bert finally admitted that, yes, he was hungry but if they could finish their business, he would like to go home to his woman.

"Where do you live?" Reed asked.

"To the north 'bout half a mile on Gramercy Road."

"Any children?"

"No, sir. No, I mean. And if I could ask. What is your business with me?"

"That's the problem. I don't know yet. But maybe we'll be able to figure it out before long if you give me a little time."

"You paid for my time, all right. So I guess you can have as much as you want till your money runs out."

"Good. So would it be okay if I met your wife?"

"I suppose so. Maybe. If you want."

"Thank you. But first let's get a little surprise for her," Reed said and walked in silence with Bert until they came to the Eatery.

"I can't go in there," the black man said, pointing at the, no colored allowed, sign in the window.

"Hmm," Reed said, not having noticed it before. Well, damn, he thought, at first determined to bring Bert in with him anyway and to hell with everyone's prejudice but then decided against it. Bert would have to go on living here after he was gone and there was enough animosity in the world without dragging him into an unnecessary confrontation.

Inside Reed asked for three full meals of pot roast and the use of a picnic basket to carry the food in. Coming out, they walked the dirt covered streets to a small, one room log cabin sitting back off the road in the trees. Bert walked to the door, opened it and looked in.

"What happened honey," the woman asked, somewhat alarmed as she came towards him once he was inside. "Is everything okay. You're home so early."

"No need to get worried," he told her. "We have a visitor and my time is paid for by this gentleman."

The woman took one look at Reed, backed up a couple of

steps, looked at him suspiciously and was quiet.

Reed stepped forward and told her his first name, said he was very glad to meet her and put out his hand. She looked at it, almost took it it and then said, how do you do, to him. The cabin windows were small and with the door now closed it was difficult for Reed to get a good look at her at first. He then handed over the picnic basket and suggested that they had best eat while the food was still warm. Then he slipped out of his back pack and set it by the door.

"And I'll just have a glass of water if I could, too," he told her.

They ate in silence in the dim evening light as Reed sensed their discomfort with his presence but the food was obviously something special for them and it was soon gone. Then the woman got up and brought a candle back to the table.

"Oh dear," she said as she realized she had let the fire go out in the wood stove and had no way to light the candle.

"Let me do it," Reed said as he reached in his jacket pocket for the matches he had used earlier in the day, got them out, scratched one on the side of the box and lit the candle, creating another surprised look on Bertram's face. Then he took a really good look at the woman's face after the candle flame grew and it finally occurred to him what he was doing there. Another close look at Bertram confirmed it because until that moment, the differences in their ages and the color of their skin had blinded him to the facts. His first reaction was one where he wanted to jump up and hug them both but he forced himself to remain still. Then he looked back at the woman who was now staring at him like she should also know who he was but was unable to figure it out.

"Well, ma'am," Reed said after finally breaking eye contact and standing up. "I most certainly want to thank you for your hospitality in allowing me into your home as a stranger."

It was time to go, he decided because he needed time to think this through. Kyara had sent him back in time to witness the two of them in a previous lifetime together. And with a different racial background. Holy Hanna. He had never considered that one before. Actually, he hadn't even considered reincarnation in itself as anything more than a passing curiosity. But here it was, one on one, and getting adjusted to the idea was going to take a while.

Taking a last look around the most humble of abodes, he went around to where Bertram was now standing. Then he dug in his pocket, took out his money without allowing Bertram to see the size of his roll, pulled off two one dollar bills and handed them to him.

"Again, my thanks," he told them both. And then he told Bert that if he was willing to come to the hotel at nine in the morning he would give him another two dollars for the day and two more for each day that they were together after that.

"There's no work to be done so wear your other clothes if you have some. And if you don't want to come and see me, I'll understand."

Obviously he was in too big of a hurry, Reed decided by noon the next day. He wanted to know everything possible about Bertram's and his woman's background but it was a matter of trust and Bertram was still reluctant to share much of it with him. About all he was able to find out was that they had come from Georgia two years prior and Bertram had been set free when his owner died and that his woman's name was Katelyn. Well, maybe that was the problem. Quite possibly they were worried that someone still had a claim to them, and they might have to go back into slavery, he decided and indeed, as he later learned, Katelyn was not actually free but had run off with Bertram on his journey north, which explained everything. But for the time being he was stalled out and ready to quit for the day. And with that he dug in his pack for the spiral notebook and pen he had brought along and began to record what little he had learned. That done, he brought out his other notebook, the one prepared at home full of notes and data about the time and place he was in to see if it might give him some ideas and quickly noticed that Bertram was looking at it very closely, as if he were able to read upside down.

And damned if he wasn't, Reed learned as he handed the

note book to Bertram and nodded his approval. Not only did the man seem able to read, he was able to read quite rapidly and quickly scanned through several pages as though completely fascinated by what the words said. But then Reed took it back when he realized it was also full of the future dates of major events in the civil war, took out his other notebook again, found a blank page and gave it to Bertram along with a pen and told him to write. "Write anything. Your name, where you live, whatever."

Bertram looked at the ball point pen oddly, made a few scribbles and then did as asked as Reed's eyebrows went up. Not only was the man able to write, his penmanship was almost as good as Reed's and he almost wanted to shout he was so thrilled. This was himself. Someone who had learned to read and write under the most dire of circumstances. How marvelous.

"Jeez, Bertram, you can read and write both. How did you learn to do that?" he asked with enthusiasm.

"From Katelyn," was all this former self was willing to say for then.

"Okay," Reed stated, letting it go. "What about tomorrow? Can we talk some more then?" Reed asked hopefully and watched Bertram think it over. Obviously the man liked and needed the money but his fears were still holding him back and it occurred to Reed that he had also been more than a little remiss in his approach to the situation.

"My apologies," he said. "I should have explained this better to you instead of just sticking my nose into your business. I'm a writer and I'm doing research for a new book I'm working on. It's a novel about the upcoming civil war and I want to be able to create my characters as realistically as possible so I'll be searching for people from all sides of the situation. North and south, black and white, civilian and military and you're the first ones."

"You said black. Mister, we're colored. And your notes already got dates in them. How do you know what happened if it hain't happened yet?"

"You're right. I don't. I was only speculating based on what I've found out so far from my studies of the government

165

and military individuals."

"And maybe there won't be no war. Then what? You going to make one up?"

"I'm prepared to do that if I have to and don't worry. I won't be using anyone's real name except for the president and the generals."

"Well, sir. If that's the truth I can stay longer for your questions or I can be back in the mornin'."

"That's great, Bert. Is it okay to call you Bert?"

"For two dollar a day you can call me any name you want except one."

"Good. And that one has never been in my vocabulary. So, why don't you go home. And what if I come by your place in the morning when I'm ready. Talk to your woman and see if I might ask her some questions too. Nothing really personal."

Reed's earlier self left with another two dollars in his pocket after agreeing that Reed could come to his house in the morning. Then Reed went back to the hotel and asked the clerk where he might find something to read. Books, magazines or newspapers of any kind.

"To borrow or to buy?" he was asked.

"To buy."

"Try the general store for newspapers and maybe some old magazines from Philadelphia. And if it's books, go down to the church and see what the reverend has. They're to borrow so maybe if you made a donation..."

"Good morning, ma'am," Reed said to Katelyn the next day when she opened the door.

"Mornin to you, sir," she replied and Reed took it as a good sign. "Bertram be with you in one moment."

"And this is for you," he said as he set down the big picnic basket he had bought to carry all the books and papers he had found that they could read.

She looked at him inquisitively before she bent and picked it up, almost without effort and he was surprised at how strong she was, but then, why wouldn't she be? She probably knew how to chop wood, carry water and do a whole range of things that were necessary for survival back then.

"What have you got?" Bertram asked as he also came to the door.

"Don't know. Best we find out," Katelyn said as she took it to the table and opened it.

"My goodness. Books and books and newspapers and... oh my. That's so wonderful. Who do we give them back to when we're done?"

"No one. They're yours to keep. Having things to read might be nice when winter comes."

"And before."

"I didn't get you a bible. Wasn't sure you wanted one."

"Not in this lifetime. How come you knew that?"

"Just a good guess, ma'am. I'm glad I got it right," he said as he watched her pick up book after book with joy. Then she spoke again, but not to Reed.

"Go with the gentleman, Bertram. And answer his questions when he asks. Then you stop at the store and bring home something he likes for supper. If he has a mind to eat with us."

"Yes, ma'am," Bert said and patted her gently. Then he moved to the door to go with Reed. But Reed had a different idea. He had also brought along a second basket of food and wanted to know if the three of them couldn't go somewhere together to talk and have a picnic lunch.

Three full days of being with Katelyn and Bertram gave Reed about as much insight into their lives as he might ever be able to get and he was astounded by it. But it was also the 13th of the month. Two more days till the 15th. What was so important about that date. What had he missed, if anything? He had no idea. But Kyara had been clear about it so what could it be? Did it have something to do with the war? He didn't see how. The only direct connection that Waynesboro seemed to have with the war was that two southern Generals rode through there on the way north to Gettysburg with their troops and General Lee came back through after the retreat. And that didn't occur until July of 1863, two years later, so it most certainly had nothing to do with that. Thinking about it, however, finally made Reed realize what he had overlooked.

He had asked a hundred questions and had an in depth look at their lives from a factual point of view but he had still done them a great disservice. How could he have been so callous? He had never once asked them how they felt about any of it on a personal level. Especially regarding the issue of slavery. Charged as the issue might be, he felt that by then they trusted him enough for him to bring up the subject and so the following day, that was what was on his mind as he set out to knock on their door. Then, once he had allowed them to give voice to that, there would be no further reason for him to stay that he could think of. He would still stick around through the fifteenth, however, just in case something did come up. But if nothing did, and he couldn't think of anything else to pursue, then he might as well go back home.

But still, he kept on. This was Kyara and himself in another lifetime. They had come there for specific reasons. Obviously, one of these reasons was to start out living the life of black slaves under a harsh set of circumstances to gain another perspective on what life was all about. Much as he might want to help, however, to what level did he dare tamper with that so as not to deprive them of the full depth of such an experience? His experience and hers in a place so radically different from his own. Maybe it was because of this one, which was actually back in his own past, that he felt the way he did about people of other races. Black people had differences in skin color and features but, to him, being black was no different than being Irish or Jewish or Arab and so what? Neither was being Asian or native American or anything else. And, thinking about it, what he was always most impressed by was, as separate groups of people, so many of them had an amazing ability to survive all the prejudice that was sometimes still being heaped upon them in the still very backwards world of the twenty first century.

So, empathizing with them and thinking ahead, his first

impulse was to give all the money he still had to them when it came time to leave. It might be counterfeit but it was undetectable in this low tech world so in this society they could buy themselves a mansion and never have to work again. But, no. That would most likely defeat their reasons for being there. Maybe a little something to keep them comfortable for a while but that was it. Let them work out the rest of it by themselves.

Jeez, he then scolded himself, he had missed something else too. Beneath his placid and relatively compliant exterior, there was another, completely different side to Bertram. He was an extremely angry young man. Rightfully so, no doubt about that. So too was Katelyn, but to a much more moderated extent, even though she was the one living with the fear of being found out. She, in spite of it all, seemed to have developed a more philosophical attitude towards life in general and was able to provide a bright and stabilizing force in Bertram's life. And, as Reed soon found out, if Bertram ever needed one, he needed it now. God damn, the impetuous young man hated the idea of slavery so much that he was determined to go off and fight in the war. He had, in fact, already made plans to do so. He was intent on saying goodbye to Katelyn and leaving on the 15th to go to Philadelphia and volunteer, convinced that he could become a black soldier. It was no wonder Katelyn was always so attentive, fussing over him all the time, trying to ease his private pain.

"Holy jesus, Bertram," Reed said when it finally came out that morning as he sat drinking coffee with them at the tiny table in their cramped little cabin. "Are you sure you want to do that?"

"Yes sir, I do."

"Well, okay. You certainly have the right to do that but do you ...."

Oh hell, Reed thought. He'd better be careful here. The issue was a very emotional one for Bertram and he didn't want to alienate him now. So instead of questioning Bertram's good sense he asked him how he thought Katelyn would be able to survive when he didn't come back.

"What do you mean? Not come back?"

"Have you ever killed anyone? Do you know how to shoot a gun? Do you know how to take orders from someone who doesn't give a damn as to whether you live or die? Do you have any idea as to how bloody this war will be? How many innocent people will get caught in the middle, black and white? How many people's houses and businesses will be burned to the ground? And no matter how it goes and who wins, do you think that will be the end of it? Or will that just be the beginning of something else? And do you realize what madness comes out of war? How many crazy people it gives a voice to? War costs lives and money and leaves the future stained with blood and animosity and ..... Well, okay. Never mind. I'm sorry to rant but you are an intelligent man and have a better than average chance of having a good future and are blessed with this wonderful woman in your life, standing by you and.... Dammit. The idea of you joining the army makes me want to weep."

Bertram didn't respond immediately, obviously thinking it over first. Then he spoke.

"Yes sir. But why do you care what I do? You're a white man. Why you care if I live or die or what happens to my woman here? How you going to answer that?"

"I can't, Bertram. But I damn well have my own reasons for caring and maybe someday I'll try and explain it. But for now just take my word for it that it will be a senseless war of brother against brother and even though it might put an end to slavery, that's not what it's all about to begin with."

"Well, Mr. Lincoln says he wants to free the slaves. That's what I heard talk about so if that ain't it, what is it?"

"A lot of talk. Lincoln doesn't give a damn one way or the other about slavery itself. For him it's a political issue. He has taken the view that seceding from the Union goes against the constitution and there is no middle ground. He said, a house divided against itself cannot stand. Something like that and he is stubbornly determined to preserve the Union even if it takes the death of half the people in it to do that. As for the south, the white landowners don't care about the morality of slavery. For them it's about cotton. They need the cheap labor to produce cotton. And it's not just the whites. Some of your own people who have also managed to become landowners, have slaves too. They own them just like you were owned. You lived in the south for most of your life. You must know that."

About to say something, Bertram suddenly looked at Katelyn and stared at her as she stared back at him for the longest time. Then they came together and put their arms around each other because the plantation Katelyn had escaped from had been owned by a black man. A colored man, as they would have put it. One of their own, this time around.

Then, when they released each other, the somewhat defeated Bertram sank into a chair and sat there looking at Reed, with Reed feeling his agony.

"But what can I do? It isn't right."

"I know it's not. And maybe there's nothing to be done except try and live through it. I don't know but I wish to god I did."

"But," Bertram said and stopped as he remembered something. "Those papers you had that I saw. They had lists of dates and places and numbers on them. What was all that about? I recognized some of them but the days were all in the future. How is that possible? Like I asked before, is it you speculating about things that might happen, or you know some folks who have that kind of vision, or what?"

Oh jeez. How was he supposed to deal with that, Reed wondered. More lies? That was the last thing he wanted to do but under the circumstances, like it or not, the only choice he seemed to have at the moment was to stick with his previous story about writing a novel. So, if he was going to fake it, might as well do it in a big way, he decided and dug around in his back pack until he found the notes Bertram had seen but a small part of before and handed them to him. Bertram took them and began to search through them one by one as Katelyn looked over his shoulder. Many minutes later they both looked at him with big questions in their eyes. He had certainly gotten their attention. Now all he had to do was to come up with some plausible sounding explanation and hoped they believed it. Before he could begin, however, Katelyn spoke to Bertram and saved him.

"I know you don't fully trust him, dear man. I know I

didn't at first either so don't ask me to explain this but why do you suppose he might be not wanting you to go off like you say you want? What good does it do him either way? I can't say I understand why but for some strange reason I believe he cares about us cause otherwise what did he ever have to gain by being so kind. Now you think about that, baby, cause if you don't, I may never see you again and that will kill me just like some stranger kills you. And for what? You want to do something, you come up with a better idea than walking off like a blind man into a ditch."

It took a few minutes for Bertram to let her words sink in.

"Well, maybe you are right, woman. You are more important than me trying to fight the people I hate. And Mr. Reed is right too. How would I do that? I don't know nothin about fighting. But how can I just let it be gone? There must be something."

"I know. But you gotta try. That's the way it is."

They talked a little longer. Bertram had been swayed but Reed still didn't think he was totally convinced.

"I tell you what, Bertram. You want proof? If you can ride a horse, I'll show you proof. Where can I rent some saddle horses?"

"None for rent round here. But if you had the money, you could buy some. Down at the livery or out on the west road there's a man who raises them."

"But can you ride?"

"Course I can ride. But why do we need horses?"

"Because we will go to Manassas. It about seventy miles south of here in Virginia. And if we go, we have to be there before the twenty first. That's just six days from now. What do you think?"

"What are we goin to do there?"

"Watch the battle of Bull Run. Once you see how many soldiers get killed there you will forget all your ideas about being in the military."

"How do you know there's a battle going to be fought there? Just cause that's what it says on the papers you just give me to look at, how can you know that?"

"Well, you have every right to be skeptical so I'll make a deal with you. Are you interested?"

"Yes,sir. Maybe. Depends."

"Starting now I will pay you five dollars a day instead of two. You come with me and do as I say while we're together. Not because I want to control you, but just so I can keep you out of trouble so you can come home to your woman. Then we'll see what you think about things."

"But what if you get killed watching? How can you be close enough to watch and not be in the way of getting hurt," Katelyn wanted to know.

"Because the battlefield is surrounded by hills so we can watch from a safe distance. And as long as we stay to the south east we will be okay."

"Why to the south east? I mean... never mind. What do you think, Kate?"

"I guess... well, maybe you should go with the man and do what he says. Then when you get back you can be at peace with yourself and not spend the rest of your life fretting about things you can't fix. How does that sound?"

"I think you are most likely right, just like you usually are, so I guess I will go."

"Okay," Reed said. "It's your decision so let's get busy. We have a lot to do first."

TWENTY FIVE

Two big roan horses with western saddles, saddle bags, bed rolls, canteens, jerky and hard tack, two big Henry lever action, long rifles, a Smith and Wesson revolver for Bertram and his own forty five semi automatic with five, thirteen round clips of hollow point ammo for Reed and away they rode, off to the south. Bertram could ride, all right. Maybe it was the sense of freedom it gave him but Reed had to hold him down to a more reasonable pace so he didn't run his animal into the ground. They made twenty five miles the first day, camped in the woods at night and thirty more miles the next day. That evening Reed gave Bertram an introduction to firearms and they ended up shooting a wild turkey for their supper. Bertram was a bit shocked at firing a rifle for the first time, the noise and the recoil making him fearful of it in the beginning but he settled down, learned how to steady himself and aim well. Then Reed had him practice with the revolver. It would be a long time before Bertram would be much of a threat with that as a weapon but the fact of his having it might serve to intimidate folks into at least leaving him alone.

Sixty five thousand troops was one hell of a lot of human beings but they had been arriving for days. Almost completely untrained and undisciplined, bedraggled looking in everything from bib overalls to dirty uniforms, some with boots and some barefooted, they carried whatever weapon they were able to come across, from swords to smooth bore muzzle loaders to shot guns and handguns. Some of them knew how to use what they had, many did not, and before the day ended the North would have nearly three thousand dead and wounded while the south would lose almost two thousand as human blood would spill and seep into the overrun ground. And that would only be the beginning of four long years of horror.

Goddammit, Reed said to himself as he thought of it. It was insane. If only there was some way to change it. But what could one man do? What could the two of them do together? Nothing. Not a damned thing but sit on an adjacent hill and watch the slaughter and then go home and live with the helplessness. What in the hell was wrong with all of these god damned people? Didn't they see the stupidity of it?

But then a thought came to him. Maybe there was a way. Not to stop the battle. It was too late for that. The battle would go on no matter what. And when it did people from Washington would bring their picnic baskets out and sit on the hilltops and have their little lunches and drink wine and watch the bodies of other humans get blown to bits as if they were going to a ballgame or a circus sideshow or... well, what the hell. Maybe that was what the country needed. Maybe that was all it deserved. Maybe even that was too good for them, the calloused, unthinking, heartless fools.

Yes, but what about all the others? The ones who cared and felt and worried and reached out and wanted something saner and better for themselves and those around them and ended up getting over run and trampled upon and had their hopes and dreams pounded into the mud. What about them? Why did they have to stand by and be victimized and caused to suffer helplessly because of a few stubborn sons-a-bitches whose egos were bigger than their brains and had the power to run civilization into the ground to support their own misguided greed and stupidity?

But yes, Reed decided, maybe there was a way to change some of that, and maybe he really had the ability to do it. But did he have the right? And did he have the ability to change the course of history? Not in an over all sense. No matter what he did, it wouldn't change any of the history books back home in his own reality. Nor in a lot of other ones either. All it would do would be to create another reality in the multiverse of realities. One that could take mankind down another probable path to be explored and experienced. And, in the bigger scheme of things, that might just be a very positive thing to do.

So there it was, he told himself, and it was just so overwhelmingly simple. One other man. All he had to do was be persuasive enough to get that other man to do one thing a little differently the following day when the main battle was over and the North was on the run in retreat. That man was none other than Confederate Brigadier General Thomas J. Jackson. Old Stonewall, as he would become known as later. But how? What could he say to such a man as Jackson that might be convincing enough. Better yet, how exactly would he ever be able to get into the man's command post without getting himself shot first? He didn't know but he felt he had to try, so with strict orders to Bertram to stay put and stay out of sight until he returned, Reed rode off into early evening dusk of the day before the first major battle of the American Civil War.

Bertram was mostly silent on the way back home after witnessing all the ungodly brutality and barbaric bloodshed as human beings senselessly blasted, bayoneted and hacked their human counterparts into eternity. Reed thought he was probably in shock and left him alone for the most part, poor man. Damned if he wasn't in shock himself. Damned if wasn't the most brutal, horrifying thing he had ever seen or ever hoped to see. Dummies, as Bertram later described it to Katelyn. Dummies standing out in the open field shooting blindly at each other, over and over again as rows and rows of them were mowed down and more stepped up to take their place in the slaughter. And then Jackson's famous charge as northerners dropped their weapons and ran off like scared rabbits through the woods, chased down, some shot and some captured. At first.

But then the difference in tactics. In Reed's history, Jackson's charge had ended there. Once the battle reached the point where the southern troops had the north on the run, they stopped short of complete victory and let them go where they eventually regrouped and reformed to continue the war. But here, under these circumstances, Reed's persuasive powers had been effective. In this world Jackson had continued the charge and by late afternoon the south had killed another thousand poor fools and had surrounded and taken captive almost twenty thousand more. The back of the northern army was broken.

Two days later General Robert E. Lee rode into Washington DC and demanded that Lincoln personally sign a letter of surrender and that was that. In one small corner of the universe, the war was over and history had been changed, hopefully for the better. And as for Reed and Bertram, they made it back to Waynesville without endangering incident because they traveled mostly by moonlight along the less traveled back roads.

Reed left Bertram alone the day after they arrived back home so he could have the time with Katelyn to sort it all out. Then the next day when he went to see them and say goodbye he found out that all along they had a secret goal they had been working towards. They were hoping to save enough money to buy a tiny little store over in the small town of Rouzerville, just a mile or so east of Waynesboro. The store was right adjacent to Stephey's Tavern and had two rooms of living quarters on the second floor, totaling more than twice the space they had in their cabin, something they didn't even own but rented from an old white widow woman. There Bertram wouldn't have to work in the grinding mill any longer either, and they could work together and not have to humble themselves to the whites. There were also several families of other coloreds in the area and it might be a place that they could begin to call home. The only problem was in swinging the deal. They were short another two hundred dollars and not completely sure that the old white couple who owned it would sell out to them because of their race.

"Well, let's go see what we can do," Reed told them after he heard about it. "Now that you have horses of your own, we can ride on over and check it out."

The old man drove a hard bargain but after half an hour of haggling and a few extra dollars the store owner handed Bertram a signed deed, along with a list and proof of ownership for all the inventory in the store. The man also agreed that he and his wife would be out by the end of the week and able to hand over the keys then. He was also able to tell them that the upstairs was already vacant and they had permission to move their household things in before that, provided they used the back stairs while they did it.

"Well," Reed said to them once they got back to the cabin. "Looks like you are all set. You have horses to ride, a business to run, guns to protect yourselves with and, I almost forgot. Here's your bank book. You'll need some working capital to get started on and money for groceries so that should be enough to tide you over. And now, the last thing I want to do is say goodbye, but I must. And, absolutely, not one word of thanks, please. No matter how you see this, believe me. I have gained far more from meeting you both than you may ever know.

Approximately two weeks after Reed had left Bertram and Katelyn, the postman delivered a heavy package to their store. A somewhat unusual one for them. They had never seen a cardboard box of such smooth and well made construction before and were somewhat baffled by the fact that it was not wrapped in brown paper and held together with twine but closed with clear packaging tape. Something else neither they or the postman were familiar with. They were also at a loss as to who might be sending them something since there was no return address on it. The postman put the package up on the store counter top and then spent a couple of pennies for some candy sticks as an excuse to hang around while they opened it because his curiosity had gotten the better of him. Bertram, however, let it set there for a while to take care of a customer and then moved it to a low shelf behind the counter so he could wait for Katelyn who was upstairs fixing their lunch.

By the time she came down the postman was gone and Bertram sat the package back on the counter and took out his pocket knife. He carefully slit the taped seams down the middle and opened the box. Then he understood why it was so heavy. It was full of books. Not books published prior and up to 1861 but books that were all published after 2010. Of primary interest was a complete set of encyclopedias. There was also a full sized edition of a JC Penny catalog, a copy of Time magazine with the picture of America's first black president on the cover, a copy of the Sunday edition of the LA Times and a variety of other publications that might present a cross section of early 21st century life.

TWENTY SIX

Unknown to his counterpart in California, Reed had brought back samples with him so he could make comparisons of their DNA and it was no surprise that, within the range of test equipment error, they were identical. What did surprise him, however, was how closely Bertram's DNA also matched his own. The correlation was nearly the same as that for identical twins. But then, why not. They were far more closely related than siblings.

Well, DNA was one thing. The thing he wondered about the most, however, was what final effect did his attempt to change the outcome of the civil war have? Did the different ending of that one battle really alter anything for the better in the long run? He certainly hoped so but the more he thought about it, the more his not knowing bothered him. He wasn't interested in all the day to day details he might get from reliving that period of history, however. Bertram and Katelyn were already doing that and somehow, on some other level he would eventually gain the benefit of it. For now he was just extremely curious about the end result. But, shame on him for not thinking of it sooner. Instead of being in such a big hurry to get home he could just as easily have jumped into the future of that reality while he was still there and found out before coming back.

With that in mind he decided that the surest way for him to accomplish his goal would be to begin by transporting himself back to the same location he had gone to the first time, simply because it had worked well enough and he didn't want to end up in the wrong place. The one just outside Waynesboro. Then he would launch himself into the future of that era from there and hopefully end up in the same place a hundred and fifty years later.

Oh, shit, he said to himself after he had completed the first leg of his journey and moved on to appear at the later date. He had ended up in someone's front yard. Waynesboro had grown considerably. But he hadn't considered that it would have expanded out quite this far. Well, thank god the house wasn't ten feet closer to the street or he would have been in real trouble, trapped in the wall of the structure. Or would he? What would happen to him if he made such a mistake and tried to reappear inside of something solid? It was something else to worry about if he was going to continue his explorations. If only Kyara were around. She might know the answer. But, then, letting himself get side tracked into thinking about her was also a mistake. It kept him from realizing that he was standing almost directly in front of the big bay window of the house where he had appeared. Bad enough, but the woman who lived there had seen him and was now yelling at him from the open front door, accusing him of something that was not very nice. He apologized, saying that he was only trying to retrieve a piece of paper the breeze had blown out of his hand, shrugged and walked off.

Paved streets were much easier to walk on than the rutted, muddy trail he had been on the previous time into town. Minutes later he asked directions to the public library, found it and began searching. There were no books whose titles directly reflected the American Civil War so he reviewed several of them that dealt explicitly with American History. What he was looking for was labeled the Secessionist Movement. After the North was forced to surrender, Southern leaders were in a position to dictate the terms of peace that followed. Instead of withdrawing from the Union, they made slavery entirely a States Rights issue instead and slavery as such, existed in that context until the late eighteen hundreds but had in effect died out almost entirely some years before, all by itself. Once that had occurred, Congress had been able to push through a constitutional amendment that gave power back to the federal government regarding all human rights issues, including slavery.

As soon as that was clear in his mind, Reed stopped reading. But then something came to mind and he again swore at his own stupidity. Yes, he had seemingly changed the course of the American Civil War and saved Bertram from joining the army and getting himself killed. Or did he? The fact was the Civil War had still occurred in his, Reed's, own reality so maybe what really happened was that Bertram, himself, did the same thing he, Reed, did when he divided wherein one aspect of himself became a doctor and another did not while yet another didn't go to college but ended up living on a charter boat in California. In spite of all his efforts, Bertram may well have still fought in the war. He might even have gotten himself killed. But, enough, he told himself. He could spend an entire other lifetime exploring all those possibilities and that wasn't what he wanted to do. Besides, something else was up. Kyara was not only on his mind again, thoughts of her were beginning to over ride everything else he was thinking of. That meant it must be time to get back home to his own reality.

TWENTY SEVEN

Unfortunately for Reed, the big house up on the ridge was empty when he arrived. There was no note from Kyara waiting for him and at first he was immensely disappointed. Obviously, it was his own thoughts of longing to be with her which had misled him. But now that she wasn't there and he knew of no way to contact her, all he could do was try to be patient and wait. But what to do in the meantime?

In spite of his decision to leave it alone, he ended up spending more time thinking about other aspects of what might have happened as a result of what he had done back in 1861. In that regard he went on line to make a check on what effect his meddling with history might have had on his own reality. His feeling was that it would have had absolutely none because that other reality would simply have split off and gone its own way, beginning at the point where he had been able to persuade General Jackson to change tactics. And, as near as he could tell, he was correct so he need not have worried about that any further. But that wasn't the main issue either. Was it. Thinking about what he had taken upon himself to do had other ramifications. It was about power.

On the one hand everyone who had ever been alive on earth had in some way, large or small, brought change to the world. Even the fetus that aborted, if nothing else, had some effect on the parent. But quite often it went beyond that. One small emotionally charged event could sometimes be so dramatic as to cause the affected one to set off on some personal crusade that ends up changing the world in some significant way, large or small. It all begins somewhere. And it begins in the human mind. No house, no boat, no highway or skyscraper or airplane was ever built without the idea first taking birth in someone's mind. No book was ever written, no organization ever formed, no war ever started that didn't first have it's conception in the mental realm. And no war ever solved any problem that couldn't have been solved in some more humane way if the effort had been made to do so.

It would be different, however, if people could look back at war and realize other possibilities but too often they did not and that was one of mankind's greatest failings. People did not seem to learn the lessons that should have been the most obvious. The real tragedy. But, the world was the way it was because that is exactly where human thinking had taken it. If society seemed to be so radically off track at times with its' behavior, it would not do any good to wait around for God to come down from heaven and do some dramatic house cleaning event that would sweep away all the sinners. Only mankind can change what mankind has done.

Not only did humanity create the great works of literature and music and art and beneficial technology and take humans to the moon and back, it also started every war that was ever fought and was responsible for every dissident act that ever occurred. And when things got off track the individuals who stood by and chose to do nothing were ultimately as guilty as the perpetrators. And so were the ones who then emulate bad behavior and continue it, as well as the ones who later become aware of it and allow it to go on. But, so what?

He hadn't come into the world to set himself up as a preacher so he could tell everyone else how to live their life. Let them figure it out for themselves, just like he was trying to do. And in that regard his most important question was, where did he draw the line in the exercise of his own power? In most respects anyone looking at him would say that he didn't have all that much to begin with and on some levels they would be absolutely right. But, unlike some, his mind was his own and so were his thoughts and no one did his thinking for him except himself. So where did he go from there?

The President of the United States was sometimes referred to as the most powerful man in the world but was that really true? Certainly he was one of a select few who could punch in a secret code or give a command and have most of the major cities of the world obliterated. But what did that prove except that, for any sane person, that kind of power would be far more of a burden than something to take pride in. As for blowing up the world, no doubt that too had happened in some alternate reality, just like Hitler had won World War II, so that on some level humanity got the benefit of that knowledge also and it was exactly the horror of that event which bled back into the minds of people in this reality in a deep, subconscious way that kept it from happening here. But again he had strayed. Now, with the knowledge he had gained from Kyara, he had another kind of power.

If he chose to do so, he knew he could sit down at his table and concentrate and project his consciousness into the White House itself. Then he could look over the man's shoulder and discover some of his personal secrets as well as pry into affairs of state and government. He could also make his way into the Pentagon or into the inner chambers of what ever the later version of the Russian KGB was, or the heads of the Chinese government. Additionally, once he knew the physical layouts of the various places, he could project himself there, sort through things and carry off documents or personal possessions. If he chose to.

He could also steal trade secrets and technological secrets, become a spy and work for the NSA, help some empire builder take over the financial world or make off with gold bars from Fort Knox and settle for becoming an inside trader in the stock market. Or he could come up with even grander plans. Become the planet's richest man and save the world from hunger. But, too, he could beat up on people who were physically weaker than he was or walk off with little old ladies' purses or do a lot of other things where he had all the advantage, so where was the challenge in any of that?

On an even bigger scale he could also keep going back in time and attempt to keep wars from happening but what would that solve? Somehow all the possibilities played out anyway. And, as he had finally realized, there most certainly had been another reality somewhere in which the civil war was also avoided, just like he had done so that trying to prevent other wars would solve nothing. While what he had done was all of good intent, it was also overly personal and somewhat selfish in its own way. Bertram had gotten caught up in hatred and wanted to deal with his situation through the use of violence. That would have gotten him killed but whether or not that would have been inconsistent with Bertram's and Katelyn's reincarnating into that time and place to begin with was pure speculation. All any of it did was to reconfirm the fact that he could move sideways from reality to reality but also jump around with regard to time.

If he could jump back and forth in time and if Kyara was now living somewhere in the future, that meant that time was the biggest illusion of all and that all time existed at once. It was somewhat analogous to being in Los Angeles. All of Los Angeles existed at once but any one individual could only be in one location in the city at any one point in time. You couldn't physically be in two places at once and you couldn't be in two different places in time at once. But, and that was a most interesting aspect of things, when it came time to reincarnate, a person had a tremendous amount of freedom in choice. What time period would best serve their present needs? In what part of the globe? Under what system of government? Who would be the parents? Someone whom one still had old business with, or someone that might provide a completely different perspective on life. In particular, what kind of challenges did one need to face? An ongoing stream that one jumped into the middle of to give dimension and validity to their own identity.

There was nothing simple about any of it. One's life in the physical world was not an accident. It was a life of choice. And if one is confused as to what they might be doing there in the particular life they were living, let them look at the challenges they have to face by being there. That is what they came to work on. How they choose to handle things from that point onward was up to them. Understanding that life is not an accident, that what one sees is not all there is and that there is great meaning and purpose to it all can give life a perspective it would not otherwise have and make the journey far more bearable. And with that realization came some bigger clarity.

Reed decided he wasn't really interested in seeing how much he could manipulate the world or how much political or financial power he could accumulate. In and of themselves, those seemed like shallow pursuits. What he wanted to understand instead was how the greater reality, the one behind the physical world, how that brought the physical plane into existence to begin with and how power of mind came to be the

184

primary driving force behind the scenes of everyday life. That was where the real challenge began. And at that very moment of realization there was a knock on the front door. A rather gentle one but he heard it nevertheless.

TWENTY EIGHT

"Alicia," he said and broke into a big smile as he opened the door. "Come on in. I've been thinking of you."

"Really? That's nice. I hope," Alicia said as she gave him a smile and a quick hug and came inside.

"Very nice," he assured her. "You've always been one of my most favorite people. More than that and you know it. I'm glad you're here," he told her as he looked her over. Damned if she wasn't just as sensational as ever. The voice with a slight husky edge to it, the eyes bright and clear, and that demure and seductive smile. Of course she was very special to him. Not only had they crossed the line way back when, they had almost moved in together. And even though she didn't know it, they were actually married in that other world and it was his having recently been around that other Alicia which made him realize how much he sometimes missed this one. But they could get to that part of it later and since it was lunch time, he asked if she was hungry.

"That's exactly what I had in mind," she said. "I came to take you to lunch. Unless you have other plans."

"No. That's perfect." he replied. "But sit down for a bit first so we can catch up. I take it you drove out. How long did it take?"

"Three days."

"Long ride. You must be tired."

"Not at all. I got here last night and slept late this morning."

"Last night? Where did you stay?"

"At the Ramada downtown."

Why didn't you come up and stay here?"

"Because it was after ten o'clock."

"Alicia," he scolded and told her he was always up half the night anyway.

185

"Okay. Next time I will."

"And tonight, too. For as long as you can stay. It's really good to see you again. You look marvelous."

"Thank you. So do you. Let me know when you get hungry."

"I'm hungry now so why don't I fix you something here."

"Okay. But I get to help," she stated and got up. "Let's see what you have."

Together they dug through the refrigerator, then took their preparations out on the patio. It was then that she told him about the divorce he was already aware of.

"He turned out to be a very distressing man," she said.

"Obviously. What happened? Except for the religion, he seemed like Mr., had it all together, nice guy to me."

"He was until he got passed over for a promotion at work. I don't understand why because he was thinking of changing companies anyway. But something happened and he became this fragile ego-ed, churlish, cranky, macho monster instead. And the last person I would have thought who would have turned into a conspiracy nut. Guns under the bed, guns under the couch, guns in the closets, guns in the car, out in the woods shooting rubber bullets at his buddies one weekend a month. Up all night on the internet downloading more war stories and, well, it's over, thank god, so no need to talk about that anymore. How about you? Anyone new in your life?"

"Yeah," he smiled happily. "Looks like it."

"What does that mean?"

"Looks like we will end up together."

"Good for you. Local girl?"

"No. She's from, ah, California."

"How did you meet?"

"Hiking in Sycamore Canyon. Which is out north of town about twelve miles."

"Really. That's very unusual. And from the look on your face I'd say it sounds serious."

"It is. We have a strong connection. Like you and I."

"Only more so. Right? It's okay, you can say it. I

understand and I think that's great. I'm looking forward to meeting her."

The conversation went on from there. Later he took her up the hill to Jerome and they walked around the old mining town, visiting the museum, the art galleries, historical buildings and gift shops and later had dinner out on the deck of one of the better restaurants before going back to the house. They slept together that night at her request. She had been through a lot of trauma and just wanted to be held. After breakfast in the morning he asked her what plans she had made, if any, and told her she was welcome to stay as long as she liked.

"I've never been to California but I always wanted to go up the coast. I understand it's beautiful. Maybe I'll even move there once I get my financial situation sorted out. Any place in particular you might recommend?"

"Several, actually. But go up the coast highway and check it all out. Then, if you feel so inclined, stop in Morro Bay for a few nights. I was just there a few weeks ago. The Driftwood Inn is a good place to stay. And then in the evening go down to the Wharf. It's a restaurant and bar. Go out on one of the charter boats for a half day fishing expedition. Have lunch at Betsies' Cafe. And then I want to know how you feel about the place. Who knows. It might just seem like home to you. If not, keep moving. I'm sure you'll connect with something out there. But I want to hear about it, regardless," he assured her, wondering if there would be enough bleed through from that other universe for her to pick up on and make her feel more than ordinarily familiar with the place. Maybe someday he would be able to explain it all to her also. Like he had to her alternate.

They spent one last night cuddled up together and her plan was to leave first thing in the morning so she helped him with breakfast. Then, when they were each carrying their own plates into the dining room, Reed noticed a piece of that distinctive light blue stationary at the place where he usually sat. Clipped to the back of it was a photograph. He sat his dish and his coffee down and read it as Alicia watched him curiously.

187

Hi, Lover, it said as before. Hope you slept well. Telling Alicia to stop in Morro Bay was a good idea. What she learns may be surprising for all of us. And since she's leaving, find your spare toothbrush and meet me on the Santa Monica pier about nine in the morning your time, exactly four weeks from now but in 2061. Visualize the area in the photo. I'll keep it clear for you. Love, Kyara.

Reed read the letter twice and then looked at the photo. Unable to help himself he glanced at Alicia who was still watching him. He smiled at her.

"Seems like you have middle of the night mail service. None of my business but that wasn't there last night. Was it?"

"No. It's from Kyara."

"Does she have a key to the house? Jeez, Reed. I'm really sorry. Do you think she knows you let me sleep with you?"

"I'm sure she does and I'm sure she also knows what didn't happen so it's okay. This is a very unusual woman."

"Obviously. Is she coming over today? I'd sure like to meet her."

"No. I'm going to see her. In a month," he responded and without hesitation, handed Alicia the letter.

Before reading it she questioned him with another look and he nodded his approval.

Alicia read the letter once, then read it again and when she looked at Reed there was a huge question mark on her face.

"2061?" she questioned and stared at him. "And keeping a safe place on the pier for you. What does that mean?"

Reed simply returned her look and shrugged, not about to try and explain it just yet.

"Some kind of private code, huh? Okay. You can explain it to me later. But what is it I might learn in Morro Bay that might be so surprising? For me and you, and her? You already know, don't you. That's why you wanted me to stop there, isn't it?"

"Yes, I wanted you to stop there. But no, I have no idea how it will turn out. It may seem quite ordinary to you. Maybe even a little boring. But you have always been a very intuitive individual so I guess we won't know until after you've been there. As for Kyara. She's another very intuitive individual so we'll see. I'm sure you'll get to meet her one of these times."

TWENTY NINE

Three more weeks and five days. Not so long, actually, but that didn't mean it wouldn't be a difficult wait. It had been months since he had seen her and then it wasn't nearly long enough. Not even close. A lifetime wouldn't be either and he was very excited about going to see her. To be with her and find out what her world was like. Fifty years into the future was also an intriguing idea. Had the human race been able to make more social progress in the next fifty than it had in the previous half century? Perhaps not. But what did it matter? It wouldn't if he could spend the rest of this lifetime with her, here or in the future. But what to do in the meantime to keep his anticipation in check? Maybe it was time to do a, wouldn't it be nice if ....? But what?

There were several things that came to mind and the first was definitely something he could work on by himself. Sure, he knew about neurolinguistic programming, body language interpretation, voice stress analysis and much of the other over-hyped but relatively useless approaches to interpreting human behavior and getting at the truth. Getting at the truth. Any reasonably intelligent person could learn to become an effective liar, to divert, mislead or cover up and who would ever be foolish enough to expect a politician to submit to a lie detector test? Or anyone else for that matter unless it was a matter of extenuating circumstances. There had to be a better, more expeditious, immediate way.

How many times had he known who was making the call before he picked up the phone? How many times had he known who he would run into somewhere ahead of time? How often does one person know when someone important to them is in trouble, next door or half way around the world? Go to a large party where people don't know each other and watch how quickly people of the same intelligence and self esteem levels find each other as well as how well those with similar backgrounds and interests are drawn to each other almost without words and from far across the room. With or without a glance. Furthermore, these same people also instinctively make an effort to avoid certain others who wouldn't be good for them no matter what. Very definitely, the phenomenon was real. Something non verbal and non visual both was happening all the time. Now if one could just develop those abilities a little further. Bring them up out of the subliminal level into full conscious awareness upon demand.....

Projection of consciousness was a fact. Kyara and he were not alone in their ability to do remote viewing. The Stanford studies and others showed that it was a teachable skill but with a wide variance in outcome dependent on the individual trainee. And then there were the stories about some indigenous peoples being able to project their consciousness into the mind of an eagle or a hawk and get a view of the earth from above for hunting or for protection purposes. Projecting it into the water of a river to let the current carry their awareness down stream to see if it was safe to go there. Projecting it into an animal and be led to drinking water in the desert. So what about projecting one's consciousness into the mind of another human being to find out what they were not only seeing, but thinking?

Reed drove down to the library, picked some newspapers off the shelf and found a chair in the corner where he could pretend to be reading but observe people instead and practice. An hour went by and then two. So had at least a dozen different individuals he tried his luck on but with zero results. Instead of making any kind of connection, he found himself falling asleep. From there he went to the nearest coffee shop, had lunch and practiced some more, again with no results. He couldn't seem to get inside anyone's head and see through their eyes at all, nor was he able to pick up on any of their thoughts. Then he went back to the library and pretended to read more papers. This time he wasn't going to try and project but was simply going to act as a receiver and see what he could pick up. Thoughts, after all, had

190

to have an electromagnetic reality of their own as brain studies implied. And just because they might still be out of the range of present technology to detect, that didn't mean they didn't exist. What it meant instead was that if one mind could generate thoughts, another mind should be able to pick up on them, and obviously did as he already knew from personal experience. The trick was to expand that capability and be able to have conscious control over it. Clearly, that was the hard part, the part he needed to work on.

Another hour went by and he was concentrating on one old man who was talking to a library worker, both too far away for him to hear and turned so he could not see their lips. Again he drew a blank but in the midst of it he suddenly felt something coming at him from the side. A low level sensation, a tingle perhaps, something that told him someone had noticed him and was coming over to greet him. Maybe a woman. He waited without looking around, to see if he was correct.

"Hello, Reed," the female voice now real. He looked up. It was a woman he had met at an art show several months back. The one who had tried to latch onto him. What was her name? Linda.

"Hi, Linda," he answered and stood up. "How are you?"

"Fine. Just fine," she said and then gave him a little smile. "You never called me. I was sure you would."

"Well, I was thinking about it but I never said I would, so I didn't lie to you. But then, my old girlfriend showed up and .... So that's what I'm in the midst of right now. I'm sorry."

"Oh. Well, just my luck," she said and went on a little before the conversation ended and she left.

Reed sat back down and thought about what had just happened. Why had he been able to pick up on her thoughts and not someone else's? Because they were directed at him? That probably had a something to do with it. Plus there had to have been some emotional content involved, also. That would give things a different slant. Wouldn't it? Time to go somewhere more evocative. The county office buildings were just a short walk away. Who might be there? People paying their taxes. That might be irritating and worthy of some emotion. Or, how about superior court? If court was in session and people were in there worrying about being found guilty of something, their thoughts might be quite strong.

He was in luck. The court was nearly full but he was able to find an empty seat in the back. The middle aged man standing before the judge in jeans, flannel shirt and cowboy boots was there because he was behind in his alimony payments and the judge was reprimanding him rather severely. Holy, jeez, Reed said to himself. Did that guy just tell the judge that he thought his ex wife was a stupid, bitching whore and she didn't deserve one penny of his money? But why wasn't the judge doing something about it? Because he hadn't heard it, he then realized. It wasn't said out loud. But Reed had been able to pick up on it anyway. How about that! He also became very aware that the man was extremely upset and having a difficult time keeping himself from telling the judge to go stuff it. And there was more. Something about Arkansas. Yes. The man was being very acquiescent outwardly, making promises to keep from going to jail but all the time knowing that he was off to Arkansas to live with ...... someone.... an uncle, maybe, up in the mountains and to hell with letting the bitch get any of his money.

The next one up before the judge was a scruffy looking young man with an attitude who was clearly guilty of running a red light and nearly hitting a pedestrian but there was nothing coming through that Reed could pick up on. Just some dumb shit that should have paid his ticket instead of arguing with the judge because it ended up costing him an extra hundred dollars.

After that a poorly dressed older woman was called to come forward. She had been accused of shoplifting a bag of pretzels from the C Market. The judge asked her a series of questions and dismissed her with a reprimand as Reed felt that he sensed some remorse on the woman's part but nothing otherwise significant. And that was the end of it. It was the last case of the session so he got up and left. Outside he saw the cowboy leaning up against an old pickup truck smoking a cigarette and complaining to another individual of about the same mentality. Since his own vehicle was parked in the same row, he had to walk past the two men. As he did so the cowboy gave him a suspicious look so Reed took advantage of the situation to verify his own success at picking up on the man's thoughts.

"Excuse me," he said to the man. "I didn't get your uncle's name."

At first all he got was a look of total confusion which then turned darkly suspicious.

"What uncle? Who said I had an uncle?"

"You did. Back in court. Your uncle in Arkansas. The one you're going to go live with so you don't have to pay your back alimony."

"What!" the man said in a loud voice and stared at Reed, then looked at his friend and back at Reed, now with open hostility.

"Take it easy," Reed said. "I don't care if you think your ex is a a stupid bitching whore because maybe she is. But before you go running off maybe you should check and see if Arkansas is a reciprocity state. Or, maybe I'm wrong. If that's not what you were thinking in there in front of the judge, I apologize. And don't hit me like you're now thinking of doing or I'll pound you right on your big nose."

With that the man's expression went from anger to complete bewilderment and he turned to his friend and growled, "Let's get out of here," his actions confirming Reed's ability to pick up on what he had been thinking.

THIRTY

Well, that was very interesting, Reed told himself, but he still had three more weeks to go before seeing Kyara. Of course he had the ability to shorten the process if he wanted. At least he thought he did. But if he got too impatient and something went wrong ... If he missed the connection... Somehow it might be best if he waited it out.

Unable to think of anything else to do during the meantime, however, he decided to go back to work on the addition he had started to put on the house. The concrete slab was already down with vertical rebar in place around the periphery and several pallets of concrete blocks waiting to be mortared into place. Nine hundred and twenty four blocks to be exact, which weighed thirty six pounds each. All together, that was about sixteen tons and while it might sound like a lot on one level, it really wasn't much more than a week or so of work. Certainly nothing remotely close to what that guy down in Florida had done all by himself back in the early nineteen hundreds. What was his name, anyway? Ed, somebody. A name he should remember but couldn't.

Reed went into his study and dug through his books. Ed Leedskalnin, that was the guy. The man who at thirty one began chiseling large hunks of coral rock out of the ground and sculpted them into a wide variety of shapes. Not thirty five pound rocks but rocks varying in weight from a few hundred pounds up to twenty nine tons. Not only sculpted but lifted up and lofted into place. And completely with hand tools nearly a hundred years ago before electrification and convenient power tools. As to how he managed, that alone would be mysterious enough. But equally impressive was the fact that this man, Ed Leedskalnin was only five feet tall and weighed a mere one hundred pounds. Regardless of all these severe limitations, this pint sized man carved out and moved over two million pounds of rock, entirely by himself over the course of several years and built a monumental site now called Coral Castle that still goes without scientific explanation as to how it was accomplished.

Reed had read about it and had visited the site some years earlier and now he remembered how perplexed he had been at the time, trying to imagine how it could have been done. What an enigma at the time, with no way to solve the mystery. But now...... To hell with the addition. Now he had a way to find out. Maybe. If he could somehow get to know Ed Leedskalnin and gain his trust.

THIRTY ONE

The first thing the following morning Reed stood before the nine ton coral rock gate and clanged the bell made of old car parts. Twice. And then he waited. Some moments later he saw someone peak through the small gap along one side and the big stone began to move.

"Mr. Leedskalnin. Good morning sir," he said politely, once it was open and he could see who was there. "If you're not too busy right now, would it be possible to get a tour of your place?"

It was Ed, all right. He looked like just like the picture of him in the brochure Reed had brought along and the short little man looked him over.

"My pleasure," Ed said after a short scrutiny. "But it will cost you twenty five cents."

"Fair enough," Reed responded, already prepared as he dug in his pocket and pulled out some old silver coins he had purchased from a coin collector the day before and handed Ed a quarter that was still in good condition. It was now the fall of nineteen forty nine, two years before Ed's death. Most of Ed's projects were completed by then and Reed was hoping to get an in-depth look at the man's achievements.

Perhaps it was Reed's sincere interest in Ed's work that helped establish some level of rapport and kept him going because three hours later Ed was still proudly showing Reed around, explaining the purpose and function of each piece of carved rock. Once they came to the east wall where they had a good view of the forty foot tall obelisk, however, Reed took the risk and asked Ed how much it weighed as a place to start something more serious. His assessment of the diminutive man had told him that if this little guy had the super-human ability to do all this, he could certainly handle what came next.

Ed looked at him curiously and scratched his head.

"A lot," he said. "Several tons for sure. Why would you want to know that?"

"Well, I suspect the exact weights of the rocks you have carved and moved aren't all that important to you personally. And why should they be. But as a matter of interest to people like me, well, it gives us some perspective on what you have done. And, as I'm sure you know, it's extraordinary. The obelisk, for example, weighs twenty eight and a half tons and is the second heaviest stone in the place. The heaviest piece is in the north wall and weighs twenty nine tons," Reed pointed out and went one to list the extreme weights of several other large pieces that Ed had personally carved out of coral.

Ed stood his ground as he looked at Reed with suspicion and remained silent. Reed slipped off his small back pack, set it down, unzipped it and handed Ed the color printed brochure full of photos and descriptions of Ed's work he had brought along. Ed hesitated at first, took it and slowly thumbed through the sixteen pages. Then he went back to the bottom on the inside of the cover and read out loud.

"Copyright, 1988." Then he looked up at Reed with a trace of growing anger. "This is nineteen forty nine," he said matter of factly. "So it looks like you went to a lot of trouble to try and trick me. Maybe you and some other people. But it won't work," he continued as he reached in his pocket, found the quarter Reed had given him and handed it back.

"No, you keep it. You earned every bit of it and a lot more," Reed said and held out a whole handful of quarters instead, most of them dated after the year two thousand.

"Look at the dates on them," he said as he dumped them on top of the stone table nearby.

Ed hesitated but his curiosity finally got the best of him and he began sorting through the coins.

"I'd be a fool to try and spend these. So would you if anyone took a close look. Besides, they don't even seem like they're made of real silver. They're fake."

"Well, they're not fake where I come from but that's okay so let me show you something else instead," Reed answered and again dug in his pack.

What he brought out this time was a palm sized transistor radio, something he already knew would work here because he had tried it out before ringing the bell on Ed's gate. He already had it tuned to the only radio station within range and when he turned it on, the announcer's voice came through loud and clear.

Ed jumped back a step in surprise and it was clear that Reed now had his full attention. Reed handed it to him and he finally took it, looking at it as though he were afraid it might blow up in his hand but he kept it and examined it carefully.

"Where does it get it's power?" Ed asked as Reed took it back and popped open the small cover and showed him the two little AAA batteries inside.

"They're rechargeable," he said, "but I brought you a charger and some extra ones in case they fail," he continued and brought out another item from his pack.

"Just put the dead batteries in here like this. Then open the top up so the sun can shine on it. It will convert the sun's energy into electricity and charge the batteries."

"What are you trying to tell me? That's not possible."

"No, but then neither is this," Reed said and waved his hand about to indicate all the work Ed had done.

"Seriously Ed. You can put people off by saying it's all about the laws of weights and levers but that doesn't explain a thing and you know it. But I also know that even if you told them the truth, they wouldn't believe that either. And, as you are obviously fully aware, if you were foolish enough to give them a demonstration, they would either shoot you or lock you up because they would think you were some kind of demon. The kind of power it takes to do what you have done scares the hell out of people so they don't really want to hear about it. Not only do they not ask, they don't even use their common sense."

Ed listened carefully, stared back at Reed and shrugged, not disputing any of it but not agreeing either.

"But," Reed said. "look a it. Take the obelisk, for example. If you were just going to lift one end of it. That would be almost thirty thousand pounds. You probably weigh about a hundred soaking wet so that means you would need a lever almost three hundred feet long to do that by yourself. Where would you get such a thing? You don't have electricity here, either, so you don't have any power tools. You also don't have a monster gas powered crane. Or a big, heavy duty helicopter or anything else, so the only way this got done was that you either had visitors from outer space come in the middle of the night or you did it all by yourself. And if you did it by yourself then it's pretty obvious you know something that no one else in today's world seems to know or has been able to figure out. Nor will they within the next sixty years, at least."

"Okay, Mister. You say your name is Reed and you have given me some things that don't seem to have been invented yet which makes you look like you might be from the future but what do I know? I live a very isolated life down here and I'm sure there is a lot of things I don't know either. So if I admitted to having some strange power I might be in big trouble. You might be from the government or maybe from some big corporation and you don't care what you have to do to get the information and then, once you had it, you'd probably use it to hurt people one way or another. So, forget it. I don't know a thing. And even if I did, I wouldn't share it with some stranger with a pocket full of quarters, real or fake."

"Good! That is exactly what I would expect. And I didn't come here to try and coerce you into doing something you don't want to do. On the contrary. I came here to share information with you, if you're interested."

"Interested in what? Except for some fancy gadgets, I can't imagine what you have that I could use."

"Well. It's a bit of a walk into town. What if I could show you an easy way to get from here to there? Or anywhere else you might want to go."

"What? You're going to give me a free automobile? Forget it. I couldn't afford the gasoline."

"No. Something much more expedient."

"Expedient? You mean like easier?"

"A lot. And I fully understand your caution so instead of a lot more talk, why don't I just show you what I mean. Then, if you think you can trust me, we can share what we know."

"I'm willing to watch but I won't commit to anything."

"Okay, fair enough. Let's see," Reed said and looked around. "See that open spot by the south wall? Keep an eye on me, then look down there," he said as he looked at Ed and disappeared from in front of him, then almost immediately called back from his new location by the far wall.

"Stay there," he told him and quickly reappeared in from of him.

Ed's eyes opened wide as he stared at Reed, seeming to be a little alarmed by what he had witnessed. Then he actually smiled a little.

"Notice that my clothes went with me," Reed pointed out. "So does whatever I can carry. Like my back pack," he said as he picked it up and went through the process once again.

"So," he told Ed. "I have a secret and you have a secret. If you don't want to go into a lot of detail, then all I would ask for is a demonstration since I already have some idea how you do what you do."

"Yes, well. Tell you what. If you are even half way right, I'll do it. How do you think I've done all this?"

"Well, first of all, I think there is something about this location that might be important. The same with your first site where you started this project. Secondly, you, yourself, are what amounts to a super poltergeist. Not only can you make things move around, you can consciously control them," Reed said, which brought a chuckle from Ed.

"You are able to generate a very intense psychic force field around objects you want to work on or move. I mean, coral is limestone and for all intents and purposes, is hard as hell. For one man to chisel this much rock out of the ground with nothing but hand tools under ordinary circumstances would take ten lifetimes, let alone carve them into shapes and move them around. But somehow you learned how to do that. Maybe create a force field which affects the molecular structure of the material. Kind of softens it up and negates the pull of gravity on it so you can work it easily and levitate it around. Maybe at night, which seems to be when you do most of your work."

"How do you know I only work at night?"

"I don't for sure but that's what the brochure says so I guess that must be what most of the people around here have reported," Reed said and went on to say more.

Ed scratched his head as Reed talked and then looked at him when he was done.

"Maybe so. Or, as you said, maybe I had some help from out there," he stated as he pointed to the sky, clearly not completely ready to share fully.

"Well, that wouldn't surprise me either," Reed responded, not to counter Ed's statement but because of his own thoughts and experience.

"It wouldn't? Why not?" Ed, said, surprised at the answer.

"For a lot of reasons. Want to hear some of them?"

"I would. I saw one of them things once and as near as I could tell, it was as real as these rocks here."

"It might take a while."

"Go ahead. The gate is locked and I got all day."

Reed went through the whole thing as Ed listened to all of his words and concluded by telling Ed, why not. Maybe ET's had helped him accomplish his monumental work to create yet another enigma to tease people with. Help them get over their superficial obsessions, set their egos aside and look at what else might be out there and what might be more important than what. But, like the Giza pyramids and all the rest of it, was it working? Not particularly. But Ed didn't seem to mind. He hadn't done what he had to try and prove anything, he said. He just did it for himself and that was enough.

"Well" he said when Reed was done talking. "There were times when help would have been nice but it's all done now so it don't make no difference. As for my part of it, I guess maybe you are right. I just never thought of it quite like that but, could be. Except for the night part. What you say is somewhat true but nights are best so I don't get distracted and have something big fall on me."

"I see what you mean," Reed said, "but the big question is how did you figure it out. I know you were around when table tipping was the big thing. Lots of people were doing it for fun at parties and stuff. Today, of course, it's almost totally forgotten and in my time period most people never even heard of it and would laugh you out of the room if you brought it up. But if one reviews the history of that early era, it was kind of taken for granted. Even so, while it's similar, it's not exactly the same as what you are doing because I doubt that you have some entity, or entities, on the other side helping you out. Or, maybe you do. So, what are you willing to share with me?"

"Seems like you have most of it right, one way or the

other. It's not table tipping like you say, either. That's a different kind of energy but it was what got me thinking. That and the pyramids in Egypt. The big ones. They're different than all the rest and they weren't built by some pharaohs no matter what the experts want to believe. They sure as heaven weren't built with thousands of slaves chopping rocks out of a quarry and rolling them up dirt ramps, either. That might have worked for all those small stones that weighed only a ton or so. But how did they get more than a hundred monster stones that weighed from fifty to seventy tons up a ramp and in place to build the kings chamber which is more than two hundred feet up inside the pyramid. Who are they trying to kid? What kid of science comes up with an explanation that stupid?"

"Well, there you have it. If you can't figure it out, make something up or just ignore that part of the enigma. So how did you discover the answer?"

"Actually, I didn't. It discovered me. All my life I was interested in Egyptian history and I read everything I could get my hands and all the time I had the weird feeling that I had been there before, in Egypt, I mean. Way back when. So maybe I was, even though I don't give much credibility to this reincarnation stuff some people talk about. Anyway, I gave a lot of time to thinking about how they built those things. A whole big lot. And then I started having dreams about it and the dreams kept getting clearer and clearer, especially once I came here to Florida. They were so clear one night that when I got up the next morning I went right outside and found a big rock and, by gully, there I was making it rise up right up off the ground. Next thing I knew I was able to make it go where I wanted, too. Well, that was nice so next I tried to chisel some rock out of the ground and use it to build something with, but it was impossible. So then I thought about it some more and found that if I just got down on my knees, held my hands out and concentrated real hard, the rock would actually soften up enough like you said so I could chisel it out using those sharpened up old truck springs I showed you back in my tool room. Well, so that was it. And, as they say, the rest is history. The more I did it, the easier it got. Until recently. Now it takes a lot out of me so I just quit."

"Okay. Good! Thank you. It would be nice if you could show me. Especially how you got those big ones you used up on the roof of your tower where you wouldn't be able to be in direct contact with them the whole time. But, if you're not feeling up to it, I certainly understand."

"Well, that wouldn't be fair at all. You showed me what you can do so I need to respond accordingly. I could even help you practice a little if you have the talent for it. Then you can show me how to disappear. Might come in handy sometime if someone bad ever showed up."

THIRTY TWO

If only he had some way to contact Kyara. Leave her a note in the middle of the night like she did him. But, it wasn't possible. He had yet to go to her world, didn't know exactly where she lived and would have a very difficult time finding her, if at all. Soon, however. Just a couple more weeks. But damn, he missed her terribly. He would so love to have her share his next adventure with him. The one inspired by Ed Leedskalnin. In addition to the companionship, she would be a great asset. When were the Giza pyramids actually built, how and by whom? Next to Kyara, that was what was foremost in his mind. And, either way, with or without her, he would need to make some careful preparations before leaving.

Concerned with his next trip after coming home from his meeting with Ed made it hard for him to get to sleep, however, so he got up, got dressed and went outside in the moonlight to see if he could put his new skill to work. Even though it had taken a while, he had been able to move a small stone with Ed's coaching before he left Florida but now, nothing worked. Again and again he tried but it was hopeless. Was it the location or had Ed in his enthusiasm, actually moved it for him? The fact that he was trying to levitate concrete blocks instead of limestone shouldn't have made any difference. Regardless, it was very discouraging. He knew very well that it was all about perception. Rocks, steel, diamond. Nothing was solid on the atomic level. Everything was composed of atoms. And atoms were composed of awarized bits which could either act as particles or waves where the electrons orbited a nucleus at relatively phenomenal distances away so that an atom was composed of far, far more space than matter, making the whole construct a massive illusion.

On the atomic level, matter was not solid at all and everything in it was always in a constant state of motion on an infinitesimal level. But, matter could be influenced by mind, that had been proven in many ways. So, why wasn't he be able to use the power of his mind to reach out and connect with the matter in his concrete blocks and get it to do what he wanted? Ed Leedskalnin was able to do that. He had seen it with his own eyes. Maybe old Ed had deliberately withheld some small but vital part of the process. Well, didn't matter for now, he decided and gave up after an intense, hours long effort. Gave up for the time being, at least. He would try it again after he got back and if that didn't work he would pay Ed another visit.

Just like Leedskalnin had said, though, Reed was also more than convinced that the pharaohs did not build the Giza pyramids. They were not capable of it. They did not build the Valley Temple that stood nearby either. Nor the sphinx, the Osirion and a lot of the other Egyptian antiquities. Falling down step pyramids, Abu Simbal, statues of themselves and on and on, all with a less demanding level of expertise, yes, but not the big ones. Different architecture, different constructions, far more grand in concept and accomplishment and far more difficult to bring into being. That meant that there was not just one ancient Egypt but at least two very distinct and separate periods in the region's history, most probably with a large separation in time. There was no way to prove that scientifically, however. But, why bother? It was already clear enough to those who had taken an objective look at the evidence. That evidence said that the sphinx was at least fifteen thousand years old and maybe older. So were the Giza pyramids. The Egyptologists, the self appointed experts in the field, just didn't want to hear it, however. Regardless, Reed wanted to know the truth, if for no other reason than for his own satisfaction.

THIRTY THREE

Overwhelmed and transfixed, all Reed could do was stare. And stare some more as moment after moment went by. Finally something barked at him and he jerked around. Standing only a few feet away, a bat eared desert fox yapped and then sat down and watched him, looking friendly enough. What a nice welcome, Reed decided and said hello back in a soft voice whereupon the fox got up and walked off. Then Reed did a full circle scan of the area around him to make sure he was safe, noting what he had not expected to see. The bedrock plateau the pyramids sat on was itself rather sparse in terms of vegetation. A few bushes, splotches of grass hanging onto life here and there, a few stunted trees but just beyond, circling the area, it changed radically. The desert he had expected, did not exist. It wasn't sub tropical lushness either but there were mature thorn trees in full bloom, loaded with pink flowers randomly dispersed across the landscape and farther to the west the terrain was savannah like, full of green grasses and small, unusual shrubs with clusters of wildflowers here and there. Back to the east, probably along the Nile river, there were tall palm trees of the Borassus variety and to the south he saw what had to be some fat, gnarly old silver barked baobab trees. While everywhere overhead the sky was a delicate, beautiful blue, even to the south east where the modern, grossly overcrowded, city of Cairo and its polluted atmosphere had not yet come into being.

Then, unable to look away any longer, he turned back to the pyramids. The so-called Giza pyramids, brilliant in the sunlight, their white, polished limestone capstones all intact and in place less than a quarter of a mile away, gleaming jewel like, fresh and new. There were none of those very poorly constructed small pyramids and other structures the pharaohs were guilty of putting up, either. The three big pyramids stood alone, clean and beautiful and awesome beyond belief against the sky. At first their presence there was a shock because he hadn't expected them to even be in existence yet. Some researchers had dated the sphinx to be ten to fifteen thousand years old, and related and dated the sphinx to the Giza pyramids, so Reed had purposely set his goal at sixteen thousand BC, a century before that. The intent was to go back to a period before they existed and then start jumping forward in time from there until he found the point where they did. Then, depending on what state of completion they were in, he would fine tune his presence so he could be there when they were under construction.

Well, he decided, as he continued to stare at them. He had obviously gotten the time wrong but he wouldn't know that for sure until it was dark out. At the moment, as near as he could tell from the sun angle, it was still morning, maybe about eleven. He had enough time to walk in closer, walk around the pyramids and then be able to see if the sphinx was also there before the sun was straight up and he could make his first set of measurements. Before he did so, however, he slipped out of his ungodly heavy back pack and found his binoculars. Looking through them full circle again, he could see no signs of human life so he hoisted the pack back up on his shoulders and headed southwest.

Maintaining caution, he stayed in the tall grass and wherever possible used the bushes and trees as cover as he swung wide around the two largest pyramids and went between the small, completely misnamed Menkaure, and Khafre, the second biggest, trying not to be overly awed and distracted by their overwhelming presence as he went.

But there was no sphinx. It did not exist at this point in time. Just one huge mound of rock from which it would somehow be carved out of in the future. It's absence did not overly surprise Reed, however. No matter how old the sphinx really was, it had always been an incongruity, quite inconsistent with the Giza pyramids themselves, even though it also seemed clear that it too, had not been built by the pharaohs, but at a much earlier date than when they ruled the land.

There was no city of Cairo, either, as he already knew, but there were small clusters of primitive looking buildings off in the distance and he could see people moving about them through the binoculars. Not Arabic. Darker skinned with loose flowing garments obviously made of cloth. Were they early Nubianes? If so, they were further north than historians had attributed them to be this long ago. And when did they invent bows and arrows? If it was this early, they could be dangerous because the Nubians were skillful hunters and used deadly poisons on their arrow tips. Well, he could do more exploring later. First he had to get into a position where he could use the west side of the large pyramid as a reference since it was supposed to be perfectly aligned north and south.

Reed attached the precision theodolite he had brought along to it's tripod and carefully leveled it. Then he put a dark filter over the objective lens and pointed the telescope towards the sun and watched as the image moved towards the center of the field of view, adjusting only the elevation as it went. Making the assumption that there hadn't been any earth crust shifts in the interval between the time of his own world and the time he was now in, all he could surmise from his first measurement was that it was somewhere around the end of July, heading towards the fall season, just as it had been back home. But northern Egypt was about four hundred miles farther south on the planet than Jerome, Arizona and for July, it should have been much warmer here than it was and that began to bother him.

It would have been easier to have found a secure hiding place for his back pack and leave it behind while he explored. But he didn't feel safe in doing that so that once he had helped himself to granola bars and a drink of his precious water, he slung it up on his back and cautiously headed off towards the Nile River. The green belt along the river actually extended out almost to the pyramids on the western side and became thicker as he went so he began to feel more secure and made his way to the river bank. There he was able to isolate himself in some high shrubs and look down on the scene below. There were strings of palm trees along both sides of the water, which, if he hadn't been so exhilarated with being there, he might have made clearer note of the fact that many were stunted and not nearly as tall as they should have been. Instead his eyes moved on to clusters of bamboo and thick stands of reeds and rushes in the inlets on both sides of the river and stopped when he saw movement.

There were people just a short ways down stream. They were chopping down reeds and gathering them together into bundles.

He studied them through the binoculars. Nubian like but also quite tall, with a Maasai quality about them, some chanting as they worked, others talking back and forth. They were too far away for him to tell what they were using as cutting tools but they had the appearance of large axes. Maybe sharp stones attached to heavy sticks. Regardless, they were tool makers, no doubt about that and then he saw something even more significant. Coming down river from behind him he was suddenly aware of boats in the water. Bamboo boats at that. Not as well crafted as they might have been, but boats nevertheless, and fairly sizable. Five of them in all, the largest about twenty feet in length with six people in it. The rest were slightly smaller, with three or four people in each, most of them paddling with fairly well made paddles as they went on by. When they came abreast of the workers on shore, shouts were exchanged, along with a great deal of chatter before they got too far away.

All of the people, both those in the boats and on shore, seemed to be wearing the same kind of clothing, very basic and style less, made of a medium grey colored cloth like material, rather sack shaped for the most part. Regardless of that there were still widely varied expressions of individuality amongst them. Almost all wore sashes of different colors, tied like belts around the waist, and some wore them like scarfs around the neck. The women further adorned themselves with beaded necklaces and bracelets and the men had a variety of white painted marks on their faces, making some of them appear rather sinister. But there was one woman in particular who seemed to stand out. Tall, almost statuesque, long black hair pulled back and tied with a red colored ribbon, almost regal, finely chiseled facial features with bright objects hanging from her ears, Reed couldn't help but stare as he kept the binoculars focused on her face and body. Then, as he continued to watch, she quit what she was doing, stood up, put her arms out to her sides and appeared to be stretching. At that moment her back was towards Reed but she slowly turned completely around and for one brief moment stopped and seemed to have been staring straight at him, well hidden as he was. Then she said something to the rest of the group and went back to work. The incident was enough for him to rethink his concealment, however, and he did so, reassuring himself that there was no way she, or any of them would be able to see him because he was down on his stomach in the brush several hundred yards away and without his binoculars they in turn, would have been almost unnoticeable to him.

Convinced of his safety, he went back to his observations but his attention was soon pulled away by another bamboo boat coming down the river. A rather large one this time but with only three people in it, two men and a woman. Again there were greetings as the boat beached itself on the sandy shore close by. The three people got out and the two men pulled the nose up on the sand, then swung the back around so that the side of the boat was parallel with the shore. As soon as it was secured people from the rest of the group began carrying bundles of reeds down to it, and started loading them on board.

If only he had a video camera with a long focal length lens, Reed thought as he continued to observe. He would also have liked to get some pictures of the one woman in particular. But where was she now, he soon wondered? He scanned the entire group carefully but she wasn't there and to make sure, he counted them all as he had first done. There was one missing. The arrival of the boat had distracted him and she had obviously slipped away. But hopefully she would be back soon so he could get one last look at her before he left. He still wanted to explore the area around the pyramids more thoroughly before night came. It was then that he thought he heard something.

As quietly as possible he got to his knees, put his binoculars in his pack and very carefully stood up and waited, still concealed by the tall surrounding bushes. There was nothing. He must have been mistaken. And from as near as he could tell without his binoculars, the group down river was still at work. Except for the one woman. Then a voice. A soft, melodic voice that spoke several words. Shocked and surprised, he turned towards it and there she stood, not ten feet away, off to his right in a clear place between the bushes. The woman from the river, carefully studying him as she looked him over. Then her eyes found his and they stared at each other. How else could it be explained? Hidden as he knew he was, damned if she hadn't somehow sensed his presence and come to check him out. There was no fear in her eyes, however, even though there might have been a trace in his, but only a deep curiosity instead. With that he stepped out into the open, looked around to make sure she was alone and relaxed a little. Then he said hello back to her as quietly as he could, hanging onto his back pack just in case he had to make a sudden departure.

She said something else in her musical dialect but he could only shrug. Then he put his hand on his chest and told her his name was Reed. She seemed to understand the concept and pointed to herself and replied. It sounded like Zirania and he repeated it after her which made her smile. Then she gestured at him. He nodded back, having no idea as to what he might be agreeing to and she came closer. Then she reached out carefully and touched his jacket. It was made of very soft micro fiber and she ran the back of her hand across it, made a cooing sound and smiled at him. Then she looked down at his feet and the hiking boots he wore and puzzled over that because her feet were bare. Next she looked at his face and carefully raised her hand and reached out to feel the stubble on his face and frowned. After that she felt his hair and then she placed her fingers on his forehead and kept them there a few moments as though she might be trying to read his mind while she stared into his eyes. Satisfied, she put her hand down, looked at him some more and pointed to the holstered automatic weapon he carried on his belt.

He shook his head no and held up his hand so she stopped and then she pointed to the embroidered design on the front of his jacket and raised an eyebrow in question. An expensive outdoor jacket, it had the name of the maker sewn into it. He didn't know how to explain it so he just repeated the name to her. She tried to say it but couldn't pronounce it, then backed up and bent down where she used her finger to draw something in the lose dirt. But it wasn't a figure. It looked like a written word with separate, distinct characters. Shocked, he reached in his inner jacket pocket and took out his note pad and a ball point pen. Then he printed his name on it, pointed to himself, wrote her name as he had understood it, showed it to her and pointed to her.

Very pleased, she motioned to his pad and he handed it to her along with the pen. She studied the pen a second, carefully felt the paper and then moved the pen across the paper and smiled at the squiggle she had made. Then she very carefully began to make figures. Except they weren't figures, they had to be letters. For sure they were not in any way symbolistic hieroglyphics. And the letters fell into groups so she had to be making words. Oddly enough, she also wrote left to right and put down what could only have been the equivalent of three sentences. Handing it back, she smiled at the wide eyed look on his face and made some comment. He torn out the page from the notebook, folded it up and put it in his pocket. Then he printed her a note in return that said his name was Reed, that he was from several thousand years in the future and that he thought she was very intelligent and beautiful and handed it back to her.

She looked at it very carefully as though trying to decipher its meaning, then handed it to him and made a motion which indicated she was asking him to tear the page out for herself. He shook his head no and gave the entire notebook and the pen both back to her. She took them with her left hand then pointed to herself with her right as a questioning gesture. He nodded and smiled as he learned she did have pockets in her garment. After she put it away he pointed to her clothing with a questioning look and she allowed him to feel the fabric. It was coarsely woven but the material itself was soft and thick. It had to be warm and comfortable. He was about to examine it more closely when a loud, deep voice rang out from behind her and she stepped back.

The man was equally as big as Reed. His eyes were dark and angry, his skin smooth without facial hair and his face decorated with white painted stripes, all of which made him look quite threatening. He was also carrying one of the axes that were being used to chop down the reeds and one thing was for sure. It was not a crude, caveman's kind of tool. It was more like a small sized battlefield weapon, clearly made of metal and very sharp. It could easily take his head off. Reed stood very still, ready to unsnap the flap of his holster as the man spoke to the woman in a harsh voice and gestured towards Reed.

She stood in front of the irate man, holding her ground and began scolding him. Unable to control himself, he grabbed her wrist with his free hand and tried to pull her around but she jerked herself lose and slapped his face with a wild swing which stopped him cold and made him take a step back. Looking at her, he seemed to have realized his mistake and spoke to her in a way that could have only been an apology. Her own anger seemed to subside and she answered him gently, then patted him on the face and smiled at him. With that he looked directly at her, bent at the waist and bowed as if honoring her. Then he turned his attention back to Reed. Frowning as though he wasn't quite sure if he approved or not, he looked him over very closely, pointed to the sky and said something to the woman who nodded as if in agreement.

Time to leave, Reed decided. He had caused enough trouble so he spoke to them even though he knew they wouldn't understand what he was saying. He knew it was much too long of a speech but he couldn't seem to help himself. First he gestured towards the woman and told her what a great honor it had been to meet her. Then to both he said he wished that he could stay longer, that he wished they could become friends and that they could teach him their language and tell him about their culture and, and... After that he apologized to the man for upsetting him, turned to the woman and said her name as best he could, bowed to her in respect, looked into her eyes and nodded. Then he touched himself on the forehead as Kyara had often done and disappeared from in front of them.

THIRTY FOUR

There is no such thing as an absolute calendar. Calendars are mankind's creation. They are, however, based upon two things that are, for the most part, quite precise. The first is the amount of time it takes for the earth to travel around the sun in it's orbit, which is defined as a year. The second is the amount of time it takes for the earth to rotate around on it's own axis from the point where the sun is directly overhead at the equator on the equinox until it comes back around to where it is again directly overhead. This is defined as a solar day even though it is not exactly a complete earth rotation due to the earth's movement around the sun. A very minor point not really worth knowing but it takes almost three hundred and sixty five and a quarter solar days for the earth to complete its orbit around the sun. A fortunate number because the whole thing is set right by adding one calendar day to the year once every four years and one additional day approximately every eight hundred and twenty five years. Regardless, days and years are still celestial in nature. Dividing the year up into months and weeks and splitting the day up into hours, minutes and seconds, however, is all purely arbitrary. We could just as well have had three weeks in a month and sixty short hours in a day or anything else. Picking some reference point to start counting the years from is also completely arbitrary since there is no such thing as an absolute day where it all began. Somehow, though, no one ever questions it when we say, for example, that this is the fourth day of month so and so, two thousand and whatever, AD.

But what about before the time when someone decided to start counting days in a formalized manner? What did those people use as a reference point. Someone living in five hundred BC did not know he was living five hundred years before Christ was born and that the formalized year count was running backwards. So how did they keep track of the passing years? Where did they start counting from? Not that it really mattered.

What did matter, however, was Reed's goal. He wanted to go back in time before day one of the modern calendar and come home knowing with some degree of certainty, where he had been time wise. At least within a hundred years or so. To accomplish that he needed all the extra equipment in his overstuffed and very heavy back pack and now that he felt safe again, he dug it out and began to set up. Another half an hour and it would be dark enough to find the stars whose positions he needed to take readings on. Then he would know just how far back in time he had really gone. This was possible because of the wobble in the earth's axis as it spun in space like a top and it was called precession. Not much, only about a degree and a half of tilt but

212

enough so the if one projected the earth's axis onto the star field, it transcribed a circle onto the sky. A long term one which repeated itself every 25,776 earth years, such that by determining where the earths axis was pointing at the moment one could establish where they were time wise, within that long interval. Unfortunately, if a person went too far back, into the previous precessional cycle, they would be unable to establish that. That could only come from carbon dating or geological study.

Okay, he decided some twenty minutes later, everything was ready. The theodolite was on the tripod and precisely leveled. His laptop computer was on and the software program he needed was pulled up and running, waiting for the numbers to be inputted. And then he would know. But, regardless of how far back in time he was, he knew it was definitely before the bronze age. Not that the black man's wicked looking axe was made of bronze, because it wasn't. No, it looked to be made of something far stronger than that, like stainless steel. Something that required a much more advanced technology than for bronze. But where had it come from? He had spent the rest of the afternoon exploring the entire area and there were no signs whatsoever of any such capability. This culture was primarily agrarian with a diet supplemented with fish taken from the river. The housing was of mud brick construction, seemingly well designed and generously sized with roofs of bamboo and reeds while the streets were systematically laid out and clearly these people were clever, orderly and very social.

And then there was ....

But what was this, Reed wondered as he looked up at the now visible stars in the northern sky. Polaris was easy to find. Just follow the two end star of the Little Dipper across the sky and there it is. Yes, but it very definitely was no longer the north star. He could tell that even with looking through the theodolite. So where then was Vega? Slightly dimmer in brightness than Polaris and much closer to true north, he found it visually. Then he moved the theodolite telescope around, found it again and locked it in position. At first he was going to record it's position in his notebook but remembered that he had given it away, so, using his small LED flashlight, he entered them directly into the computer, clicked on calculate and then sat back and stared at the final number.

At first his mind kind of stalled out and he just sat there. Then he went through the entire process again, but the numbers were still the same. He repeated it once more and had to admit that what he had come up with had to be correct. No wonder it was so damned chilly at this time of the year in this part of the world. He hadn't gone back in time to sixteen thousand BC. He had over shot his mark by about three thousand years. He was nineteen thousand years back into the past, just as the ice age was ending and the pyramids were already there. My god, he thought. What about that? There were people here, too. Civilized people. People who not only spoke fluently but also had a clearly defined written language. And what appeared to be, machine made tools of steal. And what else? He could only wonder.

He got to his feet, turned off the laptop, took down the theodolite and put everything away in his back pack. Then he looked south across the plateau and saw the fires. Camp fires, no doubt. And a lot them, spread across the landscape, flickering away in the night. Who was lighting those? The people who lived in the houses or were there others not as civilized? Would he dare light one too? Maybe, but he decided against it and crawled into the small shelter he had put together using dead branches and leaves, wondering if it would be warm enough to get him through the night. Inside the tiny structure he laid there thinking for what seemed forever. Thinking about the woman with the bright flashing eyes who had stood up to the man with the axe. The woman who had most certainly sensed his presence when he was spying on them from a distance and had come to him. Was she the only one or were there others who had that kind of ability? What if some man had the same skill or innate psychic talent or whatever it was? Some other man with an axe who might feel as threatened by him as this one had been? Did they already know where he was at? Would it even be safe to go to sleep?

Finally, after what must have been an hour or more, he drifted off. But not for long. Then he was wide awake again, shivering badly. While the temperature was still far from freezing, it was much too cold to be sleeping here the way he was dressed. Crawling out of his makeshift hole he stood up, stomped his feet and thrashed his arms about in an attempt to warm up but it was not enough. Digging through his pack he found his flashlight and matches, dragged the brush from his shelter to a clear area and set it on fire. It took a while but eventually he was warm again. Then he looked at the north sky. The Big Dipper had rotated around at least sixty degrees. It had to be about three o'clock in the morning. He had slept longer than he thought but the big question he faced was, what was he going to do now?

The enigma of the Giza pyramids was unsolved and as desperately as he wanted to know when they were actually built, by whom and how, he didn't dare try to go back any further the way he was prepared. It was just too damned risky. And then he began to feel that there was something out there just beyond the rim of the firelight. People or animals, it didn't matter. He had never transported himself at night either. Another mistake, but what choice did he have? Still, there was one last thing he had to do. He scratched around the edges of the fire with a long stick and dragged out a few pieces of wood that had burned themselves out, felt them to see if they were cool enough, wrapped them in some socks and put them in one of the zippered compartments on his pack. If he could afford it, a laboratory could carbon date them and confirm the time period he was in. That done, he wrestled his pack up onto his back, held his small flashlight in his hand, turned it on and thought of home.

THIRTY FIVE

As things came into focus, there was Kyara smiling at him, ravishing as ever in spite of the fact that she was dressed in some rather bulky looking jump suit kind of thing that almost completely disguised all the curves that he knew. He gave her an immense grin and in less than a second they were in each other's arms with a somewhat dismayed audience looking on. Then,

215

without words, she took him by the hand and led him through the surprised onlookers up the pier. At first he didn't notice because he was so taken by her presence. But, even after leaving the small group behind who were shocked at his sudden appearance, he realized he was still being stared at. Was it his clothes? Or the haircut? Or did he just generally appear to be out of place in this future world?

"God, I must look really dorky. Are you sure you want to be seen with me?" he asked.

"What do you think?" Kyara asked as she stopped and gave him a quick, hot kiss on the mouth, then took his hand and pulled at him.

"Damn, woman. Do you have any idea how much I missed you?"

"Not as much as I missed you."

"Oh, yeah," he responded as he stopped her and kissed her back although she now seemed a bit nervous. "This won't get you in trouble, will it?" he asked.

"It might, if we keep doing it here."

"Oh, oh," he said as he looked at her expression, then looked around at the crowd. "Let's go. You can tell me later."

What was wrong, he wondered. Obviously a lot more had changed than the new pier they were standing on. And the level of the ocean as she led the way, now starting to hurry a little.

The sea level had risen, what? At least eight feet. The almost quarter mile wide strip of sand he had once walked on was now almost completely gone and the water was lapping over what once used to be Pacific Coast Highway. But he could find out about all that later. Right now Kyara was pulling at him. They even darted between the traffic to get across the street, went on to the promenade where the streets were still blocked off as he remembered them and hurried into a clothing store. Inside, she led him over to a corner and stopped.

"We'll be okay but until I get a chance to explain, just think in terms of big brother is watching. And I mean almost everywhere except that the cameras are so small they are almost impossible to locate. There aren't any in this corner though, so slip your back pack off. Good. Now shield me a little from other customers," she said as she unzipped her jump suit and quickly stepped out of it to expose a completely different style of clothing underneath. Then she removed a floppy cloth hat from one of her pockets, quickly piled her hair up and stuffed it under the hat. Next she unzipped his back pack, dug through it quickly, found his light weight, blue colored jacket and had him put it on to cover up the shirt he was wearing.

"Do you have a hat?" she asked and when he said no, she told him to wait there. A minute later she was back.

"Okay," she said as she jammed her gray jump suit into the pack. "I'll take this. You stay here and count to ten. All the stores on this side of the street are connected so go from store to store until the end one. It's a cafeteria. I'll wait for you out front but don't come to me. I'll cross the street but you stay on this side and follow. Do a little window shopping along the way. Three blocks down is a parking structure. Wait just inside at the ground level. My vehicle is light tan. I'll pick you up."

"Got it," he assured her wondering what it was all about. So far it seemed rather serious. "See you in a bit."

At first sight it didn't look as though things had changed that much and Reed still recognized many of the buildings. Stores were still stores with window displays and people were still out walking around but something was certainly different. There was still a burden of traffic but the noise levels were way down. And the cars didn't look at all like one would imagine them to be fifty years in the future. Instead of seeming exotic, most of them reminded him of an unpopular Volkswagen model from back in the 1970's called the Thing, something about as basic as a car could get. But still, some of the differences were notable. They were all electric powered which accounted for the low noise levels and had solar panels covering the roof and the hood.

Kyara's auto was also one of the most popular look-alikes but was surprisingly sports like in acceleration and agility and, as she explained later, breakthroughs in solar cell technology and battery efficiency contributed to increased versatility and range. Meanwhile she drove like a pro.

"Sorry about all the intrigue," she said, once they were under way. "But I made the mistake of disappearing on a surveillance camera a while ago. Unfortunately, I didn't realize it was there until I was stopped on the street a week later and taken in for questioning by Internal Security."

"Internal Security? That sounds pretty ominous."

"It can be if you take it seriously, which I guess I'd better start doing."

"How did it come about?"

"It's a later day branch of Homeland Security. Over the years Al queda and all the other foreign based fringe groups were systematically obliterated but instead of downsizing the organization as should have been done, its paranoid proponents literally invented internal threats to replace external ones and turned a segment of the federal government against its own people, just to keep themselves in power. Normally that wouldn't seem possible but there are still enough disenfranchised, mentally deprived people around doing bad things to give the whole scenario some semblance of plausibility. When that is mixed with the fears of the few remaining extreme Christian fundamentalists and far right conservatives who want nothing less than complete control over everyone's lives, there is a problem. The general public is also badly informed, rather directionless and prone to believe all the propaganda, so it's becoming a difficult time."

"But getting stopped on the street. That couldn't have been much fun. What happened?"

"I got lazy and made a mistake. I didn't feel like driving clear across town so I popped over to the clothing store, bought a few things, went outside where no one was around and disappeared, not knowing about the camera. The entire camera complex is rigged with facial recognition so a couple of days later another one picked me out and alerted the police. As it turned out the problem wasn't that they actually believed I had disappeared. They thought I had hacked into their data system and deleted information. Then when I didn't have any ID, they locked me up. Under the circumstances I might have been there a long time so I took the easy way out and went home in the middle of the night. Now they are seriously looking for me."

"Jeez. Not good. What now?"

"I take you home, get undressed and let you chase me around the house."

That evening after their special game of hide and seek, Kyara sat him down and asked him about his recent adventures.

"Intriguing," she said as she examined the note the black woman had written for him.

"Very," he agreed. "So was everything about her. Especially that uncanny sixth sense. Too bad we couldn't communicate better. Maybe if there had been more time but I felt a definite connection. Any chance she was another aspect of you?"

"Not that I'm aware of but it's something we could find out about. I also like the idea of being able to move heavy objects around mentally. The question is, once they are all in place and mortared in, could they be taken apart. Could we somehow dis assemble the Federal Building?"

"Do you think it would be worth the effort?"

"Probably not. But, if nothing else works....., she said and asked if he was hungry and would he like to eat out on the deck.

"Is it safe," he asked as he stood and looked over the railing at the step slope below which the stilt supported structure hung out off of.

"Don't worry," Kyara told him. "It's been here for over a hundred years and never been seriously damaged in any of the earthquakes. Not even the Big One."

"The Big One?"

"Sorry. I forget you didn't know. It was in twenty nineteen. Before I was even born. Even so, a lot has happened in the last fifty years. But all that is for tomorrow. Then I will show you some of it first hand."

"Good. I'm excited about seeing L.A. again."

"If you want, we can see a lot more than that. How about Vancouver and Seattle, San Francisco, Los Angeles and St. Louis."

"In one day? Is that possible?"

"I'm borrowing my father's jet."

"Your father has a jet? Must be a military plane if it can fly fast enough to cover that much distance in one day."

"No, it's private. A little four place thing that can cruise at about a thousand."

"Miles per hour? Jeez. And your father's? Isn't that interesting. But, that's right. I remember you telling me that he was rich. And you the only child."

"Just me. This time around I'm a totally spoiled brat. You'll get to meet them one of these days. After I get done monopolizing your time."

"So why are you here while I'm back half a century?"

"Because that's what we chose to do. Meeting my parents should help you remember that. Unfortunately, they are in England on business but they should be back in a couple of weeks. If meeting them doesn't evoke some old memories, I'll tell you. As for what I'm doing here in this time period, you would probably call me an activist. Not a demonstrator. I try to work behind the scenes as much as possible and so far no one in government knows who I am."

"Have you ever met anyone else who can do what you do? Besides me, who learned it from you?"

"The disappearing? Fortunately, no. Not yet, anyway. As for Internal Security, I'm hoping they will just consider me to be either an escape artist or a visitor from outer space and let it go at that. If not, maybe you can help me think of something."

"Nice," Reed said as he looked over Kyara's father's small jet which was kept at the Santa Monica air strip. "Very nice. Looks like a killer whale with wings on it. Big wings, though, for something that goes as fast as you say."

"I know. But it can also take off and land at forty miles an hour so it only needs a very short airstrip. But look closely," she said and ran her hand along the rear edge of the airfoil.

"They fold?" he questioned. "Of course, or you'd never be able to get past the speed of sound. Is it hard to fly?"

"Probably wouldn't be for you."

"Really?" he said as he looked at her with her crazy hat on and monster sun glasses to hide her face. "I thought by now planes would be able to do everything by themselves, totally unaided."

"Essentially they can. But I prefer to be in control during takeoff and landing. Anyway, I'm hungry so let's get aboard. We'll have breakfast in what's left of San Francisco."

Thirty five minutes later Kyara dropped the plane down from twenty five thousand feet to five thousand, slowed their speed and extended the wings to full lift position, then slowed to just a few miles per hour over stall speed as she came into the bay area from the south. Air traffic was very light and every craft in the area was shown in live mode on a three dimensional holographic display on the instrument panel as everything in the sky transpondered back and forth in real time updates. At first, viewing the metro area from above, it appeared to have changed little from what Reed remembered. San Jose, Sunnyvale, Menlo Park and then, what happened to the Redwood City area?

"Gas line fractures and fires caused by the quake. Almost everything from here up to San Mateo went up in smoke. I think the fires killed more people than collapsing buildings did."

"What was the toll?"

"For the entire area, I believe it was almost a hundred and forty thousand."

"A hundred and forty thousand? My god. When?"

"Nine years ago. So, as you will see, there's still a lot of reconstruction going on. But if you want to see how really powerful an earthquake can be, look what's coming up."

At first, Reed didn't know what he was looking for but as Kyara did a loop over the area it suddenly occurred to him. He shook his head in dismay.

"That's not supposed to be there, is it?" he said. "And it goes all the way from the ocean to the bay. Holy... jeez," he exclaimed as he looked down at the jagged, zig zag, unobstructed rift that varied in width from about fifty feet to nearly a hundred and ran all the way from Pacifica on the coast to San Bruno on the bay, separating San Francisco proper from the rest of the peninsula. There were already several bridges that spanned the new channel but...

"It looks like the north side of the rift is lower than the southern side, too," he said as he thought about it.

"About eleven feet."

"But then.." he said, thinking about what must be ahead.

It was worse than he could possibly have imagined. The quake had been so powerful it had actually shifted the whole of San Francisco proper the same amount of distance as the rift was wide. The entire area was nothing but an immense pile of rubble with nothing left standing. A city without man made landmarks. The only thing that appeared to have been cleared was 19th Avenue which connected the lower peninsula freeway system through the disaster area with north bound highway 101. Almost the entire twisted and destroyed length of the Oakland Bay Bridge was still in the water and there was nothing being done to rebuild it. The original southern span of the Golden Gate Bridge was also beneath the water but an emergency span was in place and under use. One that was now fifty seven feet shorter than the old one had been.

At first all Reed could do was stare as Kyara circled the area. Finally, she told him that the quake was a ten point three in magnitude and that the epicenter was just a half mile off the coast. The northern end of the land mass the city sat on was also tilted up over twenty feet and rotated inland about the same amount. The radius of the quake's severe damage area extended nearly thirty miles inland and was felt as far away as Reno, Nevada. Immediately after it was over and long before the aftershocks had ceased, people had abandoned the surrounding region in droves, many of them leaving with nothing but their personal possessions and few ever came back. The one time population of the previously thriving city that had been nearly a million souls was now down to an estimated few thousand and what was left of the civilized portion of the once city was now the home of derelicts and scavengers, still scratching through the devastation looking for things to salvage in order to stay alive.

Shocked and speechless, Reed kept his face tight against the window as Kyara banked and circled. Finally he said it was enough and Kyara righted the craft, came around to a westerly heading, pushed forward on the throttles and went into a step climb out over the ocean.

"Are you okay," she asked when she looked over at him.

"That was pretty damned gloomy," he said.

"My apologies. I should have warned you."

"No. It's okay. I think it was important to get the full impact first hand."

"But you don't need to have fifty years of tragedy dumped on you in one day so we'll skip Seattle and St. Louis."

"Were they as bad as this?"

"Seattle was worse."

"Wow," Reed said. "I can't imagine. But I'll take your word for it."

"All right. We'll do something else instead."

"Like what?" Reed asked as Kyara leveled the craft off and punched some numbers into the on-board computer before answering.

"Hawaii. It's still intact and beautiful. We can be there in two hours. Lunch instead of breakfast."

"And then?"

"Dessert?"

"You look very yummy this morning."

"Still? After last night?"

"Damn right."

"How many times did you wake me up?"

"As many as you did me. Actually, I don't remember sleeping. How's that for a guy who is technically fifty years older than he was two days ago?"

"Well, I like older, more mature men. And for the record, this plane also has an auto pilot."

"Then we'd better see if it works."

"Marvelous," Reed said later. "Now I feel like I'm able to cope again. What else has happened in the last fifty years?"

"Where do you want to start? Global warming, other natural disasters, wars, politics, religion, fashion design or prime time entertainment?"

"None of that just yet. I want to know more about you? I bet you were cuter than hell as a kid. Probably a precocious little trouble maker who made all the boys crazy and was two steps ahead of her teachers all the way. Public school or private?"

"Some of both. Plus some of the best home tutoring money could buy."

"And where were you born? I think you said it was a ranch."

"Up in the San Rafael Widerness area away from everything for many years. Then we moved to Malibu and lived in an ocean front house that is no longer standing, thanks to a tsunami. But by then my father was very successful and bought a house in Holmby Hills where they still live. He gave me my house as a college graduation present so, as I said, I am a bit of a spoiled brat."

"Well, I'm not complaining," he replied and kept her busy with questions until the big island came into view. Kyara punched more buttons on the control panel and quickly received a synthesized voice call back giving them permission to land on the Oahu strip. She then put the nose down, slowed the craft until the wings were fully extended and sat the plane down so softly he couldn't even tell when the wheels actually hit the ground. She then taxied in to a small plane parking area near the terminal and shut down the engines. Getting out of her seat, she opened the cabin door and they stepped out into the sun and warmth.

THIRTY SIX

Shocking as the sight of the destroyed city of San Francisco had been to him, once they had returned to Kyara's home, Reed still wanted to know more. In particular, how had Los Angeles fared in the last fifty years?

"Okay," she told him. "Back to the airport, first thing tomorrow. Tonight I want to make sure you feel very welcome being here."

"I already do. But that doesn't mean... I think your couch looks very comfortable. And I love how thick your carpet is...."

"What do you notice that's different?" Kyara asked as she cruised slowly over the down town area through the north-south flight corridor at five thousand feet.

"Well, to begin with, there is no smog. I always loved this part of the world on those few days of winter when that dirty blanket went away and you could see the mountains and the ocean both. Like now. It's absolutely beautiful. Is it always like this?"

"Almost always. Thanks to wind, solar and other alternate sources of energy. But what else?"

"Except for freeway and street locations, almost everything is changed. Especially the skyline. And, isn't that where it was? The old city hall is gone, too. But Century City looks about the same. What happened?"

"Sub surface coupling and resonance. The epicenter for the so called big one was just off the coast of Long Beach which was almost totally destroyed, like San Francisco. But as you can see, it also coupled into the downtown area. That was forty years ago so there is almost no visual evidence left. I believe the death toll was over forty thousand at the time. The next biggest one was nine years ago, right after San Francisco. It was epicentered at Newport Beach and only killed about three thousand. Other than that it has been relatively calm, even though geologists say we could have another big one at any time."

"Which is what they have been saying for over a hundred years. Can't go wrong on that one. But Seattle and St. Louis too."

"Also New York City."

"New York City? With all the tall buildings? That must have been devastating."

"Extremely. But as I said, so was Seattle and St. Louis. The St. Louis quake even changed the course of the Mississippi River, again. Just like back in the mid eighteen hundreds. Are you sure you want to hear this? It must sound pretty morbid coming all at once."

"It does. But still, if there has been this much activity in the United States, there must have been some serious stuff happening globally too."

"Japan, of course. South America, and the Philippines in particular, with huge death tolls but none of it comes close to what the effects of global warming have done. Especially in the last twenty some years with accelerated temperature rises. And, as you saw, coastal flooding. The most ominous thing about Attic ice melt however, is its affect on the Atlantic Gulf Stream. It 's dropping in temperature and changing course."

"So Europe must be slipping into an ice age all its own. Has anything good happened?"

"Although it's too late and totally irreversible at this point, the human race finally got the message. Birth rates have dropped to almost zero in some parts of the world so, all in all, present world population is now down to about four billion."

"In fifty years. That's very significant."

"It's certainly better environmentally. Politically, not so much. While there is less reason to haggle over resources, it still goes on because some countries were so completely depleted in the past. There are still a few dictatorships in the world, too, and some countries are as extremely nationalistic as ever. Tyrants posturing over nonsense and religious differences with religious issues still the main cause of conflict around the world."

"Good grief. Has anything good happened?"

"A little. On the up side the U.N. is slowly gaining in its ability to intervene in things and there is a world body of law slowly coming into place. But, as always, the wealthy and the powerful still have a way of corrupting the outcomes in their favor. Even here in this country."

"But you still have free speech."

"That's what we are told. People still seem to disappear from time to time, however, and I don't mean voluntarily and the message seems to be that some things are better left alone," she said as they approached Santa Monica airport once again, leaving him to think about that.

Once on the ground and back in her car, she asked if he would like to see something else of interest on the way home.

Their first stop was at the big Catholic Church by Lincoln Park in Santa Monica.

"Really?" Reed said with surprise as they went inside, paid the fee and took the tour. "It's a damned museum."

And when Kyara stopped at the old Mormon Temple on Santa Monica Boulevard in west L.A.. and Reed found it was also a museum, he could only say that it seemed appropriate.

"What happened," he asked once they were back outside.

"For the Catholics, self destruction. But it was a long, slow death. Primarily because its patriarchs could never get past their own ego bound stupidity and put an end to all the internal corruption. They also hung onto papal infallibility and were against birth control to the last dying breath and never dumped any of the wayward priesthood or the hypocrisy along the way so eventually much of the membership moved over to other Christian sects, primarily Episcopalian. Between lack of contributions and court awarded payouts in the molestation cases, it went legally bankrupt. Even with their tax free status at the time many Catholic churches couldn't even pay for building maintenance, let alone handle other expenses, so in most cases the sites were donated to cities or to the state."

"And the Mormons?"

"Not just the Mormons. Religious organizations all gradually lost their tax free status over the years because of all the abuses. There are still a lot of churches around, as you will see, and even though they struggle financially. Cults haven't disappeared either and the portion of the population that seems to need someone else to do their thinking for them is still appalling. But there is a growing disinterest in religion for the middle and upper classes which has created some sharp divisions in the country. The believers still think Jesus is coming to save them and damn the rest of us, so the ranting continues even though he's sixty years overdue. And, if you think congress is stalled out over political differences in your time period, you should see it now. Except it's not party lines but religious opinion that divides it. The rest of the world hasn't done any better and religious differences are still the major source of conflict."

"Well, I was hoping things would have changed more than that."

"Unfortunately, no. But on the up side there are some healthy trends. For a lot of people in the middle, it's not religious guidance that they seek so much as the feeling of community they get from belonging to something. Once that exists, the need for religion begins to go away. It's starting to happen. Name some interest or need that you might have and there are more and more community groups out there to provide it. At least in this part of the world."

"But I don't see you as a joiner. You seem very independent."

"I think so. There is only one group I'm associated with and that is an entirely different thing. Our goal is to be socially disruptive and undo all the intrusions into people's personal lives."

"Is it working?"

"Not yet. We don't even have a solid core group of trustworthy people. And right now I can't be of much help. If there isn't a warrant out for my escape, I'm at least wanted for questioning."

"So, we need to work on getting your face out of the system. Anyone in your group that might be of help?"

"Highly unlikely. Want to go to a meeting tonight and see?"

"So this is what some of the churches that didn't become museums are now being used for. What kind was this?" Reed asked as they parked in the adjacent lot of another old church early that evening.

"Baptist. The city owns the property now and rents it out. It's used for everything from poetry readings to craft fairs."

"Sounds appropriate. What's the topic? Oh, there it is on the kiosk. Life after liberation? Really? Liberation from what?"

"Pacificity, I think."

"Honestly?"

"Yes. We have an ongoing series of these silly events just to muddy things up. Although they do keep an eye on them, the Feds write most of the group off as misguided and harmless so it serves as a great front. Plus, we have a good time making all this garbage up but if it's hard to sit through so, my apologies in advance."

"No problem as long as we can leave early if it's too bad.

"We can. Just try not to laugh out loud in the meantime."

Inside, Kyara first staked out two aisle seats and then introduced Reed to several different people.

"What's with the ginky clothes and crazy hat?" they all wanted to know.

"Tell you later," she responded as they agreed to meet at one of the women's houses after the program.

"I think I need to tape my mouth shut," Reed whispered in Kyara's ear about half way through the man's speech as she suppressed a chuckle. Then something suddenly came to him.

"Where's the men's room?" he asked.

"That bad, huh?"

"No. It's something else I need to check out. Be right back," he said as he got up and headed towards the rear of the small auditorium.

Damn. It was happening to him again, just like it had back in the courtroom where the man was lying to the judge but this time it involved Kyara. There was someone there who thought they had recognized her and it wasn't good.

Reed moved down the aisle, purposely not looking at anyone in particular but still able to notice one man's eyes tracking him. Once he was in the rear and out of sight, he stopped and moved back to where he could just see his person of interest who was sitting several rows behind their seats and was now looking back in Kyara's direction. He studied him briefly, trying to see what he could pick up on, went to the men's room, stayed a minute and came back out and returned to his seat.

"What's going on?" Kyara asked as the person in front of her turned around and glared. Kyara glared back at her for a second then dug in her pocket for her phone and handed it to Reed.

"Internal Security???" he typed in and showed it to her.

She gave him a concerned look.

"Explain later," he typed.

"What now?" she responded.

"Put hat on," he answered. "Go to lady's room, check him out."

Looking worried, she nodded and he took her hand. Then he leaned over close and whispered to her.

"Sixth row from back. Right side. Fourth person in. White, mid thirties, long hair, sloppy clothes but faking it. Pretending not to look, but looking."

"What if he gets up and follows me?"

"I think he'll wait. If not, go in the women's room and disappear outside to your car. If you're not back in five minutes, I'll meet you there."

"And what if he waits until after and calls for backup in the meantime?"

"We'll figure it out."

Four minutes later, Kyara was back.

"You're right. He's a little obvious," she typed into the phone. "Now what?"

Reed gestured to her, tapped himself on the forehead and closed his eyes.

"He's visualizing how he's going to put the cuffs on you," he whispered.

Kyara looked at him and raised her eyebrows.

"Alone," Reed typed. "No backup. He thinks he'll be a hero."

"Like hell," she sent back.

"Right," he replied. "See the exit sign by the stage?"

She looked and nodded.

"Wait till everyone stands up," he whispered. "I'll go out the front and try to slow him down. You take the back exit. Disappear if you have to. Meet you at the car."

"Well, that was close," Kyara said as they drove away. "Guess I won't be going to any of those meetings for a while?"

"Do you suppose he was there specifically looking for you?"

"I don't think so. Just routine. But he must have seen my photo and recognized me as being wanted."

"How come they can't track you to your home? Don't you have a drivers license with your picture on it?"

"Yes, the one I carry does. But I hacked into Vehicle Records and changed the one that's on file. And even though it's illegal, I never carry ID on my person."

"What happens if you're driving?"

"It's in the car, just in case. But the car is registered to a phony company I invented. If it weren't and they had my name, I'd be back in jail because all private vehicles are equipped with GPS tracking systems and it's legal to track someone without a warrant. All in the name of national security, of course."

"Even so I'd bet your GPS has been disabled."

"Modified. It stays switched off most of the time. But if a patrol car comes along and they decide to check out the vehicle by interrogating the tracking unit, it switches back on. It's something they do routinely to make sure people aren't tampering with the devices."

"But you also have license plates."

"True, and the license better match the GPS identity code."

"Okay. But what if someone decides to check up on you and your system is turned off?"

"Well, unless you are on a list somewhere, there's almost no reason to do that. But if they can't find you, it could also be because you have driven the car out of the area. Or the batteries died or something else failed. And then, it's like everything else. There are at least twenty five million vehicles in the metro area. Probably more, so it becomes a data handling problem. So, unless there is some reason why they might have a special interest in someone, there is little reason to worry about it. But that's not the point. It is still an invasion of privacy and personal freedom."

"But there don't seem to be any travel restrictions."

"Nothing formal. But there are GPS monitors along major highways also and check points at all state borders and they are not for agricultural reasons."

"Next you'll be telling me the Patriot Act is still in effect."

"Very much so. And with even more restrictions than in your time."

"Which seems so unnecessary."

"So it would. As I said before, the threat of terrorism from sources outside the country has almost completely gone away. There is no Taliban, no neo Nazis or new world order revolutionaries, no zealots or overly ambitious nationalistic, power grabbing despots. They were all run down and exterminated long ago so the whole system has re directed itself inward."

"Which you and your friends are trying to change. Or your group."

Kyara kept looking in the rear view mirror as she talked. "Group," she said. "It's best not to think of them as friends because it's hard to tell who to trust."

"Anyone following us?" Reed asked.

"Doesn't look like it. Anyway, we're almost there. I'll park down the street and we'll walk back just in case."

"Okay. But how are we going to get your picture out of the system and you off the wanted list?"

"I was hoping you might have some ideas. I've tried to hack in like I did with Motor Vehicle but these files are protected by encrypted passwords that are beyond my ability to break."

"Okay. We'll figure something out. How many people will be here?"

"Maybe a dozen," she said after she had the car next to the curb and shut it off. "But don't let me forget to ask you how you knew the security man was there."

The house was big. Two stories on a large, well landscaped lot and set back from the street. It was also in Brentwood and would have been very expensive back in Reed's time. But now, in the new world with only half the people in it, quality real estate was far more affordable. Of course that hadn't matter to the present owner. She got it in a divorce settlement.

Kyara immediately took Reed to meet Jenny, the owner of

the property and a long time friend.

"At last I get to meet your mystery man," she said warmly. "The one she says she's known forever but I never got to meet. But I forgot where you're from."

"Arizona," he replied.

"That's not so far. Why don't you move here?" she asked, her outgoing welcome clearly indicating that she liked him.

"We're trying to work something out," he responded as he gave Kyara a firm hug. Then everyone was introduced, first names only. Four men and seven women. One of the women who Kyara did not know then asked Reed why he had gotten into a confrontation with Barton, acting as though she had the right to do so. Her name was Madge.

"Barton? You mean the guy back at the, ahh, church?" he asked as he looked at Kyara. "Do you still call it that?"

"It's good enough," she assured him before turning to the woman, clearly offended by the attitude. "Why? What did he do?" she asked her, ready to do battle.

Reed smiled at her, pleased with the idea of her willingness to jump in.

"Well, deliberately bumped into him for some reason."

"Really? Did you do that?" she asked Reed with a fake frown.

"Probably," he said with a grin. "But I apologized. I think. Or maybe not."

"And why is it important to you?" Kyara asked the woman, suspiciously.

"Because he comes to the public gatherings."

"So do a lot of people."

"But he's very interested in the material," Madge said in an attempt to defend the man.

"How do you know that?"

"I talk to him sometimes after, ahhh.. and he told me so."

"And this time he asked if you knew the person who bumped into him."

"Well, yes."

"Which you didn't. So, do you like the lectures?"

"Of course. I find them very stimulating."

"Really?" Kyara said, a little shocked. "Why?"

"Because I'm interested in raising public awareness and I agree with what I think you are trying to do and... So what's wrong with Barton, anyway?"

"Nothing," Kyara lied. "I'm glad you like him. Did he ask for your phone number?"

Madge blushed heavily and stammered as Kyara took Reed's hand, motioned to Jenny and led them aside.

"Barton is with Internal Security," she told Jenny.

"Oh, oh," Jenny responded.

"Yeah," Kyara said. "And how did that one get in here?"

"Good question," Jenny said. "I think Corrine invited her."

"Dammit. That's the second time she's done something like that."

"I know. Now what do we do? We don't dare just throw them out."

"So we revert back to stupid mode for tonight. Then we tell Corrine we're leaving the group, wait a while and start over. Might be best anyway."

"How so?" Jenny asked.

"Internal Security is after me for questioning."

"Really? That sounds exciting. Why?"

"They think I deleted some footage from a surveillance camera file and escaped from jail."

"What? You escaped from jail? God, Kyara," she laughed. "Tell me about it. This has got to be good."

Kyara laughed too but then said, shhh, as she looked at the rest of the people in the group. Then she came up with a story about how there must have been a camera failure that showed her disappearing on camera which meant that she had to have tampered with the system and how disorganized the jail personnel were. Some one left her cell unlocked and she just walked out in the middle of the night.

Jenny chuckled again. "You just walked out? That's really....Do you think they did it deliberately?"

"I don't know. Maybe," she lied.

"Is that why Barton was at the meeting? To arrest you?"

"No. I think he was just playing spy as usual until he

recognized me. Thank god Reed .... got suspicious and interceded enough for me to sneak out the back door."

"Do you think this person, what's her name, Madge. Do you think she knows about why Barton is really at the meetings?"

"No. She's totally clueless. Anyway, we should leave for now. No point in dragging you into something. So, I'll give you a call. Maybe we can have lunch on Thursday as usual?"

"Of course," Jenny said and smiled at Reed.

"Unless you get out of here early. We'll be down on Pico."

"I'm glad Jenny likes you," Kyara said to Reed as they walked back to her car.

"Think so?"

"I do. Want to stop for some food before we go home?"

"What's down on Pico? A place without cameras?"

"No. But it's a place where we can jam one."

"I was wondering if that were possible. How do you do it?"

"Most of them are wireless and they are all digitally encoded for location. There are far too many to do any kind of blanket interference on though. But I can do it for several places I like to go."

"Too bad you didn't do that before you got caught disappearing."

"I know. But that was outside the courthouse and those cameras are all hard wired in."

"That would be a problem. So, how does your system work?"

"I have a very sensitive receiver which I take to a place where I don't want to be seen. It picks up the data stream sent out by the camera so we get the location code along with picture information and record it ahead of time. With that I can shut down the camera and turn on the pre recorded data at the same instant. Unless someone were watching that particular camera very closely it's highly unlikely they would ever notice. They probably don't even watch unless their spy software picks up a face or a voice they're interested in," she finished saying as they got to her vehicle. "Well, here we are. I don't see any cars that weren't here before. Would you like to drive."

"No. I love the way you hot rod around."

"So, I've been meaning to ask you," Reed said after they were under way and it was clear no one was following. "Your picture is in the system. What about your fingerprints and your voice?"

"Picture, finger prints and no doubt my DNA by now, none of which were in the system until I was detained. Probably my voice, too, although I refused to say almost anything, which was a good thing because they got tired of trying to interrogate me and just put me in that cell."

It was a small, all night restaurant on Pico Boulevard and, after she parked in the back, they went toward the building. Before entering she took out her cell phone and pointed it inside, up high on the far wall and punched some numbers into the keyboard. Immediately a little green light came on and she said it was okay to go in. After they sat down, Reed asked her how long they could stay.

"It has an hour and a half of video on it," she said. "And I can reset it if I need to, so, no hurry."

"Okay, tell me how you picked up on the security guy," Kyara said after they had ordered.

"Barton. Well, I was having a difficult time waiting for the day to come see you so I decided to see if I might be able to project my consciousness into someone's head and find out what they were thinking."

"How did you do it? It never worked for me."

"It didn't work for me either. Nothing. So I tried to tune into their thoughts instead, in a passive way. And for a long time that didn't work either. At first I thought it was because there probably wasn't much going on in most people's heads to begin with. But then I decided I couldn't pick up on it because none of it had anything to with me, which was one of the problems. The other even more important part was emotional intensity. So, in general I am completely unaware of what anyone is thinking but if they are in a strong emotional state or their thoughts may somehow affect me personally, it seems to come through. Which, in Barton's case, it certainly did. Other than that, nothing."

"What about when I'm thinking about you and it makes me horny?" she asked as she reached over and took his hand.

"Like now?"

"Like always," she said as she moved his hand down to her leg.

"Ohhh jeeez. Be careful," he responded. "I have enough trouble behaving myself as it is."

"I know. I can read your mind too. But what you did went beyond that. I could have been back in jail. You, too."

"So we were lucky. Let's hope it stays that way."

"How about at Jenny's house?"

"Only one thing. The tall blonde."

"Nancy."

"Yeah, that one. Be careful. She's very jealous of you. I wouldn't trust her one bit."

"That's very good. I've had the same feeling. And, actually, except for Jennie, I wouldn't trust any of them very far. I don't share everything with her either."

"What about your camera jammer?"

"Just you. Too bad because it would be nice to think someone really had your back if things got tough. Like you do. And my parents. But the rest of them.... well, if Jennie comes, see what you can pick up. If you think it would be okay to give her one I always carry an extra. After all, it's just a silly game anyway. That's how I've learned to look at it. Except I messed up."

"Looks like it. But it's fixable. We'll think of something."

"Thanks. I'm sure we will."

"So where did get your camera jammer. Looks just like a cell phone."

"It is. I stole a camera and took it home to find out how it works. Reprogramming my phone to disable it was a bit of a challenge, however, but everything is there. Receiver, transmitter, lots of memory and now that I have the software, I could do as many as I wanted."

"Really? You did that by yourself? That's very clever. I'm impressed. Obviously you didn't take art history in college."

"Actually, I did. Among other things."

"Damn," Reed said as he looked at her with admiration. "Now I'm even more impressed. And on top of all that you are just so overwhelmingly beautiful. I.... god Kyara..." he said and stopped, unable to go on.

She took his hand, returned the look and stared back at him.

"And I also know how to fly a plane," she said as the spell was broken by the waitress who brought their drinks.

"Well," Reed said after taking a sip of his beverage. "The possibilities are astounding. You could go into business modifying peoples' phones."

"Except most people don't care if they are being monitored. They think it actually makes them safer so, that's that. What I'm trying to do is hack in and disable the entire system, instead."

"Your own form of civil disobedience."

"Exactly. And now that you are fifty years into the future, what do you think? Is it what you expected?"

Reed thought for a moment. "Technologically, yes. Lot's of advances but again, so much of it still seems so frivolous. After all, how many features can a cell phone have or how many options are there for an automobile and who cares. Some of it makes life easier but certainly not any better. The thing I don't understand on the human level, however, is that after everything that has happened like the big earthquakes, rising ocean levels, climate changes and all the millions of people who have died from disasters and starvation, is that there hasn't been some mass change in perspective. Life should be valued more and have a different emphasis but so far I don't see it."

"What do you mean?"

"Look around. How many people do you see actually talking to each other, for example. At least half have their earphones on and a lot more are still doing the tweet or twitter thing. Whatever they call it now. Where's the real communication?"

"Yes, you're right. People are in as much denial as ever, trying to escape from their lives every way possible. But, their choice, their problem. As for me, the present day issue of civil liberties is still a very twisted one. For some reason the nation just can't seem to shake itself free of that old, ongoing paranoia on the governmental level. Once those kinds of people become entrenched, they need intrigue and conspiracy to justify their existence. Even if they have to create it themselves. So this is what I like to work against."

"Without much support."

"Exactly."

"But a challenge you decided to get involved in. Otherwise you wouldn't be here."

"I know. No complaints. But if it weren't for people like Jenny I might leave it all behind."

"And, speaking of Jennie," Reed said as he gestured.

Kyara turned and looked. Jennie was coming through the door.

"Hi, people," she said once she was near and slide into the opposite side of the booth.

"Well," she said after they had gotten the waitress to take her order. "Did I interrupt anything?"

"Nothing serious," Kyara said. "We were just speculating as to how much life might have changed in the last fifty years. What do you think?"

"I don't know. I guess people are living longer. But that's a big, totally irrelevant, so what?"

"You're right. How did the meeting go? It's only been forty five minutes."

"There's more than one situation where getting a headache serves a purpose. And then before she left Corrine asked me how I liked Madge. I told her it was her choice because I was dropping out of the group."

"How did she take it?"

"Not too well but, too bad. I'm with you, I didn't like her friend."

"Yeah. If that one had more than two brain cells, she could be dangerous."

The two women continued to talk between themselves for a few minutes as Reed listened. Then he took a drink of his coffee, leaned back and chuckled.

"What?" Kyara said.

"You two. The stuff your speaker was giving at at the church lecture. You revived the new age movement from over sixty years ago."

"What's that?" Jenny asked.

"Well, think what would happen if you took pantheism, polytheism, astronomy, ecology, environmentalism, psychology, Buddhism, Taoism, Hinduism, Theosophy, Universalism, Esotericism and a dozen more isms, put them all in a blender together and turned it on."

"Yuck!" Jenny said.

"Exactly. A whole new dictionary of meaningless buzz words, inane practices and garbled nonsense. It was supposed to raise the consciousness of the human race, whatever that meant."

"Did it?"

"Not exactly. It just added to the ongoing confusion of the times and eventually faded away due to complete lack of substance."

Kyara and Jenny looked at each other and laughed.

"Is that what you think we are trying to do?" Jenny asked, not knowing that Kyara had already told him what it was all about.

"If all the lectures are like the one tonight, it would certainly look that way because the speaker just went round and round, as if trying to deliver some highly important inspirational message. But other than use it as a cover up, what other purpose does it have? You two are much cleverer than that so, what am I missing?"

"Well damn, Kyara," Jenny said with a pleased smile. "Why have you keep this man hidden so long?" Jenny asked.

"Okay if I tell him?"

"Of course."

"Well, as you saw, we have a question and answer session after the talk. The people we are looking for are the ones who ask critical questions and criticize the material directly. The smart ones. We check them out and see what follows. Then we invite them to our other meetings. Like tonight. Except that went totally sideways."

"Big time," Kyara added.

"So, I'm guessing, but yours is probably not the only group out there."

"No. We have nine more in southern California."

"I'm surprised you never told him any of this before," Jenny said to Kyara.

"Well," Reed put in. "No need to until now. We live in very different worlds. In a lot of respects you might say that the place where I live is about fifty years behind in a lot of respects."

"Really? I wouldn't have thought that. Must be kinda nice."

"In some ways. But fundamentally I don't think there's much difference."

"How so?"

"You had a very large audience tonight. If that's typical, that means that there are still people out there seeking answers to bigger questions."

"And not finding any," Jenny said.

"Yes," Kyara said and looked at Reed. "It's what? What did you call it? The philosophical void?"

"Sounds appropriate," Jenny said. "Care to elaborate?"

"Well, religion is essentially obsolete but never gave anything but super simplistic answers to important questions anyway. As for science, science still sees the universe as an accidental and therefore meaningless happening. And, on the academic, intellectual side of things there hasn't been anything new or refreshing come out of there in half a century. The medical community still sees life as mechanistic bio chemistry and psychologists think that if they can just collect enough brain scan data they will have the answer to everything behavioral. And the government, they short circuit everything by making people live in fear. So, most people are confused and adrift because there is no sound underlying philosophy that gives them any idea as to what life is all about and what they are here for to begin with."

Jenny was silent for several moments as she considered what Reed had said. Then she spoke.

"Can you imagine what things would be like if we could just have open discussions about these kinds of things? Wouldn't that be something?" she said and triggered by the idea, looked up and around, trying to see where the cameras were.

"Jeez," she said. "Maybe we'd better change the subject. God, what a way to live."

Kyara then gave Reed a questioning look. He nodded in the affirmative and Kyara put her hand on Jenny's arm and spoke to her.

"Not to worry," she said. "We're safe here so you can say anything you like."

"What?" Jenny asked. "How.... aren't the cameras on? How do you know that?"

Kyara then reached in her pocket, took out her cell phone and set it on the table. Jenny shrugged and shook her head, not understanding.

"I jammed the cameras in here," Kyara said and went on to explain how it had been done.

Jenny was wide eyed. Then she smiled a most satisfied smile as the entire truth sank in.

"Where did you get it?" she then wanted to know and Kyara told her the rest of it.

Then Kyara showed Jenny in detail how to find the locations it was presently good for, how to gather data from other sites she might want to go to and everything else about the device. Then she explained how the thing warned her before their time was up so it could be reset if need be and handed it to Jenny.

"It's yours," she said. "I have another one. Now see if you can run through the operation by yourself."

Excited, Jenny brought the different functions up on the screen and punched the keys until she felt satisfied.

"I can really keep it?" she asked with genuine enthusiasm and said wow again as she let out an immense sigh, feeling the freedom it gave her.

Reed patted Kyara on the hand and nodded. Kyara smiled and nodded back. Then the waitress arrived with their food.

"Are you really going to eat that?" Kyara asked. "Whoever heard of a chili cheeseburger for a late night snack."

"I know. Pretty gross, huh? But that's what happens when you get involved with someone from out of the uncivilized past."

"Yeah. Sad story. Which reminds me. I also volunteer at the homeless shelter on Fridays. Would you like to come along and help me in the kitchen?"

THIRTY SEVEN

Barton had purposely kept Madge's phone number, but not because she in any way appealed to him and called and asked her out to dinner the following night after the meeting. And, being the gullible woman that she was, she gladly accepted and met him at an out of the way little restaurant in Westwood.

He flattered her through the main course as she blushed and giggled. Finally, by the time they got to dessert, he asked her if she knew who the man was that had so deliberately bumped into him at the meeting in the old converted church.

"Not really," she replied. "But I ..." and then she faltered because she remembered how she had been admonished for having thought about asking Barton to come to Jenny's house.

"Well," she continued, however, believing it was okay to share a little of what she knew with this man who seemed to be so interested in her.

"His name is Reed. Someone said he was from Arizona and he's a friend of Kyara's. A boyfriend, I think. They seem pretty involved."

"Kyara? Is she the dark haired one with the ......" He was going to say, with the great body but realized that would be a little unproductive and went on to describe the way Kyara was dressed instead.

"Yes, that's the one," Madge answered.

"Is she from Arizona, too?" Barton asked as though it were an innocent question.

Madge said she didn't know but thought she would say something nice about Kyara even though she was privately a little jealous of her.

"I heard she volunteers at the homeless shelter in Santa Monica," she told him and that was all he needed.

Barton had never admitted his previous screw up to his colleagues but this time he came prepared with a two man backup. One of them went around to the rear to prevent Kyara from exiting that way again and the other came in with Bart. Unfortunately for Reed and Kyara, Reed was having some difficulty cutting up the whole chickens as he had volunteered to do and didn't pick up on Bart's presence until it was too late. By then they were surrounded. This time, however, Kyara was very verbal and began insisting that her rights were being violated.

"And why are you arresting him?" she also demanded to know.

"Obstruction of a federal agent," Bart smirked as he jerked Reed around and put the cuffs on him. "Where 's your ID," he then demanded.

"In my wallet which is in my left front pocket."

"Arizona, huh?" Bart said after a first look. Then, "What the hell is this? Look," he said to his backups. "What we have here is a real smart ass. His license says that he was born in 1961. Does he look ninety years old to you? Wait till we get him downtown. And as for you, Miss. I'm betting you're not carrying any ID either. Am I right?"

"Good guess, lunkhead. So stop hassling us and take us to see someone with some brains."

In the back of the government vehicle they whispered to each other and discussed whether or not they should just disappear but Reed said no.

"We can do that anytime and I'd rather wait until the

244

handcuffs are off. Let's see why they really want you so badly first so we can come up with a plan."

"But I'm sure they will try to separate us."

"Do you still have the right to have an attorney present during questioning? Tell them I'm your attorney."

"Advocate. We call them advocates now. But, yes. I do. But how do we prove you are?"

"Well, they can't disprove it so maybe it will work. Would they dare take the chance?"

"It's worth a try. And once we are out of this, you have to teach me how to do the mind reading thing."

"Yeah. Sorry. If that knife wasn't so damned dull and I had been paying better attention to what was going on around us, this might not have happened."

"Possibly. But you're right. We need to find out exactly what they are going to charge me with before we do anything else."

Bart smirked with satisfaction as he booked them in but was a little dismayed when he was told to take them both into the rear interrogation room, take their handcuffs off and get them some coffee. He almost protested but soon learned that the order had come directly down from the Division Chief himself, who was on the way.

The division chief was a man old enough to be Kyara's father. Well dressed, well groomed, well mannered but very direct and to the point. He began by pointing out to them in a sympathetic voice that they should know better than to be out and about without proper identification. That was in violation of federal law.

"I realize that," Kyara said, now speaking clearly, knowing that they were being recorded. "But as an American citizen I think that is an infringement on my civil rights and I choose not to do that."

"Really? My, my, young lady. What have we here? You sound like a sovereignist militia member."

"How could I be? The government locked them all up

when I was in grammar school. I just said that to irritate you."

"All right, maybe you did and maybe you didn't, so think about how you really want this to turn out. And even though I might have a little sympathy for your stand, you must know that the courts no longer support that view."

"Unfortunately, I do. But hopefully someday that will be changed. Along with all the rest of the Machiavellian tactics used by the government in today's world," Kyara responded and squeezed Reed's hand under the table as she deliberately took a protest position to see what that might elicit from their interrogator.

"Well, perhaps you are right. But that is not the issue and that is not the reason why we wished to talk to you."

"Really? Then why are we here?"

"Well, you are here for one reason and he is here for another. And if he really is your advocate as you claim, then why doesn't he at least have proper identification of his own to prove that? Giving my agents a drivers license that says he was born ninety years ago and was issued more than fifty years ago is a poor attempt at a joke. But maybe, if things go right here, we can afford to over look that."

"So, get on with it," Reed said. "Why did you have her picked up in the first place so I can decide if it's wise for her to answer any more of your questions."

"All right then, let's proceed. Even though we can't seem to prove it just yet, surely you are both Americans and as such you must feel some loyalty and sense of duty to your country. Am I right?" he asked and looked at them intently. But since neither replied, he acted as though it were still true and continued.

"So," he said. "The reason she is here is a matter of national security. And before we continue I must point out that at this moment you are not in any kind of trouble in that regard. To the contrary, you may instead be in a position to be of serious help to us in terms of the greater good of our nation."

Kyara looked at Reed and smiled. It was now clear to them as to what this was all about, ridiculous as it seemed at the moment.

246

"Keep going," Reed said. But then, before the man could continue, he interrupted.

"Sorry," he said. "But first, if I might. You identified yourself as the division commander but you didn't give us your actual name or show us any ID either. I'm not trying to insult you but it might help if you could do that now."

"Division Chief," their interrogator said in correction and pulled his ID and badge out of his inside jacket pocket and let them see it. Howard Johnson, it said as Reed suppressed a smile, thinking of the chain of hotels and restaurants with the same name that had existed back in his own time.

"Thank you," Reed said politely. "Okay with you?" he then asked Kyara who nodded in the affirmative. "Well, sorry about the interruption. Let's continue. You wanted to talk to her because... ?"

"Yes. Let me get right to the point. We have reviewed the security footage from the Santa Monica site where she disappeared. Not only reviewed it but examined it in great detail and it very clearly indicates that it was not edited or tampered with in any way," the chief said with great seriousness as he looked directly at Kyara who simply shrugged and stared back at him.

"So," he continued. "What we are hoping for is some kind of plausible explanation. We might even be able to compensate you in some way if you could help us out because, as you must realize, this could be a very valuable tool in our ongoing battle against terrorism."

"Or maybe you think I am some kind of terrorist instead. Is that it?"

"I seriously doubt that you are but you do need to know that we are in the process of learning your true identity, thanks to one of your associates."

Kyara looked at Reed.

"You were right," she said. "That bitch."

No sooner had she said it than the door to the room opened and a woman came in, handed the chief a piece of paper and left.

"Well," he said after he looked it over. "Miss Kohnan, is it? My, my. Guess I had better be a little careful here. It seems you father is Arthur Kohnan. He's the CEO of Kohnan International. Is that correct?"

"Yes it is and he's the sole owner. It's a private corporation."

"And a very big one. An American based company with a high security rating that builds everything from jet aircraft to, well look at this. Security surveillance equipment. Is it possible that he even makes the security cameras like the one we seem to have had a problem with? Now that would be interesting."

"Of course it's possible but I honestly have no idea. Like you said, it's a very big company."

"Okay. Well, there's that but then your advocate here is also of interest, but for a different reason. We just completed an archival records search in Arizona and there was indeed a Reed Jahneke back then who's photo matches his face but who seems to have mysteriously disappeared somewhere around the end of two thousand fifteen. My goodness. Where is this going?"

"Nowhere, I hope," Reed said. "So if you don't have a bona fide reason for holding us, we request that we be released."

"And I would be happy to oblige you under normal circumstances if this were the end of it. But, as you yourself well know, Miss Kohnan, you were detained a while back, totally refused to cooperate and somehow escaped from your cell in the middle-of-the-night. As you must realize, disappearing from in front of a working camera is one thing. But also disappearing from a jail cell is very bothersome to me and I dearly hope you will be kind enough to give us some kind of explanation. Like I said earlier, we would be most willing to work with you on this matter and you could be doing us all a great service here because, as you must know, the security implications of such a thing are of grave importance. We would also like to believe that neither your father nor his company are in any way involved."

"Well. Whether you are willing to accept it or not, I can assure you that my father is in no way involved but go ahead and check it out. Right now he is on an extended business trip and has been gone for nearly a month but should be back in a couple more weeks. As for where we go from here I wish to consult with my advocate, Mr. Jahneke in private. Not in this room which I'm sure is wired, but let's say your office instead. If you have drapes or privacy screens, they can remain open while we are in there."

"I don't know. Certainly you are allowed to talk with counsel. But in my office? Well, if you feel that way then that's the way it has to be. Just please don't do anything rash."

There were two large upholstered chairs in front of the chief's desk which Reed pulled around so they faced each other and they sat down. Half an hour later they were still talking and it was clear that the chief was growing impatient. Finally Reed got up and signaled.

"So what have you decided?" the chief asked once he was inside and back in his private chair behind his oversized desk, as he looked from one to the other.

"At this point Miss Kohnan has decided not to cooperate with you," Reed told him bluntly. "She is also not sorry to have been such an inconvenience in this matter. Nor am I, and again we ask that you release us immediately."

The chief gave Reed a hard look, scratched the back of his head and replied. "That might be a possibility in your case. But as for your, so claimed client, jail break is a serious offense and I am afraid that if she does not decide to put herself in a more cooperative frame of mind, she will again be booked and charged. And as you know, she has already proven that she is a flight risk, so she can be held without bond until she can be brought to trial. Is that what you want?"

"Not exactly. But at the same time I don't understand how she can be charged with a crime that you, yourself should know is impossible to commit. Clearly, if she was able to leave a locked cell in the middle of the night, it has to be because someone released her. Look at her. You don't seriously think she was able to walk through the wall or something. Do you?"

"Of course not. And I'm sure there is a rational explanation for everything that has happened. My only request is that, in the interest of internal security, you share this information with us. But, since she seems reluctant to do so, my only choice is to keep her incarcerated until we are able to figure it out for ourselves, which I assure you, we will do sooner or later. Hopefully sooner, for her sake. So, with that in mind, this is her last chance to reconsider."

"Well, chief," Kyara said. "Maybe it's your last chance to reconsider. Because, what if instead of being able to mess with your security system so that I can not only disappear off of a single camera somewhere, what if instead of that, I simply have the ability to just plain disappear entirely? What then?"

"Then I would say it's time to put you in lockup until we can get a judge to order a psychological examination," the chief said as he scowled at her.

At this point Kyara and Reed looked at each and they both shrugged and gave each other a, why not, expression. Then Reed turned his head and looked out of the window into the open area outside the chief's office. There was no one in the immediate vicinity and all of the desks there faced away from the chief's office so he got up and whispered into Kyara's ear and she stood up also.

"Sorry, chief," she said. "My apologies for having to put you in such an embarrassing position but you give us little alternative."

"Yeah, good luck with that, Chief." Reed said. "Maybe we'll drop in on you one of these times."

"Good idea," Kyara said to Reed. "Ready?"

"Ready," he replied and before the chief could even blink, Reed was gone.

"Well, Chief," Kyara said to the shocked man. "Now you know the real answer. I can't wait to see how you explain it to your superiors. Just be careful or you may be the one being evaluated. Bye for now," she said and also disappeared.

THIRTY EIGHT

"Home just in time for lunch," Kyara said with a smile as she appeared in the living room of her house where Reed was waiting.

"I'm thinking the same thing," Reed said. "But first, tell

me how the Chief looked when I left."

"Speechless and flabbergasted."

"Flabbergasted?"

"Well, you would have said the same thing if you had seen his face."

"Good. So what do you think he will do now? Give it up?"

"Pursuing me? Certainly he'll have to cover his tracks somehow. Probably by saying he let us go for lack of evidence. But privately, once he gets to where he can handle it psychologically, he will be after us with a vengeance because he will see what we can do as a means to power. His own. Maybe we should just go back to your time and live there for a few years."

"What about your parents? Your father? What if he thinks your father is involved? Maybe he thinks your father invented some mysterious device that allows us to do that."

"You're probably right. With his mentality he'd never be able to accept it for what it is. He'd have to believe it's some kind of technological breakthrough and that's he's the person who needs to have control of it. By now I bet he's cussing himself for not doing a strip search on us because the only thing that would make sense to him would be us having some advanced device. Like the transporters in old Star Trek movies."

"So the best thing to do is to stay here and deal with it," Reed told her.

"But how?"

"Totally discredit him so that he ends up unemployed. But in the meantime he knows who you are now, so he can track you down?"

"Not really. That's almost impossible. With the exception of my driver's license which has a phony address on it, I am not in the system. As I said before, the car and the house are owned by fictitious companies and are almost untraceable. So as long as no one spots us and follows us back here, we should be safe."

"What about friends? Do any of them know where you live?"

"No. Not since I bought this place. Of course if he put my

photo on the news I'd be in trouble. I try to avoid my neighbors but I'm sure some of them would recognize me if that happened."

"But your parents know. Don't they? What if he puts the pressure on them?"

"I'd hate to put them in that position. But we still have two weeks before they're back. Do you think that's enough time?"

"Easily."

"So where do we start?"

"See if we can remote view ourselves inside his office. Now might be a good time because he'll probably want to clean things up on his end as soon as possible. Stand behind him and try to catch him using his computer password."

"Of course. Then we can go there tonight when the place is empty. Delete ourselves from all the files and get us off all the camera footage."

"And, if we have time, get creative with the Chief's personal records."

"I love it. And once that's resolved I think we need to make a decision."

"About what?"

"Your world or mine. I want us to spend more time together," Kyara said as she put his arms around him.

"I couldn't agree more," he responded and gave her a quick kiss. "How about a doubly long life together."

"If only it were possible."

"But it is. We could lead a double life together in the true sense of the word."

"And how would we do that?"

"Spend six months here, then six months in my time, back and forth. And do it so there would be an ongoing continuity in both worlds without time gaps in either life. No one would know the difference."

"True. My parents wouldn't be wondering if I was okay like they do when I'm gone because, to them, I wouldn't be gone at all. But what about us? We would know. Would we be able to handle it psychologically?"

"Well, you're right. Our lives would seem to flow together

for the people around us, but get pretty disconnected from our point of view trying to keep picking up where we left off after that much time away. So..."

"So, it was still a nice idea. We'll work something out."

"Good. I was hoping you would feel that way. Now we'd better see if we can look over the chief's shoulder."

"Do we have to do it right this minute?" Kyara asked as she put her arms around Reed and snuggled up close.

"Well, maybe not. On the other hand, if we find his password and get that out of the way, then we'll still have several hours to mess around in before we have to go down there in person."